DO YOU ENJOY BEING FRIGHTENED?

**WOULD YOU RATHER HAVE
NIGHTMARES
INSTEAD OF SWEET DREAMS?**

**ARE YOU HAPPY ONLY WHEN
SHAKING WITH FEAR?**

CONGRATULATIONS ! ! ! !

YOU'VE MADE A WISE CHOICE.

**THIS BOOK IS THE DOORWAY
TO ALL THAT MAY FRIGHTEN YOU.**

GET READY FOR

**COLD, CLAMMY SHIVERS
RUNNING UP AND DOWN YOUR SPINE!**

**NOW, OPEN THE DOOR–
IF YOU DARE !!!!**

Shivers™

FOUR IN ONE SHIVERS

By

M. D. Spenser

Published by Peter Haddock Ltd., England, by arrangement with River Publishing, Inc. All right, title and interest to the "SHIVERS" logo and design are owned by River Publishing, Inc. No portion of the "SHIVERS" logo and design may be reproduced in part or whole without prior written permission from River Publishing, Inc. An application for a registered trademark of the "SHIVERS" logo and design is pending with the Federal Patent and Trademark office.

30840

Shivers™

FOUR IN ONE
VOLUME TWO

THE ANIMAL REBELLION

GHOST WRITER

THE HAUNTING HOUSE

TERROR ON TROLL MOUNTAIN

M. D. Spenser

Shivers™

THE ANIMAL REBELLION

M. D. Spenser

Chapter One

Uncle Bob and my cousin Brad had just picked me up at the airport to drive almost 100 miles out to their remote farmhouse. This farm was supposed to be a really cool place, nestled among beautiful rolling mountains. And very far away from any neighbors.

My parents thought it would be good for me to spend two weeks on a farm during summer vacation. But now I wasn't so sure I really wanted to go.

I'm pretty much a city kid and I'd never spent even one hour on anything like a farm. Give me city life any day — buildings and buses, concrete and computers.

Who ever heard of a computer on a farm?

"This is going to be a great time," Brad said to me in the car. "We'll have a blast!"

"Oh yeah, absolutely, Brad. I'm really happy to be here. It's going to be lots of fun," I answered politely.

But really, I was starting to wish I'd never left home.

Everything seems exciting in Chicago, where I live. And there are lots of computers in Chicago.

Some kids call me a computer geek because I'm good with computers. And I do look a little geeky, I guess. Big black glasses and short brown hair and large ears. And I'm not very big or strong for my age.

Even my name sounds like a computer geek. Winston — and please don't ever call me Win or Winnie! Winston is just fine, thank you.

So here I was, a city kid named Winston riding off to who knows where in Uncle Bob's dusty pickup truck. I already was sure everything was going to be boring here in this place called Vermont.

I didn't know then just how wrong I was. Vermont turned out to be a lot of things, including terrifying. But it was never boring.

On the way to the farm, we drove through Burlington, Vermont's largest city. It's incredibly small by Chicago standards but looked like kind of a cool place to live.

At least there were sidewalks! And lots of restaurants and stores and pretty New England churches. All of it sitting right on Lake Champlain, which sparkled brightly in the summer sun.

I wished Uncle Bob and Brad lived in Burlington.

But we were heading out into the country now, farther and farther away from the city. I have to admit that everything seemed very pretty to me. The woods lining the roads were thick with green leaves and the mountains beyond the woods looked like they were covered by a dense green carpet.

And that's when I heard it.

Thump! Tha-thump! Thump-tha-tha-thump!

It sounded really weird, almost like an animal. It was coming from somewhere inside the truck.

But Uncle Bob and Brad weren't making the sound. And I knew I sure wasn't making it. When I turned to look through the rear window, I saw there was nothing in the back of the truck.

"Wh-wh-what was that?" I asked Uncle Bob, trying to sound as brave as possible. I suppose I was

3

just a little afraid.

"That? Oh, Winston wants to know about — you know. The *sound!*" Uncle Bob said to Brad. "Should we tell him?"

Then we heard the sound again. *Thump! Tha-tha-tha-thump! THUMP!* It was louder this time. It sounded like this animal was angry. And getting angrier.

Brad and I were both sitting in the back seat. I looked over at Brad. His face was wrinkled up as if he was frightened. And I could see Uncle Bob's eyes in the rear view mirror. They looked worried.

"Oh, yeah. Sure!" Brad said. "The *sound!* I don't think we should tell him about it already, Dad. We don't want to scare him before he even gets to the house."

"Tell me what?" I asked. "Come on! You've got to tell me now! What's that sound, Brad?"

"I think you'd better tell him about it. He may want us to bring him back to the airport before it's too late," Uncle Bob said seriously.

"I guess you're right, Dad. You see, Winston — that sound comes from a ghost," Brad said, looking totally scared. "An animal ghost. It lives inside our truck. And it can take over the truck whenever it wants and make us drive right off the road. Right into a tree or something at 80 miles an hour!"

"Yeah, sure it can, Brad. Tell me another one," I said, as if I didn't believe him. But inside, I wasn't so confident. I might be smart, but I can get as scared as anyone else.

"It's true, Winston! This truck is possessed by an evil animal spirit. It came from the house to the truck," Brad said.

"From the — the house? What do you mean from the house?" I asked.

"I hate to tell you this, Winston. I guess I should have told you and your parents before you came all this way," Uncle Bob said sadly. "What Brad told you is true. The truck is possessed by an evil spirit. And our old farmhouse is haunted, too. The whole place is full of the ghosts of dead animals!"

Chapter Two

"What do you mean, ghosts?" I cried out. "Your entire house is packed with animal ghosts? And this truck, too? And you let me come here? Why would you do that? Why didn't you tell me?"

Uncle Bob and Brad burst out laughing.

"We're just having a laugh at your expense, I'm afraid," Uncle Bob admitted. "We're just teasing you, Winston. There are no ghosts at our house. Or in this truck. No animal ghosts or ghosts of any other kind."

"No, but there *could* be," Brad laughed. "Maybe we'll have our first ghost while you're visiting!"

"So what was that sound?" I asked.

"Just a loose connection under the truck. It makes our muffler bang against the metal truck bed sometimes," Brad said, holding his sides from laughing so hard.

"You stink!" I said to Brad. But I was laughing too. I had to admit it was a pretty good joke.

"Gotcha geekhead!" he shouted with a laugh. Then he punched me in the arm.

Even though I am a bit nerdy, I punched Brad back on his arm. And we both laughed over how scared I had become about the "animal ghosts."

I don't usually play rough with other kids. When I'm not with my computer, I prefer to read or talk with friends or maybe play on the swings at the park. I try to fit in with everyone at school as best I can, but I'm definitely not a jock.

But I always feel comfortable when I'm with Brad. We like to roughhouse together. And he can get away with calling me names like "geekhead" because I know he's kidding.

Brad might even be my best friend, even though he's my cousin and lives so far from me. We're both almost the same age — I'm 12 and Brad is just a few months older. And we talk often on the phone and spend lots of time together in Chicago during all the big holidays.

Brad's more of a jock type, I guess. He's big and athletic, with a lot of muscles and blond hair and blue eyes. He's always the best at every sport he tries. Just like I'm always the best on a computer.

So I was really surprised when we finally got to Brad's farmhouse. Because there on a desk in his room was a new gleaming computer, Pentium with 16 RAM and CD-ROM and a 28.8 modem! And a whole pile of computer games.

"Excellent!" I shouted.

"I wanted to surprise you. Pretty cool, huh?" Brad said proudly.

"Wow, I didn't know farms ever had computers. Man, this is totally cool," I said, looking over the computer. "This thing has got everything on it, Brad. It's loaded!"

"Most farms have computers these days, Winston. Dad's had his own computer for years to keep track of the milk he sells and the animals we slaughter for food and everything," Brad explained. "But we just got this one for me a week ago. I talked Dad into getting it early because you were coming. And he bought all these awesome games."

"Just too cool. Now we can have all kinds of fun," I said.

"We were going to put the new computer in the room across the hall. That's where you'll be staying. But we decided that wasn't such a good idea," Brad said slowly. It was as though he didn't want to tell me about something.

"I guess you'd rather have it in your own room anyway, huh?" I asked, hoping that was the only reason it wasn't a good idea. But I could see by Brad's expression that something was wrong.

"No, really I'd rather have the computer somewhere else. But Dad didn't want me to spend so much time in the guest room. At least — not all alone!" Brad said.

"Why? What's wrong with the guest room?" I said to Brad. I was getting worried now.

"Nothing. Not really — I *guess*," Brad said. "It's just that it can get kind of scary over there. Especially if you have to be in there alone for very long."

"Won't I be sleeping alone in there?" I asked, fear slipping into my voice.

"It's the only room we have to put you in,

Winston. I'm sorry. I don't have another bed in my room," Brad explained, avoiding my eyes. He looked scared.

"If you're trying to scare me again, you jock-head ..." I said. And then I admitted the truth: "If you're trying to scare me, you're doing a really good job!"

"There's no reason to be scared, Winston. Not really," Brad said worriedly.

"What's wrong with that room!" I almost shouted. I was sweating so much my heavy black glasses almost slid off my nose.

"It's just that the last person to spend a night in there alone was murdered. Slaughtered with an ax in his sleep. He was hacked to death on the neck, just like we kill the chickens," Brad said, his voice shaking with fear.

Chapter Three

"What? Hacked to death!" I yelled at the top of my lungs.

"Yeah, it was awful! Blood everywhere!" Brad explained sadly. "It happened right before we bought this house. And no one has slept in there alone since then. Until tonight."

"Who did it?" I demanded.

"Nobody knows. But the state police think there's a crazy man who lives out in the woods just past our pasture. He's all hairy and smelly. He's like some kind of animal. And they think he has something against anyone who tries to sleep in that room," Brad said.

"Maybe I could sleep in your room, Brad. Or in the living room. I don't care. Any place is better than the Death Room," I said quickly.

"The Death Room! Yeah, that's what we call

it, too. And you *have* to sleep in there tonight. And every night for two weeks. *Alone!"* Brad said.

"But why? Why? I don't understand if it's so dangerous — why?" I stammered.

"Because all scaredy-cat geekheads who come to our farm have to sleep there until they stop believing stupid stories!" Brad laughed. He almost fell on the floor from laughing now, holding his stomach and bending over as if this were the funniest joke in the world.

"Ha, ha, ha, ha," I said. But I wasn't laughing. "You think you're so funny. Sure, pick on the city kid who doesn't know any better. I've never been in the country in my life. How do I know what happens on these farms? There could be ghosts or murders or anything. You stupid jockhead!"

"I'm sorry, Winston. I don't mean to be nasty to you. You're my favorite cousin!" Brad said, still laughing. "But you know how I like to kid you. I can't help it. And when you're so new to everything around here, it's just too much fun to pass up."

"Yeah, well, don't keep doing it, all right? I've had enough to scare me for one day," I said.

I probably was feeling a little too sorry for myself right then. So to make us both feel better, I tried Brad's trick. I punched him in the arm. For a geek, I punched pretty hard.

"Ow!" Brad said, wincing with pain. "You nerd!"

Then he chased me from his bedroom, into the living room, down the stairs to the dark, damp basement and back up. Then I ran into the guest room where I was staying, the "Death Room."

"Now you die! Die in the Death Room, Winston!" Brad shouted.

But he was smiling. And with his fist clenched to hit my arm, Brad lunged at me in one great leap. For once I was quicker, though, and moved aside in time.

Brad flew through the air like a guided missile shot from some powerful fighter jet. He completely missed me. And with his arms flailing wildly, he soared right over the bed and hit the wall with his head.

Brad crumpled to the ground, unconscious.

"Brad!" I screamed.

I knew he was knocked cold. But I couldn't

tell if he was even breathing. If he was even alive!
Maybe this *was* the Death Room after all.

Chapter Four

"Brad!" I shouted again. "Help! Uncle Bob! Help! Brad's hurt!"

No one came.

I could see Uncle Bob walking around in the barn below the Death Room window. He was talking to one of the farm hands beside a group of black and white cows.

The window was closed and Uncle Bob couldn't hear me. I was alone with no one to help me. And my cousin might be dead.

I ran over to Brad. There was no blood on the wall where he had hit his head. Internal injuries, I thought. Maybe Brad had knocked his brains loose! He could be bleeding to death internally right now!

"Brad!" I yelled, trying to shake him awake. "Say something! Are you okay? Brad, say something to me!"

Suddenly, Brad opened his eyes. Then he punched me on the arm. Hard!

"Geekhead!" he said with a laugh. "Gotcha again!"

"You jerk! Ouch, that hurt!" I said, standing up and moving away from him. "I thought you were really knocked out. Or maybe worse than that."

"I bumped my head a little but it didn't really hurt. So I figured I'd get you over here instead of chasing you anymore. I pretended to be knocked out so I could get you back with a good punch in the arm," Brad explained, chuckling to himself.

"You're really being a jerk! I hope you're not going to do this stuff to me for the next two weeks," I said, feeling a little angry.

"Nah, I'm just having fun. I'm sorry, Winston." Brad said softly. "Really. I promise I won't fool you about anything the rest of the time you stay here. Honest! Cross my heart and hope to die."

"Don't say 'hope to die' in here. Not in the Death Room," I said, smiling. "Come on, let's go check out your computer."

We walked across the long, narrow hallway of

the old farmhouse into Brad's room.

The house was excellent — really old, with lots of dark wood everywhere. It was built in 1849 and was even attacked by Indians once.

The wooden floors of the house creaked when you walked and the furniture smelled like the inside of your grandmother's attic. It almost felt like you had stepped inside some museum or something. The whole house might be an exhibit called The Pioneer Period.

In the daytime, the house seemed sunny and happy. But I soon learned that at night, the moon cast heavy shadows in each room and everything looked silent and spooky.

Brad's room was pretty cool. He had pictures of Michael Jordan and Charles Barkley and a lot of other sports guys on his walls.

And he had some colorful sports team pennants pinned up, too — the Boston Red Sox and the Detroit Tigers and the New England Patriots and the Boston Bruins. He even had a pennant for my favorite team, the Chicago White Sox. I'd given him that one for Christmas.

Just because I'm a computer geek doesn't

mean I don't follow sports, you know. I like to watch baseball and football, too. It's just that I prefer playing with my computer.

"Maybe you can help me set up some of the computer games, Winston. Dad said you could do better at installing them than he could," Brad said.

"Sure. That's easy," I answered. "I'll show you how to do it. But you do have to be careful. These computers can be dangerous if you don't know what you're doing."

"Really? I didn't know that," Brad said, his voice concerned.

"Oh, sure. I knew this kid who turned the wrong switch just once and he was fried like a hamburger. Electrocuted right in his bedroom," I explained.

"Oh, wow! Man, I didn't think something like that could happen," Brad said, moving a step away from the computer.

I flipped on Brad's computer and the black monitor screen glowed red and then blue and soon was ready for my keyboard commands.

"Hey, cool! You've got an online service.

You're hooked up to the Internet," I said.

"Yeah, it came with it. I guess we can send each other messages, huh?" Brad asked.

"Sure. That'll be excellent. But let me just adjust this one little switch in back of the computer monitor first and then I'll …

"AAAAAAAAAAAGGGGGHHHHHHHH!"

I let out a blood-curdling scream. My arm shook violently and the spasms of pain raced through my entire body. My eyes grew wild with agony and drool fell off my lips.

I had touched the wrong switch. I was being electrocuted!

"Winston! Oh no!" Brad shouted. "What do I do?"

The computer bounced and thrashed and finally with an electronic whine of complaint went completely dead.

I tumbled onto the floor as if my legs had no muscles.

Brad could see right away that I wasn't faking something, like he had done to me.

My eyes rolled into the back of my head and a

low groan of torment fell from my mouth. Brad knew I was trying to breathe, but couldn't.

I had been jolted by thousands of volts of electricity in the computer line. I had been fried, just like my friend. And I was dying.

Chapter Five

What can a kid do when he sees his cousin dying?

Brad became frantic. He actually whimpered as he ran to the window to look for his father, then ran back to my limp body to see if I was breathing yet.

I wasn't.

"Winston! Winston! No, no, no, no!" Brad hollered.

He bent down to my chest to begin giving me CPR, looking wildly toward the window. Should he run to the barn for help? Should he start the CPR? What should he do?

And just then, Brad felt a sharp jolt on his own arm. But this pain didn't come from electricity. It came from me. A good hard punch below his shoulder.

"Gotcha, jockhead!" I hollered. And then I

started to laugh.

"Aw, I don't believe it! You stupid dweeb!" Brad said, standing up and covering his face with his hands. "I was so sure you weren't faking me out! I thought you were dead, man! How did you do that?"

"Simple. I just started shaking and screaming, then I kicked the computer plug out of the wall behind your desk to shut the monitor down. It looked like the electricity shorted out the computer," I said proudly, still laughing.

This time, Brad was the one who wasn't laughing.

"You deserved it," I said. "You got me bad a few times already!"

After a few minutes, Brad finally admitted he'd had it coming and laughed along with me. But we agreed our games had gotten out of control. No more false stories or phony injuries, we decided.

One of us might really get hurt sometime and need help from the other one. How could we ever know what to believe if we kept on playing these stupid kid tricks?

We shook hands on our agreement and I installed Brad's new computer games. All of them were way cool, too. *Terrible Battle II* and *Karate Fighters* and *Dogfights to the Death* and other great stuff.

But we didn't play anything for too long because Brad wanted to show me around the farm.

Really, I would rather have played more computer games. But I went along on a tour of the farm just to be nice to my cousin. He's a great guy, even if he is a major jock who likes to kid around with me all the time.

The farm was really pretty and everything, I guess. All I could see everywhere around me were acres of fields, surrounded by dense woods and gentle green mountains. Not another house in sight.

Uncle Bob grew corn and soybeans and hay on his land, mostly to feed his animals. And he sure had plenty of animals to feed!

He had a newly built, red wooden barn full of cows that his farm hands milked every day. And he had another barn that badly needed a fresh coat of red paint. It was an older building, with most of the paint weathered off by the harsh Vermont winters.

That old, creaking, tumble-down barn was

right outside the window of my room, the Death Room. This was the barn where Uncle Bob kept a few horses, along with several bulls he planned to slaughter for food.

And there were lots of other animals on the farm — sheep and chickens and goats. Uncle Bob and Brad used the animals for everything, one way or another. The sheep for wool and skins, the goats' milk for cheese, the chickens for eggs and meat.

I told Brad his farm was really awesome. And it was! I'd never seen anything like it before.

But I still missed city life.

Pretty soon, I would miss the city more than ever.

As we walked through the old rundown barn near the house, Brad showed the animals to me.

"See this gray horse? Look at the spots on him. He's really pretty, isn't he? He's called an appaloosa, a great horse to ride," Brad explained. "We named him Demon because my dad says he's as strong as the devil. I ride him all over the farm and he never gets tired. But he's really nice and gentle. You can pet him if you want."

But I'd never touched a horse, so I was nervous.

Brad reached out to Demon, stroking his back. Demon shook his head as though a fly had landed on his ear.

Then Brad moved his hand up to Demon's face, gently patting the horse's nose and mouth. Demon shook his head again, almost like he was angry at Brad for touching him.

"Oh no, Demon!" Brad suddenly shouted. "No, Demon! No! Owwww, nooo!"

"Brad, what's wrong? Are you all right?" I asked worriedly.

And I ran two steps toward the front of Demon to see what had happened.

"Stay away from Demon!" Brad warned me. "Winston, don't come any closer!"

"What's wrong, Brad? Tell me what's wrong!" I demanded.

"Demon started biting me and wouldn't let go," Brad said, looking down at his right arm. "This gentle horse tried to bite my arm clear off."

Chapter Six

"Brad! You promised!" I scolded. "We said we weren't going to fake each other out anymore with these stupid games!"

But when Brad moved away from Demon, I could see this was no game.

Blood was streaking down his right arm, running in little rivers on to his hand. From his hand, the blood dripped to the barn floor, staining the sandy dirt and yellow hay.

"Brad, you're really hurt! You weren't fooling!" I blurted out. I ran for him so quickly my glasses almost fell off. Now I was the one who was growing frantic.

"Owwwww, man this really hurts! Demon bit me hard!" Brad complained. "He's never bitten anyone before. What got into you, Demon?"

Demon didn't move or make a sound.

"What's wrong with that horse? He's always so gentle and easygoing," Brad said as we walked back to the house. He was holding his arm and wincing from the pain. Blood still seeped down his arm, dropping on to the earth.

"Maybe he doesn't like me," I said, worried about Brad's arm. I wondered if he'd have to go to the hospital for stitches and shots or something.

"Naw, it's not that. He didn't even look at you. It's something else. Something weird. I've never seen Demon act so strange before," Brad said slowly. "It was almost like he was angry with me for something. Demon didn't want me touching him at all. And when he bit me, he chomped down hard. It was like he didn't want to let go until he bit my arm right off!"

We cleaned up Brad's injury with some alcohol and antiseptic ointment, and wrapped his arm in a large bandage. The bite didn't look deep enough to need stitches, Brad decided.

But he warned me to stay away from Demon.

"Don't come near him." Brad said, his voice full of dread. "I think that horse is dangerous! It was the way he acted, not just the bite. Demon might even be crazy."

But at dinner, when Brad told his father about the horse, Uncle Bob just chuckled.

"Don't worry about Demon, Brad," Uncle Bob said. "He's a good, sweet horse. Something just spooked him and he reacted. Any animal will do that if they get scared. You go right back to Demon tomorrow and put a saddle on him and ride him. You and Winston both. He'll be just fine."

We finished our meal of fresh corn and chicken and steak, all of it grown or slaughtered right there on the farm. The food was great. I was starting to like this country life better and better.

After dinner, I went to my room to unpack my suitcase while Brad started up the computer. We wanted to play some more of the cool games Uncle Bob had bought for us.

I put my clothes in the closet and in the chest and tucked my suitcase under the bed. And I decided that I didn't want to think of this room as the "Death Room" anymore.

Not even when kidding around with Brad. Not if I was going to sleep there for two weeks — all alone. I was sorry I had ever called it the Death Room in the first place.

I looked out the window at the old barn where Demon and the other horses and bulls lived. And I could see the new bright red barn farther away from the house. It looked like several farm hands were still hard at work, even though it was past dinner time.

When I walked into Brad's room, the computer was turned on. But my cousin wasn't sitting in front of the monitor.

Instead, he was looking at the back of one computer game box. And he looked really frightened.

I wondered if this was another one of Brad's jokes — even though we had agreed to stop fooling each other. Sometimes Brad gets carried away with things and doesn't know when to quit.

"Hey Winston! Come here and check this out, dude," Brad said worriedly. "This just totally weirds me out."

"It's only the back of a computer game box. Big deal! I know all those games anyway. I can show you how to play any of them," I said, probably sounding like a know-it-all. Sometimes geeks like me have a hard time remembering that we don't know everything.

"You didn't install this game, geekhead. I forgot Dad even bought it. I just found the box under those books beside my desk. I guess it just fell off the pile of other games and got buried by my books," Brad explained.

He held out the box for me to take. I looked at the front of it first. My heart seemed to stop beating for just a moment. And I couldn't find any way to take a breath.

The game was called *Animal Killers*. The cover illustration showed a bunch of animals — all of them eating people.

Except they weren't just any animals. They were all horses, spotted horses just like Demon!

They were inside an old red barn, a barn that looked a lot like the one right outside my bedroom window.

And every horse had a human arm or leg sticking out of its mouth, with blood dripping from the chewed-off limbs on to the dirt and hay below.

Chapter Seven

"This is so scary, Brad! I don't get it," I said. My voice quivered with fear. "Its just too bizarre to find this game called *Animal Killers* on the same day your favorite horse tries to eat you alive! I've never even heard of this game before."

"Wait a minute, Winston. Let's not totally weird out over this thing. Dad bought this game a long time before Demon bit my arm. And Demon didn't try to eat me. He just got spooked, like my dad said. Any animal will attack if they're scared," Brad said.

Only, I could tell from his voice that Brad wasn't sure he believed what he was saying.

The coincidence seemed very strange. *Too* strange! But maybe it was just one of those weird things that happen sometimes. You know, the kind of things that make you feel like you're in a scary movie — only everything is real.

This was real, all right. The *Animal Killers* horses looked just like Demon, inside a barn that looked just like the one outside my bedroom window. The Death Room window. And the horses on the game box were eating people!

Brad and I talked about all this a little more and then tried to laugh it off. We agreed that we were too old to be scared by goofy stuff like horses eating people. But we decided to play some other computer games for now anyway, just to take our minds off everything.

Somehow we didn't feel like playing *Animal Killers*. We didn't even install it on Brad's computer.

But Brad and I couldn't play any game very long.

We heard noise coming from outside somewhere. Then the back screen door to the house slammed hard. And we heard Uncle Bob running around the house. He sounded upset.

Brad and I walked to the front room and found Zeke, one of the farm hands, sitting in a chair and holding his arm.

Blood was running down the muscles of his

left arm, dripping on to his pants. Uncle Bob ran out of the bathroom with bandages and antiseptic.

"Dad, what happened?" Brad shouted. "What happened to Zeke?"

"You won't believe it if I tell you," Uncle Bob said, hurrying to stop the bleeding. "I don't know what's gotten into those horses."

"Did Demon bite Zeke?" Brad asked. He sounded horrified. Demon was his favorite horse.

"It wasn't Demon this time. It was Tornado. That's another appaloosa we have, Winston. Looks just like Demon," Uncle Bob explained to me. "And he didn't just bite Zeke. Worse than that."

"Worse? What could a horse do that's worse than biting people?" I asked.

Uncle Bob stayed silent, pursed his lips, and looked at Zeke.

"Well son, first ol' Tornado bit me real hard on the arm, see?" Zeke said. "For no reason at all. I've been around that horse a thousand times and he's always been sweet as pie to me. But I thought he was going to bite my arm clean off."

"Tornado did that?" Brad said, shocked.

"Yes sir, Brad, Tornado sure did," Zeke replied as Uncle Bob bandaged his wound. "Then when I moved back behind him to get away from his biting, he attacked again. He kicked me! Kicked my leg so hard I think it's broken! I'll probably have to go to the hospital."

With his right arm, Zeke lifted the leg of his jeans. He revealed a large bloody break in the skin — an injury exactly the size of a horse's hoof.

<u>Chapter Eight</u>

Brad and I were back in his room now.

And I have to admit that we were both scared.

"I've never been around horses before, Brad." I said. "Maybe I just don't understand them. But I didn't know horses went around biting people so hard they made them bleed."

"They don't," Brad said. "At least our horses don't. And I've never heard of a horse biting people as hard or long as Demon and Tornado did. It's really weird, Winston. This is definitely strange."

"It's almost like on that game, isn't it? Like on *Animal Killers*. It's as if the horses are trying to attack people. Almost as if they want to eat us or something," I said.

I was trying not to sound worried, but it wasn't working.

I knew that what I was thinking was impossible. It just couldn't be true. But I had to tell Brad anyway.

"Don't be a scaredy-cat geekhead now, Winston." Brad said. "We can't let ourselves get too afraid. They're just horses. Something has to be bothering them. We just need to think like a horse and understand them. We need to find out what's bothering Demon and Tornado — and then fix it."

"*You* think like a horse! I'll think like a geek," I whined. "I don't care if I am being a scaredy-cat. At least I have a good reason. My first day on a farm and the animals start turning into killers! I like it a lot better in Chicago!"

"The animals aren't turning into killers, Winston! Don't be ridiculous," Brad said, a little annoyed with me now. "You worry too much."

"I don't worry enough," I replied.

"Of course, Demon *could* break loose from his stall. And he could even kick right through the walls of our house and come in after us!" Brad teased. "And then he'd eat all of us while we were asleep."

I could see from the look in his eyes that he was just trying to scare me again. So I decided not to let myself appear afraid at all — even though I really was. Sometimes it's hard to be a computer nerd.

"Yeah, yeah. Sure, Brad! Ha, ha, ha, ha," I sneered. "I'm not *that* dumb about horses! Even I know that no horse could kick through an old strong house like this one. And besides, you're not supposed to fake me out anymore and scare me. We agreed!"

"I'm not trying to fake you out, Winston. I'm just teasing you," Brad admitted. "I knew you wouldn't believe a really lame story like that. There's no way a horse could kick through this house and hurt us. And no horse would ever try to do that anyway."

Right then, we heard it! The sound of hard pounding against the outside of the house! Pounding, just next to the window of Brad's room. Pounding, just beside the bed where we were sitting together.

The beating was sharp and powerful. *Thwack! Thwack! Thwack! Thwack! Thwack!*

The whole wall of Brad's room rattled with each blow.

Thwack! Thwack! Thwack! Thwack! Thwack!

It sounded exactly like the hooves of a horse, battering the outside of the old house. Stomping wildly against the wood. Trying to kick his way inside!

Thwack! Thwack! Thwack! Thwack! Thwack!

And then we heard the loud, furious whinny of a horse gone completely crazy.

Chapter Nine

Even Brad yelled and jumped back from his bed.

I was already hiding behind the door of his bedroom, trembling. I was trying to figure a way to run across the room into Brad's closet before Demon kicked his way through the walls of the house.

A mad horse was on the loose! A killer horse! A *people-eating* horse!

Terrified, I peeked around the corner of the door to see if Brad was all right. That was when Zeke, the farm hand, put his face in front of Brad's open screen window. He was smiling broadly.

"Heh, heh, heh," Zeke laughed. "I scare you boys a bit?"

"Zeke, you goonhead!" Brad snorted. "Was that you? What were you trying to do? Besides, I thought you were hurt."

"Believe me, son, I am hurt. My arm and leg are torn up good. But I'm not hurt so bad I can't play a little trick while I'm standing right here," Zeke explained, laughing until the pain in his broken leg made him wince.

"What are you talking about?" Brad asked. "Why did you do that?"

"The window was open. I heard when you boys talked about Demon kicking through the house to eat you. So I just grabbed an old rock sitting here and whacked the house with it a few times. Then I gave you my best horse-whinny imitation," Zeke said. "Seemed to work pretty good. That you hiding behind the door there, Winston?"

This country humor was starting to seem pretty weak. Did farm people pull these kinds of tricks all the time? City people didn't do stupid things like this. I couldn't wait to get back to Chicago.

I came out from behind the door, feeling really embarrassed. I'd been scared out of my wits by a rock!

At least Brad had been scared too. He had jumped off the bed just as fast as I did. That made me feel a little better about running for my life.

"Your dad is going for the pickup truck. He's taking me to the hospital to get this leg set," Zeke said, wincing with pain again. "It's a long drive and we won't be back until late tonight. Your dad told me to have you boys get to bed before long. It's dark now and you have to get up early to help with the chores."

"*Chores*?" I sputtered. "Nobody mentioned anything to me about doing chores."

"It's all part of staying on a farm, Winston," Brad said. "I've told you about that before. Helping to clean up around the barns and feed the chickens and doing everything else that has to be done. Everyone on a farm has to do chores."

"Yeah, but I didn't know *I'd* have to do them. I'm a city geek, cousin. I do computers. I definitely don't do chickens," I said firmly.

"Starting tomorrow morning, you do!" Brad answered, just as firmly.

Great! I come to a farm for the first time and the animals starting chewing off arms. And then I find out that I have to get up at dawn to help do chores.

If this was farm life, it stank.

At home, I got to stay up pretty late in the summer to watch TV in my room, or play *Death Commandos* or some other game on the Pentium computer I have. In the country, I found out that everyone goes to bed soon after it's dark in the summer. Never later than 10 p.m.

Whatever happened to kids getting to play around on their break from school?

What about late-night computer games? What about TV until midnight? Geez, my cousin's house didn't even have cable!

Where was I anyway? I was beginning to feel like an earth man who had landed on another planet. Everything on a farm seemed bizarre and dreary and kind of spooky.

Where was all the fun? And how could Brad stand to live here?

I had lots of questions. But I knew there was no use in arguing about anything. When you're an earth man stuck on Planet Zorgon, you have to live like the Zorgons, I guess.

So when Brad insisted that we brush our teeth and get ready for bed at 9:30, I didn't complain. I just pretended I was a space commander on some kind of dangerous mission.

Suddenly, I felt like Captain Kirk exploring strange new worlds, going boldly where no man had gone before. Maybe I could survive two weeks on Zorgon better than two weeks on a farm.

Beam me up, Scotty!

We were already in our pajamas, just Brad and me alone in the large farmhouse. Miles from another human being.

It really was almost like visiting another planet. At least, that's how it seemed to me.

There were no streets. No people. No lights.

Everything was black, except for the moon and the millions of stars you could see in the sky.

My cousin and I said good night and went into our own rooms to sleep. Even though I didn't know how I could possibly fall asleep so early.

I laid in bed and tossed and turned. It was warm, with no breeze coming through the open screen window. And I couldn't sleep.

I got up and looked through my window at the moonlit pastures and woods. At the tractors and farm equipment. And at the barn.

That's when I suddenly got brave for some reason. That's when I got the idea to go outside. By myself. In the dark.

I knew I wasn't supposed to, but I went anyway. And it turned out to be a very dangerous mistake.

Chapter Ten

I don't know what got into me.

This wasn't typical Winston, computer-geek behavior. Maybe feeling like Captain Kirk made me braver than usual.

But whatever the reason, I climbed out of bed and found myself getting dressed again. After slipping into my shoes and putting on my glasses, I slowly opened the door to my bedroom.

It squeaked, just like everything in the house: *Cccccrrrrrrrrrrrraaaaaaaaaaaaaaaa!*

I peeked around the corner to see if Brad was up, and saw nothing. Only the dark, frightening shadows cast by the moonlight that poured through the windows.

I crept quietly down the hallway — as quietly as possible, anyway. The floor creaked with each step, like in a scary movie. I half expected some crazy guy with an ax to jump from behind the furniture to attack me.

Maybe somebody like the crazy guy Brad invented to fake me out. The man who was hairy and smelly, like some kind of animal. The man who hacked someone to death in my room. The Death Room.

To tell you the truth, I was a little spooked as I walked through the old, creaky farmhouse. Even if I did feel like Captain Kirk. I think Captain Kirk gets scared sometimes, too. Don't you?

I pushed open the back screen door, which groaned and squealed no matter how gently I tried to move it. And I stepped out into the dark night, my way lighted only by a half moon.

But before I could step off the porch, I saw the terrifying shadow.

It was clearly in the shape of a man, a very large and very hairy man. A man who had to be hiding around the corner of the house, hoping I would walk near him.

A man who was holding an ax raised high over his head, waiting for his next victim.

Chapter Eleven

My whole body trembled with fear.

I tried to move my feet but I couldn't. Not forward to run away. Not backward to escape into the house.

I was sure the madman was going to come around the corner and kill me with his ax.

A hairy, smelly, animal-like crazy person!

But then a gentle breeze blew over the farm from the mountains, finally cooling off the warm, still night. And with the new wind, the shadow changed shapes.

The dark form on the ground didn't look like a man anymore. It looked kind of like — well, a tree.

Actually, it turned out to be a tall, furry bush planted beside the house. And the raised ax was nothing more than a piece of farm equipment that was left behind the bush for the night. It was a backhoe, with its long arm and jagged shovel still high in the air.

So much for my new-found bravery.

But I have to give myself some credit for courage that night — because I didn't go back inside after I discovered the mad killer was only a bush and backhoe. I went to explore more of the farm.

I went into the barn. The same barn that sheltered Demon and Tornado, the people-biting horses.

To this day, I don't know why I wanted to walk inside that scary, broken-down barn alone. Especially at night.

But something made me open the weathered barn door.

I admit that I was afraid. Very afraid.

The large, heavy door scraped the side of the wooden barn as I slowly slid it open, waking all the animals. The horses and cattle complained with annoyed whinnys and moos, shuffling their hooves.

I left the door open. The moonlight carved out deep shadows inside the barn. And I stepped into this unfamiliar world filled with farm sounds and farm smells.

I heard eerie crunching and grunting. I heard

strange, heavy breathing. I could smell wet hay and fresh manure and cool, moist earth.

As I walked still further into the dark barn, I followed the beam of moonlight coming through the door. Beyond the pale light cast by the moon, I could see almost nothing.

All the animals were in shadow, suspicious of their intruder. Now and then, an eye was visible, staring at me, watching every move I made.

I felt like running back into the house and hiding under my covers. I was so afraid that my hands started shaking and my legs felt weak.

But I kept walking into the creaky barn.

Further and further inside. Further and further away from the barn door — and any hope of escape if one of the horses began to attack me.

What would I do if Demon tried to eat me? What if Tornado started to kick me? How could I fight back?

But I didn't get a chance to answer those questions. Because something else attacked me first.

Without any warning, I saw a huge white creature of some kind, flying furiously out of the black shadows. I didn't know what it was. But I knew it was coming directly at me!

It was flying straight at my face!

It had long, fierce claws that looked like a dozen daggers. And all the claws were extended, gleaming in the moonlight, trying to rip out my eyes!

Chapter Twelve

What was this big white creature? And why was it attacking me?

I ducked, bending wildly to get out of harm's way in time. I almost made it.

The flying white attacker missed my eyes — but just barely caught the top of my head with two of its sharp claws. I reached for the wound and felt the warm, sticky blood trickling from my scalp.

Then I heard a frantic flapping of feathers and an angry clucking — and saw that my attacker was a great white rooster that had lunged at me from the shadows of the dark barn.

I didn't know anything about farms or farm animals — but I sure had never heard of killer roosters before! Then again, I had never heard of killer horses either.

At that moment, I knew I didn't want to find

out any more about them — not killer roosters or killer horses or killer anything else. I turned and ran from the barn as fast as my frightened, shaky legs could move.

As I tore from the rundown barn, the animals all stirred in their stalls, stamping their hooves and snorting. The rooster cackled and flapped its wings fiercely.

It was as if all the animals were saying, "This is what you get for disturbing us! Don't come back! Unless you want worse from us next time!"

Believe me, I had *no* plans to go back! Except back to Chicago and my familiar city life — as soon as possible. Brad could keep his fresh country air and delicious country food and different country ways.

I didn't like any of them. I wanted to go home to the security of my parents and my computer games.

But before the night was out, I would hope for something else even more. I would hope to see Chicago and my parents and my computer again *just once* before I died.

I would hope and pray with all my heart for enough luck just to stay alive.

Chapter Thirteen

I raced back to the house at a full gallop. Demon or Tornado couldn't even have caught me if they had tried to chase me down. I didn't know I could run so fast.

And I didn't slow down for anything until I was safely inside the back screen door.

Then I crept quietly through the creaking old farmhouse into the bathroom, where I cleaned up my bleeding head with soap and water and antiseptic. My injury looked like nothing worse than a little scratch.

But that rooster attack had been too close! I knew it was no accident. And I felt very afraid.

What was happening to the animals on my cousin's farm? Did farm animals always act this way? I'd never heard Brad talk about anything like this before — and he had seemed as surprised as anyone when Demon and Tornado began to bite people.

I slipped back into my bedroom without waking up Brad and quickly was under the covers, shivering with fear. I tried to answer all the questions that zoomed around like laser beams inside my head.

I believed that I was smart enough to figure out why the animals wanted to hurt people — and smart enough to decide what we should do about it. But I wasn't. And I'm not sure anyone else could have figured it out either.

No matter how hard I attempted to understand them, the animal attacks were a complete mystery.

Uncle Bob and Zeke still weren't home from the hospital. But I felt too tired to wait up for them — even though I wanted to tell them about the assault by their rooster.

I wanted to tell Brad about it, too. But I couldn't wake him up over something that sounded so silly. Would my cousin really believe the rooster had tried to claw out my eyes?

So I tried to put aside all my fears and let myself fall asleep. Maybe things would look less scary in the morning.

I took off my big, black glasses and set them

on the night stand beside the bed. And I closed my eyes.

I noticed the house crunched and groaned all on its own — without anyone walking along the old wooden floors. Odd noises echoed down the long hallway that led from the living room to the bedrooms.

Plat! Twick! Pop!

Ggggrrrrrrreeeeeeeeeeeeeeeeeeeeeeeeeeee!

I couldn't sleep with all these strange sounds. Our home in Chicago didn't make sounds like that. Why did they have to happen in Brad's house — especially tonight? Things had been frightening enough already.

I put my glasses back on, crawled out of bed and slowly opened the door to my room.

The door squeaked a little and I peeked around the corner carefully, afraid of what I might find.

But I saw nothing.

Only the heavy shadows in the living room at the end of the black hallway.

I closed my door and tiptoed back toward my bed. I knew there was nothing dangerous inside the house now. No crazy men with axes. No people-eating horses. No eye-gouging roosters.

Maybe I could finally get some sleep. Even if I did have to sleep in the Death Room.

I started to climb back into bed. But that was when I noticed the most terrifying sight I had ever seen.

Outside, just beyond my window, the farm animals had gathered into small groups. Dozens of animals in dozens of groups. All of them were free and loose in the farmyard, milling together.

I had left the door to the old barn open, and the animals had simply walked out into the moonlight. The horses and the cattle and even the roosters.

And somehow all the other animals had gotten out, too. The black and white cows from the new barn. And the sheep and the goats from their pens and the chickens from their coop.

And the farm animals looked as if they were talking to each other in some way. Planning something.

Something terrible.

They neighed and clucked and bleated and mooed together, nodding their heads and scratching at the ground.

The horses seemed to understand the cows and the bulls seemed to understand the chickens and the goats seemed to understand the sheep. They moved together, all the different animals, in little restless gatherings.

And sometimes two or three of the animals turned their heads at exactly the same time, looking toward the farmhouse.

And I was sure the farm animals were looking right at me, looking straight into my face through the window.

Dozens of killer animals were watching me, plotting something awful against the city boy who slept in the Death Room.

<u>Chapter Fourteen</u>

I felt sure the animals were plotting against me somehow. They wanted to hurt me — the computer geek.

But what could I do?

I knew the only thing to do now was to wake up Brad. Even if he thought I was nuts for telling him the animals were talking to each other.

He could see for himself how they had collected into little clusters, making quiet sounds and looking toward the Death Room. He wouldn't have to take my word for it. He could come and look out the window and find out the truth.

"Brad, wake up," I said, slowly opening his door. "Brad. Psssssssssttt! Brad! It's Winston. You've got to wake up!"

"Huh? Hmmm? Wha's it — Huh?" Brad grumbled sleepily. "Winston, is that you? What's wrong? Why aren't you asleep?"

"Brad, you've got to get up quick. Come into my room for a minute. Hurry," I begged him.

"What for?" Brad replied, annoyed now. "I was sound asleep, Winston. It's the middle of the night. Whatever it is, it can wait. Tell me about it in the morning!"

And with that, Brad rolled over and covered his head with the pillow.

I walked inside his room and shook his shoulder.

"Brad! Come on! You've *got* to get up! Right now," I ordered. "This is serious! It's a matter of life and death!"

That got Brad's attention. And this time, it was no dumb fake-out game.

"Huh? Life and death?" Brad said, sitting up in bed. "What are you talking about, Winston?"

"Brad, listen — I'm not kidding. I'm serious this time!" I said, speaking quickly. "I couldn't sleep so I walked outside to the old barn. And some big white rooster tried to scratch out my eyes!"

"Scratch out your eyes? What? Winston, this

isn't funny!" Brad said, laying back down on the bed. "We said we weren't going to pretend things to scare each other anymore."

"No wait, Brad! I swear to you — cross my heart and hope to die! I *swear!* I'm not lying! And now the animals are all out of their barns and everywhere else and they're in the barn yard. They're — They're — well, the animals are all talking to each other!" I explained, embarrassed at my own words.

But I knew I was telling the truth!

Brad groaned and tried to go back to sleep. Now I decided that I couldn't afford to wait any longer. I had to do something to get Brad into my room.

So I grabbed my cousin's arm — the one Demon hadn't bitten — and *pulled* him out of bed!

Thwunck! He flopped on to the floor. Brad looked a little like a fish dropped on to the deck of a boat.

"Winston!" he shouted angrily. "I'm going to kill you!"

And Brad jumped up off the floor, chasing me into my room across the hall. I held up my hands to show him I didn't want to fight — and then I pointed through the window to the barn yard.

Brad stopped and looked out. Then his face got even angrier than before.

"You think this is some big joke, Winston? We have to get up early and do chores! See if you think it's so funny when you have to work in a few hours," Brad shouted.

"What are you talking about?" I asked. "Don't you see the animals — Right outside, they're all gathered — "

But when I looked out the window, I saw only a still barn yard illuminated by pale moonlight. The animals were gone.

"Brad, I *swear!* Why would I lie to you?" I protested. "All the animals on the farm were loose, right outside my window. They were all talking together in little groups, looking at me inside the Death Room. They were plotting against me, Brad. They wanted to kill me!"

Then Brad suddenly understood something and he didn't seem as angry anymore.

"Winston, you were only dreaming. I thought

you were just trying to get even with me again for scaring you today. But you must be having night-mares. You probably just got all scared because of the horse bites and that stupid computer game, *Animal Killers*," Brad said.

"Then what about this?" I said, showing Brad the scratch on my scalp. "You see? I got that from the rooster. I ducked when he attacked my eyes with his claws. I just barely got out of the way in time."

"Hmm, that does look like a scratch from a claw," Brad said.

"You see, I told you. It's all true. Everything I just told you," I replied.

Brad seemed like he was starting to believe me. At least a little. But he didn't have to wonder very long whether I was trying to fool him.

With loud whinnies and the stamp of ap-proaching hooves, Demon and Tornado raced by my bedroom window. They were running side by side.

The two gray appaloosas circled the barn yard, rearing and kicking their hooves at the half moon. They shook their heads wildly, heavy drool dripping from their mouths. Then they reared again and ran off into the night, still side by side.

"Winston! You did go outside! And you left the barn door open!" Brad hollered.

"But Brad, you don't understand. *All* the animals are out! Even the ones — " I stammered. But Brad interrupted me.

"You geekhead jerk! Now Demon and Tornado are loose! Come on! We've got to go get them and bring them back to the barn before Dad gets home!" Brad said.

We each rushed to put on our clothes and then tore outside, looking for signs of Demon and Tornado. For a moment, we saw nothing in the moonlight.

The only sound was the crickets in the distant fields. And the rustling of leaves in the wind.

Then a terrifying dark shape appeared over my cousin's shoulder.

"Brad, look out!" I screamed at him.

I suddenly saw that the shape was the two wild horses racing from behind the house. They ran shoulder to shoulder. And now they were only six feet away from Brad.

They instantly began to throw their front hooves high into the sky, above my cousin's head.

Demon and Tornado were trying to bash in Brad's brains!

Chapter Fifteen

*AAAAAAAAAAAAIIIIIIIIIIHHHHHHHHHHHH
HHHHHH!*

I screamed at the top of my lungs.

At that very moment, Demon and Tornado came crashing down with their powerful feet toward Brad's head.

Luckily, my cousin was a good athlete. He hit the dirt and rolled under the horses' legs. Demon and Tornado missed him by no more than an inch.

"Run, Winston!" Brad yelled at me. "Run into the house!"

The horses kept rearing, rising up on their hind legs and trying to smash Brad with their front hooves.

But Brad was too quick for them. He rolled on the ground — to his right, to his left, to his left, to his right.

The blows from Demon and Tornado missed

again and again and again.

"Run away, Winston! Get inside and lock the door!" Brad shouted.

But I couldn't leave my cousin alone with two mad horses trying to trample him.

I grabbed a light, metal lawn chair off the porch nearby and flung it as hard as I could toward Demon and Tornado. It didn't hurt them. But it was enough to frighten them. They backed away from Brad.

He scrambled to his feet and sprinted toward me. Pulling my arm hard, Brad dragged me onto the porch and inside the back door as Demon and Tornado reared and raced away. They disappeared into the blackness.

"Winston, this is crazy!" Brad said breathlessly as he locked the screen door. "This has never happened. Nothing like this. Not ever! I've never even *heard* of horses behaving this way! Not tame horses like Demon and Tornado. What could be wrong with them?"

"I don't know. But I know I've never been so scared — ever!" I answered. "I've been scared practically the whole time I've been in the country."

"This isn't what the country is like, Winston! The country is a peaceful, beautiful place. I'm telling you, this has *never* happened before. We take good care of the animals. And the animals are good to us. They give us milk and wool and meat," Brad explained.

I could tell he was very upset by all of this. And I knew something very strange was happening. Farm life couldn't be like this all the time.

Farm life had never been like this anywhere in the world before! For some reason, everything had changed on this farm. Now it really was as if Brad and I were stranded on a foreign planet.

I began to feel like Captain Kirk again, looking for a solution to our dangerous problem.

The transporter wasn't working! The communicators were knocked out! Brad and I were alone on a new, bizarre world! Surrounded by aliens! Faced with death!

What would Captain Kirk do?

"Let's get to our computer, Spock!" I ordered.

"Spock? Huh?" Brad asked. "Is that what you

called me?"

"Uh, I meant Brad. Sorry," I said.

We hurried to Brad's room and I flicked on his computer. Then I picked up the *Animal Killers* box.

"What are you doing with that? This is no time to play stupid computer games, geekhead! We've got a big problem," Brad said. "Demon and Tornado are on a rampage. And we have to get them back into the barn before Dad and Zeke get back from the hospital."

I knew Brad still didn't understand how bad the problem really was. Demon and Tornado were the only animals we had seen when we were outside. The other horses and the cattle and sheep and goats and chickens all were out of sight.

I was sure Brad hadn't believed me when I said every animal on his farm was roaming free.

But there was no time to convince him now.

I took the four disks from the *Animal Killers* box and began to install them on the hard drive of Brad's computer. It only took a few minutes, but Brad kept trying to pull me away the whole time.

"Leave me alone, you jockhead!" I snapped at him.

After I finished installing the software, the computer walked me through a sample game of *Animal Killers*, giving tips on how to play. This was just what I was after.

"Jerkbrain! Why won't you stop this? I need you to help me," Brad said. "We have to go bring back Demon and Tornado!"

"Just a minute, Brad. Just one more minute and I think — *Wait! Aha!*" I said excitedly. "Here it is, Brad! This is it! This is it! I knew it! I was right!"

"What? What are you talking about, Winston? What were you right about?" Brad asked.

"I think I've figured out why the animals are rising up against us. It's a rebellion, Brad!" I answered. "The animals are rebelling! And the answer was right here on your computer all day long!"

Chapter Sixteen

"The animals are rebelling? That's nuts, Winston!" Brad said. "Rebelling against what? You must be losing it after being so frightened by the horses. Come on! We need to go round up Demon and Tornado!"

"No, wait! Read this and you'll see what I'm talking about," I explained. "It's too strange not to mean something. Look at the game, Brad! Just look! It explains everything!"

Brad leaned down toward the computer, bending close to read the game instructions off the monitor. This is what the *Animal Killer* instructions said:

"Animal Killers is a computer game of imagination, skill and bravery.

It brings you to a small New England farm, where the cows and horses and chickens outnumber

70

the people by 50 to 1. The farm also has many sheep and goats. You will be forced to defend your life against the attacks of these beasts — without injuring even one of them.

In the game, the farm animals begin a rebellion against you and your family, who live in an old house on the land. The animals have organized themselves into an army against your family — intent on eating you and your loved ones before any more animals are slaughtered for food.

You suddenly find yourself in a strange world where gentle animals become deadly, where grass-eating horses and hay-crunching cows begin to eat people. You can hide. You can run. You can attempt to capture the animals.

But if any animal is injured or killed, ten more animals from surrounding farms will take its place to attack you."

"Wow! This is so weird!" Brad exclaimed. "Do you think this is what's happening to Demon and Tornado?"

"And all the other animals on your farm, Brad. Keep reading," I answered.

Brad and I continued looking over the *Animal Killers* instructions:

"The animal rebellion begins when a tame riding horse named Devil bites one of your family members on the arm. Another gentle horse named Twister soon bites and kicks a farm worker.

The attacks continue with chickens and roosters trying to claw out the eyes of your family. Then, all the farm animals gather in a mass meeting late at night to plan the destruction of everyone in your house.

As the animals launch repeated surprise attacks, anything can happen."

But Brad and I couldn't read any more of the computer game instructions. We were interrupted by a fierce banging against the side of the house, right next to Brad's window.

It sounded as if something was trying to break through the wood, just like when Zeke fooled us with the rock.

Then we heard the wild whinnying of horses and the furious *crack, crack, crack* of hooves against the house. Demon and Tornado were trying to smash through the old building to eat us.

And this time, we knew Zeke wasn't anywhere around.

We were alone and under attack by a deadly army of animals.

Chapter Seventeen

This time it was a real attack.

We could hear Demon and Tornado crashing their feet into the house, neighing and snorting as their hooves thundered against the wood.

But for some reason, I didn't hide behind the door of Brad's room as I did when Zeke played a trick on us.

Instead, I shut off the computer. Then I ducked behind the bed with Brad to decide what we should do. A geekhead and a jockhead against a farm full of killer animals.

"I'm really scared, Winston!" Brad said breathlessly. "The animals want to eat us! And Dad's not even here to help! What should we do?"

"We need to be calm, Brad," I answered softly. "We need to come up with a plan. Somehow, we've got to try to get away from here."

"How can we do that? The nearest neighbor is five miles from here. And we have killer farm animals every step of the way in between," Brad said. "We'd never make it if we tried to run."

"I think we need to figure out some way to outsmart the animals," I replied.

"How can we do that?" Brad wondered.

Demon and Tornado smashed against the house and whinnied furiously as my cousin and I talked. We didn't have any time to waste.

"I don't know for sure yet. But I don't think we should hurt any of the animals," I said firmly. "Remember, Brad — everything that happened in the game has happened almost exactly the same way on your farm. If we hurt any animal, maybe ten more animals from other farms will take its place."

"I agree with you about that, Winston," Brad said, nervously looking toward the wall of his room. "We can't take a chance on hurting any of them. But we need to think of something to do!"

"And we'd better think of something quick!" I yelled, pointing toward the wall. "The horses are getting inside!"

Hooves were breaking through the wall of Brad's room.

Clack! Clllaaaaaammmth! Spuuuuzzz!

The wood was breaking, giving way beneath the powerful feet of deadly horses. And now the plaster in Brad's room was chipping away in great clumps as Demon and Tornado hammered through the wall.

Brad and I looked at each other, sheer terror in our eyes. We knew this could be the end.

Demon and Tornado were hungry. And we were about to become breakfast!

Chapter Eighteen

The plaster was smashed to bits.

We could see through to the outside. The hole grew quickly larger, showing the fierce eyes of Demon and Tornado.

The murderous horses bucked and reared and slammed their feet into the wall. Soon the hole would be big enough for them to squeeze inside the house. Big enough for them to get through and eat us!

"Come on, Brad," I hollered, grabbing my cousin's hand. "We've got to get out of here! NOW!"

We bolted down the hallway into the living room. What we saw there shocked us so badly we almost couldn't move!

Goats were gathered at every window of the living room and kitchen, even at the doors. They were eating through the metal screens! Eating their way inside to allow the rest of the animals to come after us!

Outside, beyond the goats, the scene was wild — like something from a nightmare.

Sheep and chickens by the dozens shifted back and forth across the ground, nervously waiting for the goats to finish their work. Now and then, an impatient chicken would fly at one of the screens, its sharp claws extended to tug angrily on the metal.

The animals seemed like football players before the Super Bowl — pumped up and ready to get into the game. Only this time, Brad and I were the footballs.

Past the sheep and chickens, other animals ran around as if they were insane. Horses and cows and bulls ripped through the farmyard in a frenzy, running at top speed, then stopping and suddenly spinning in crazy circles.

Brad couldn't believe his eyes.

"I don't believe this! I just don't believe this! This can't be happening," he kept repeating. "I must be asleep. This has got to be some terrible dream!"

"It's no dream, Brad. It's real. We're under siege by a farm full of killers," I answered quickly.

"But why? Why now? We've always slaughtered animals for food on our farm," Brad said. "It's just the way things are on a farm. Farmers grow vegetables and raise animals and they eat some of the vegetables and some of the animals. It's the way we live. Why are they attacking us for that after all these years?"

"I wish I had some clue, Brad. But we can't stand around worrying about that now. Those goats have almost eaten through the screens," I said. "We've got to find some place to hide!"

Brad looked fearfully toward the windows. The goats gnawed on the metal screens. Another few bites and the hens and roosters could flap their way inside.

Lots of hens! *Lots* of roosters!

And we both knew their claws would go straight for our eyes!

"Come on, Winston! Follow me," Brad said, running down the long, black hallway.

Even though I had my glasses on, it was hard to see where I was going. We were moving too fast in the dark hall, racing for safety.

That was when it happened. Running full tilt, I

smacked into a small table that held a planter of flowers. I tripped over the table, end over end, tumbling head first to the ground.

My head banged hard against the wooden floor — *Whamp!* And the ceramic planter fell on top of my head right after that, spilling dirt all over me.

I was knocked cold. Unconscious. Motionless.

Just then, Brad heard the first chicken claw its way into the living room, flapping its wings to wiggle through a hole in some screen. Then he heard another chicken squawking angrily as it squeezed through another window.

Then another chicken. And another!

Four bloodthirsty chickens were in the house, running down the hallway, ready to rip out our eyes!

And I was completely helpless, lying on the floor in a heap!

Chapter Nineteen

Brad had to do something — fast!

As the chickens ran down the hall, he picked my glasses up from the floor, grabbed my wrists and pulled me into the bathroom.

Then he slammed the door shut and locked it, just in time. The chickens began to scratch and claw at the heavy wood separating them from us.

"Winston, wake up! Are you all right?" Brad was saying. He splashed cold water on my face. Then he lightly slapped my cheeks. "Winston, Winston! Wake up! Please, please wake up!"

"Owwww," I said, slowly moving and rubbing my forehead. I had hit the floor very hard. And the ceramic planter hadn't helped my head any, either. "What happened? Was I kicked by Demon?"

"You were kicked by the table in the hall, you clumsy nerdbrain!" Brad replied. "You almost got us killed."

"Where are we? What's that noise?" I asked, still groggy.

"We're in the bathroom. It's the strongest room in the house. Dad always said to hide here if we had a tornado," Brad explained, handing me my black-frame glasses. "And that noise is a bunch of chickens scratching and pecking at the door, trying to get at us. At least there's no window for the goats to eat through!"

"Yeah, and no window for us to get out, either," I said, sitting up carefully and squinting to look around. It was hard to see anything because Brad didn't want to turn on the lights. It seemed safer in the dark somehow. "We're trapped in here, Brad. Once those horses break through the wall of your room and get into the house, we're dead. They'll kick down this door faster than you can say *Animal Killers*! And then they'll eat us alive!"

The beaks of the chickens pecked incessantly at the door. They sounded like four machine guns firing at the same time.

And then there were six machine guns. Then

eight! Then twelve!

One by one, more chickens and roosters clambered into the house — and joined the others to peck and claw at the wood.

The pecking was getting louder and louder: *Tut! Tut! Tut! Tut! Tut! Tut! Tut!*

The scratching was growing angrier and angrier: *Scraw! Scraw! Scraw! Scraw! Scraw! Scraw! Scraw!*

Finally, one beak poked through to the inside of the door. We could hear the wood splintering now, giving way with each new peck. The chickens were slowly getting inside.

Suddenly we heard a different sound: a hard thud against the door. Then another thud, even harder than before. And another.

In the darkness, I could barely see Brad's eyes looking fearfully into mine, his mind horrified by the same thought. The horses were in the house!

It was only a matter of minutes until their powerful hooves would break down the door. Only minutes until the door came crashing down around us, letting in the hordes of crazy chickens with eye-ripping claws!

The hooves banged harder and harder against the door. *Blump! Blump! Blump!*

The door rattled with every hit.

"This door can't last long against those horses," I said.

Sweat ran down my forehead. It wasn't only dark inside the bathroom, it was hot.

"And the chickens are already pecking through the wood," I said. "We've got to make the door stronger!"

"There's no way, man!" Brad answered. "There's nothing in this bathroom that can hold out against the horses! But, wait a second, Winston. Shhh! Shhhhhhhhhhh!"

We turned our ears toward the door and listened again to the banging. Brad touched my shoulder.

"That's not the horses, Winston! Listen. It's not hard enough for that. And it's too low to the ground," Brad said. "I think it's the goats butting their horns against the door. That's a pretty thick piece of wood. Even with the chickens pecking through it, we still have some time. It's going to take a while for a bunch of goats and chickens to get into this bathroom."

Brad and I tried to think of some way to get out of this mess. But we weren't having much luck.

Then from farther away, we heard a different noise. A huge crash and banging and clomping in another room. Something had made a terrific racket.

Demon and Tornado! They had bashed their way through the wall of Brad's bedroom at last.

They really were inside the house now!

Brad and I shook as we heard the heavy clattering of hooves walking down the wooden hallway floor. *Clack! Clack! Kwomp! Kwomp!*

The horses were coming our way!

The chickens stopped pecking and the goats stopped butting. All the other animals must have cleared a path for the great appaloosa horses to approach the bathroom.

There were several loud, ferocious whinnies, like the sound two horses might make if they were fighting each other. But we knew they weren't fighting each other.

Because right after that, we heard the first

house-shaking attack of horse hooves against wood. Demon and Tornado were battering the door.

Even that heavy old piece of oak couldn't stand up to so much punishment for long.

Brad and I were trapped inside the dark bathroom, no possible way to escape! And people-eating horses were coming in after us!

Chapter Twenty

The powerful front hooves of Demon and Tornado rammed the door over and over.

Kraaaagg! Kraaaag! Kraaaag! Kraaaag!

We heard one hoof rip through the door. Splinters of wood skittered across the tile floor of the bathroom. A few more hard smashes of horses' feet and Demon and Tornado would be inside! Eating us!

I tried hard to think. What would Captain Kirk do *this* time?

"We can hide in the bathtub and cover ourselves with towels!" I said frantically. "Maybe the horses can't eat through the thick cotton. It's our only hope, Brad. Come on!"

"No, it's not!" Brad said. "I didn't want to use this unless we had to. But we have to! Come with me, Winston! Hurry!"

Before I knew what had happened, Brad had

jumped up to grab a small cord that dangled from the bathroom ceiling. He pulled it hard with both hands and a narrow staircase dropped down — a staircase that led to an upstairs attic.

The oak door crashed into the bathroom with an ear-splitting bang.

Brad yanked on my arm and dragged me up the stairs. Then he grabbed a handle and pulled the stairs shut behind us as Demon and Tornado charged into the room.

The horses were looking for victims. Looking for food!

And they weren't happy we had escaped. They fumed and sputtered and spit, clomping around angrily on the tile.

I couldn't believe it! We were safe! It really was as if Scotty had beamed us aboard the Enterprise just in the nick of time!

"Excellent, Brad!" I shouted. "I was sure we were horse-food that time! You saved our lives. But I don't get it. Why didn't we come up here right away instead of waiting inside the bathroom? This is an awesome place to hide!"

"Well, uh, er — just forget it, geekhead!" Brad said, a little nervously. "I have my reasons. Let's just think of some way to get out of here."

"Why should we leave? Let's wait here until your dad gets home. Maybe he'll know how to stop the animal attacks," I said.

"No way! I want to get out of here as fast as possible. Come on, Winston! There's another staircase on the other side of the attic. Let's go over there and see if it's safe to get down," Brad said.

It was dark in the attic, but not as dark as the bathroom. There was one small window where moonlight entered, casting a pale, eerie glow around the filthy attic.

Everything was covered with a thick layer of dust. Spider webs hung from old wooden beams. Big, black spiders dangled near our heads.

Still, it seemed the safest place on the farm.

Below us we heard frustrated whinnies and bleats and moos and clucks. The house was full of animals now — horses and goats and sheep and cows and chickens. All waiting for us to come down.

They stomped around, knocking over lamps

and furniture. Horrible sounds echoed up to us — the sounds of light bulbs breaking, of tables shattering, of chairs thudding to the ground.

The animals were tearing the house apart.

"We've got to get out of here!" Brad said. "Let's get to that other staircase right now!"

He sounded scared, but I didn't understand why.

"Brad, you're crazy! We can't go downstairs. Even if we use that other stairway, the animals will see us," I said. "They'll bite and stomp and claw us to death! And then Demon and Tornado will eat us, one limb at a time! We have to stay here!"

"We *can't* stay here!" Brad shouted angrily. He began to walk across the attic to the other staircase. "Just trust me, Winston! Follow me!"

"Brad, stop!" I said, grabbing my cousin's shoulder. "Listen to those sounds downstairs! Do you want to walk down into that? You're losing your cookies! There's no way I'm going down there with those killer animals!"

"And there's *no way* I'm staying up here!" Brad yelled, breaking away from my hand. "I'm not crazy! Just follow me!"

Then I spotted it: the reason Brad wanted to get out of that attic so fast. And the reason he didn't want to go there in the first place.

Actually, there were *lots* of reasons. Probably more than three dozen of them!

Because that's about how many fat, greasy gray rats were in the attic!

I could see their little rat eyes shining in the moonlight as they moved out of the shadows. They squeaked and squealed and scampered around the end of the room.

They were all gathered on one side of the attic. A great gray mass of fat rats!

They were looking directly at us, all of them at once.

And then in one large wave, the rats began to move. It was like they were marching — right at us!

They looked angry! And hungry! Their sharp front teeth glinted in the light.

Maybe these rats are part of the animal rebellion, too, I thought. Maybe they want to eat us alive, just like the horses!

Downstairs, the animals were still bounding and bashing and breaking everything. Brad and I would have no chance if we tried to escape down either staircase.

But we had no chance if we stayed in the attic, with hungry rats ready to swarm over us!

Things looked as bad as they could get.

I hoped Brad had another trick saved, something that would get us out of this horrifying mess.

When he looked over at me with tears in his eyes, I was sure he had some plan to save us.

But instead, my cousin only opened his mouth — and screamed!

"*HEEEEELLLLLLPPPP!*" he hollered at the top of his lungs.

Chapter Twenty-One

I have no idea why, but that bloodcurdling scream actually calmed me down.

I just knew I had to think of something all by myself. Now!

I didn't have time to imagine that I was a star-ship commander or anything. I was just Winston, the computer geek. And I had to figure out some way to save our lives before the rats chewed us into bits.

I ran over to the attic window and looked outside. The only animals in sight were some horses and bulls, racing in wide circles far out in the corn fields. All the others seemed to be in the house or in the barns or maybe just running wild somewhere else.

I flung open the window. There was nothing below us except the ground. Nothing to stand on at all.

But I had no time to come up with some fancy

plan. We had to move fast.

"Brad, come here! Stop screaming and come here. Right now!" I hollered. I must have sounded like I was his father or something.

Brad obeyed my instructions and ran to the window, ahead of the approaching tide of rats.

"Crawl out the window and hang by your hands," I ordered. "It's won't be that far to drop to the ground that way. And wait for my signal before you let go!"

Without a word, Brad nearly leaped out the window. He grabbed the ledge and hung on as tightly as he could. Then I squeezed through the window beside him, letting my legs hang down toward the ground.

Both of us held on, dangling above the farmyard. I could see the wave of rats sweep across the floor in front of the window. For now, at least, they were confused.

But I knew we didn't have long before the rats would find us and crawl up to the window ledge.

I looked around carefully as I clung to the window. I was looking for any animals.

Still no sign of them close by.

"When I give the word, let go and start running, OK?" I asked Brad. "Run to the old barn. But don't go inside until I get there."

I knew Brad was a faster runner than me. I didn't want my cousin rushing inside to find a barn full of human-eating animals staring at him.

"OK," Brad answered. "You give the word."

I glanced around one more time. I still didn't see any animals — and I couldn't hold on much longer anyway. My hands were starting to slip.

"All right — JUMP!" I shouted.

Brad and I let go of the ledge at the same instant. We flopped on to the ground, banging our shoulders together as we landed.

But we were all right. Brad got to his feet right away and started running for the old barn.

My glasses fell off when I jumped. I found them quickly, blew the dust off, put them on, and started tearing after Brad, moving my feet as fast as they could go.

I was running for my life!

When I reached the barn, Brad was waiting. I

was puffing hard but he was hardly out of breath. Sometimes I wished I was a jock like him.

At least there were no animals anywhere near us.

"We made it this far anyway," Brad said worriedly. "Good work, Winston. This time *you* saved our lives! But now what do we do?"

"Remember what the game *Animal Killers* said? We can hide. We can run. We can try to capture the animals," I recalled.

"We've been hiding and running! You don't mean we should try to capture them, do you? How could we catch all those farm animals? They're strong and some of them are really big. They'll kill us if we try to capture them," Brad said.

"I think the computer game will tell us how to capture them. I'm sure the clue we need is in that game," I said.

"But — But the computer is *inside the house!*" Brad said. "The animals are running around crazy in there. You can't go back inside!"

"Yes, I can," I said, sounding a lot braver than I felt. "I have to!"

"But how, Winston? How?" Brad asked.

I looked down for a second, trying to figure things out. Then I snapped my fingers and smiled.

"I think I just came up with a plan!" I replied.

Chapter Twenty-Two

Quickly, I explained everything to Brad.

My plan had to work! If I couldn't get back inside the house to the computer game, we had no chance of ending the animal uprising. I was sure of that!

Armed only with my idea, my cousin and I split up. Then we put the plan into action.

Brad hurried to the new red barn, which was just a short run away from the old barn where we had stopped to talk. He grabbed a long ladder that lay alongside the new barn. Then he set it up so he could climb to the barn roof.

As he did this, I tiptoed toward the house, watching for the first signs of any animals coming my way.

When Brad was done setting up the ladder, he ran back toward me, stopping halfway between the old barn and the house. And he stood there, waiting.

By now, I had sneaked onto the back porch of the house. I could hear the animals still banging and crashing inside, expecting us to come down from the attic at any moment.

I took off my glasses so I would look a little more like Brad. Then I waved to my cousin. He waved back.

That was our signal. Everything was ready.

Now we had to hold our breath, try out my plan — and hope we didn't get killed!

Without warning, I jumped in front of the back door and stared inside at the animals through the ripped screen. I shouted at them and wiggled my hands by my ears.

"Hey, stupid!" I yelled at them. "You can't catch me! Can't catch me!"

Then I turned and raced off the porch at full speed, shouting as I ran.

"Can't catch me! Can't catch me!" I hollered.

The animals stormed out of the house, knocking the screen door off its hinges.

Cattle and chickens and goats and sheep. And

then two horses. All charged out the back door as though they had only one thing in mind: murdering me!

Their nostrils flared and their eyes flashed hatred as they clattered after me.

Or rather, the boy they *thought* was me.

I had run around a corner of the house after leaving the porch. I was hiding.

It was Brad who was running toward the new barn, using his speed to tear across the farmyard well ahead of the animal assault. And he was yelling, just as I had.

"Can't catch me! Can't catch me!" Brad shouted.

The animals thought it was really me they were chasing, exactly as I'd hoped they would.

Brad made it to the ladder and scrambled up to the barn roof. I knew the barn was newer and sturdier than any other building on the farm. He would be safe from the animals on the roof — even if the horses kicked the barn with their hooves and the bulls battered it with their horns.

It would take a long time for any farm animals

to knock down a whole new barn!

Brad grabbed the ladder and pulled it up after him. Then he waved to show me he was all right.

Quietly, I stepped inside the house and walked down the long, dark hallway to Brad's room.

The house was eerily silent. There were no sounds, except the awful creaking of the wooden floor as I walked. I felt sure all the animals were gone.

At least, I prayed they were gone!

Inside Brad's room, I picked up his computer from a pile of books scattered around the floor. Demon and Tornado had knocked over his desk and cracked the computer monitor.

I plugged everything on the computer back together and turned on the power. Then I called up the game *Animal Killers* on the broken screen. I breathed a sigh of relief. The hard drive wasn't damaged.

I desperately needed to find some answers!

I scrolled through the game instructions that I hadn't had time to read before the horses chased us out of the bedroom. Something in these instructions would have to tell me how to capture the animals, I thought. There must be some way to win the game.

But I was wrong! This is what the instructions said:

"Animal Killers is a computer game with endless fun because the game itself is endless.

Players score points by skillfully hiding from the unpredictable animal attacks. Or by running away from the animals in time after an attack begins. Quick and clever decision-making by players is required.

Some points also may be scored by capturing the animals. But this tactic is only useful as a way to locate new hiding places. The animals always are strong enough to escape any place that holds them.

No barn or fence will stop the Animal Killers! Nothing can stop them! And there is no escape!"

That was when I heard the scratching, like fingernails clawing at cement.

I turned my head and felt a flash of terror through my whole body!

A huge white rooster was perched on the broken plaster of Brad's bedroom, right where Demon and Tornado had kicked through the wall. It was probably the same rooster that tried to tear out my eyes in the old barn!

But this time, the rooster knew it could get me for sure. I was only three feet away from its long, sharp claws!

And I was sitting at the computer, frozen with fear!

Chapter Twenty-Three

So this is how everything would end for me, Winston the computer nerd. I would die at the computer.

The mad rooster would pluck out my eyes and then Demon and Tornado would eat me alive!

All while I was reading the rules for a computer game called *Animal Killers*.

But I wasn't ready to give up yet!

I reached down with my hand and grabbed one of Brad's books. Then I threw it at the rooster.

I missed. And now the rooster was really angry, squawking loudly and ready to leap for my eyes with his claws.

So I grabbed the next thing my hand could find — the box that held the computer disks for *Animal Killers*. I was ready to throw the game box and run.

But I never got the chance.

For some reason, the rooster suddenly looked afraid of me. The furious look was gone from his eyes. He seemed tame and gentle now, the way roosters are supposed to behave on a farm.

The great white rooster tilted his head to look at the box in my head, then turned and walked away. He was clucking softly and bobbing his head back and forth.

I couldn't believe it! What had happened?

But I had no time to think about anything. Because right then, I heard Brad shouting at me from the barn.

"Winston, come quick! Heeellllpp!" he hollered.

I ran out of the house through the hole in Brad's wall.

Brad was still on the roof. But he was surrounded by *every animal* on the farm. They had come from everywhere — from inside the barns and from the fields and from the woods.

And they were all bashing against the red wooden barn, trying to knock it down.

But the barn was still standing strong, just as I had guessed it would. I felt sure it could take the animal-bashing for a long time. So why was Brad shouting for me now?

"What's wrong?" I yelled.

"Get the gun, Winston! Get the gun in my dad's room! We have to shoot them or there's no hope for us!" Brad hollered. "Look, over there! On the hill! There are more animals coming!"

On the hill that overlooked the farm in the moonlit distance, dozens of animals were marching toward Brad's farm. There must have been another twenty horses and thirty bulls and maybe forty or fifty goats.

I knew what it meant. Brad had done something to hurt a few of the horses and bulls and goats below him. And now new animal killers were coming from surrounding farms to join the attack against us — ten more for every one Brad had injured.

"I'm sorry but I got scared," Brad shouted at me. "I don't think I hurt the animals very bad! I just threw my shoe at Tornado and bruised his eye a little. Then I threw the other shoe at Demon and maybe bruised his back. And I threw the ladder at the bulls and goats and it landed on their heads."

"I can't get the gun, Brad," I yelled toward the barn. "We'll just get ten more killer animals for every one I shoot. Besides, I don't know how to shoot a gun anyway!"

But I had another idea.

"Brad, don't do anything to hurt the animals again," I shouted. "I'll be right back! I have a new plan!"

Most of the animals were interested only in knocking Brad off the barn roof and eating him. But I saw that two black-and-white cows and a goat finally had noticed my shouting.

They were breaking away from the barn. And they were walking slowly toward the house — toward me!

I hurried back into Brad's bedroom and grabbed the *Animal Killers* game box. Something about this computer game is very strange, I thought.

I remembered how so many things that happened in *Animal Killers* were like things that happened on Brad's farm. And I also remembered how the rooster reacted with fear when I picked up the box to throw it.

I was positive the rooster wasn't afraid of being hit by the box. He was afraid I would do something to *damage* the box.

I had a hunch about what to do now — but not much time to do it. The cows and goats were getting closer and closer to the house.

I opened up the *Animal Killers* box to make sure all the computer disks were inside.

They were.

Then I ran to the fireplace in Brad's living room. I took down a box of matches from the mantle over the hearth.

My parents taught me never to play with fire but this was an emergency. Even they wouldn't mind me lighting a match to protect my life! And my cousin's life, too!

So I struck a match and held it to the cardboard *Animal Killers* box. And when it was on fire, I threw the box into the fireplace and watched it burn.

The box and plastic disks popped and crackled and sizzled.

Pizzzzzz!   Kew!   Zzzzzzzzzzzzzrack! Ssssssssssssaaaaaaaaaaaaappp!

As the box shriveled and folded under the flames, I heard Brad shouting again from the barn.

"Hey, Winston! Come here! Quick!" he screamed at me.

When I ran outside, everything had changed.

In the moonlight, I could see dozens of farm animals milling lazily around the barnyard. None of them were banging against the red barn anymore.

None of them seemed interested in eating Brad — or in anything else for that matter. They looked tired, moving around slowly as if ready to sink to the ground and sleep.

This is more like it, I thought. This is how farm animals should act.

And I noticed that the animals on the hill were gone now, probably walking back toward their own farms. Everywhere, things appeared quiet and normal.

I walked carefully out to the red barn, looking worriedly at all the animals. But the animals paid no attention to me at all.

I put the ladder up for Brad and he climbed down from the roof, smiling and patting me on the shoulder.

"You did it, geekhead! You're a genius, Winston!" Brad said. "What did you do?"

But as I opened my mouth to explain everything, I noticed Demon staring right at Brad. The horse had a funny look in his eyes again — the kind of look he wasn't supposed to have anymore.

A strange, angry look. A hungry look. A people-eating look!

Then, slowly, Demon began to walk toward my cousin. The horse's teeth were bare and gleaming in the pale moonlight.

How could this be happening? The *Animal Killers* box and computer disks were destroyed. That should have made everything on Brad's farm peaceful. It should have, but it hadn't!

"Brad, look out!" I screamed.

As I shouted, though, I could see it was already too late.

Demon was charging toward my cousin at a gallop, ready to take the first delicious bite out of Brad's leg!

Chapter Twenty-Four

Demon lunged at Brad's leg, his big teeth ready to chomp!

Luckily, Brad was quick enough to leap on to the ladder just in time.

Demon roared past my cousin, then turned to make another run for Brad's leg. But Brad just scrambled part way up the ladder.

"Winston, run! Go into the house and hide! I'll keep Demon busy!" Brad hollered.

That was when I suddenly understood!

I thought I knew why Demon was acting crazy again!

"Stay there, Brad! Don't let Demon get you! I'll be right back!" I shouted, racing back toward the house.

Brad stood halfway up the ladder to taunt Demon, keeping the horse's attention away from me.

Then when he saw that I was safe, Brad climbed all the way up to the barn roof and waited for me.

Behind me in the barnyard, I could hear all the animals beginning to stir, shuffling and clawing the ground. They were getting restless, moody, angry. One by one, the farm animals were turning into animal killers again!

I had to hurry.

I flew into Brad's room and saw that *Animal Killers* still appeared on his cracked computer screen.

That was it! The game was on the computer's hard drive! Only the box and disks were destroyed!

I knew just what to do. This was one time that being a computer geek really paid off!

I cleared the screen of *Animal Killers*, then called up a list of all the files on Brad's hard drive. I clicked his computer mouse furiously, then wildly typed letters and punched in keyboard commands.

Finally, I hit one last key — *Bocka!*

Then one last click of the mouse — *Ticka!*

And it was done. *Animal Killers* was completely deleted from Brad's computer!

Erased!

Gone forever!

By the time I got out to the red barn, Brad was already back down the ladder.

He was beaming a big smile and quickly shook my hand.

"My cousin, the genius geek!" he said proudly.

"My cousin, the lightning-fast jock!" I answered, just as proudly.

Brad and I agreed that we made a great team.

I helped him put the animals back into their barns and coops and pens for the rest of the night. And as we worked, I explained the whole thing to Brad.

We decided our biggest problem now would be getting Uncle Bob to believe our story about an animal rebellion! The farm was a disaster! And the house was a total mess!

Uncle Bob and Zeke would be back from the hospital very soon. At least they could help us clean up. As you can imagine, there was a lot of work to do.

"This place is so dirty it looks like a bunch of animals live here," I joked as we straightened up the living room.

Brad and I both laughed for the first time all night.

But I knew everything was really back to normal when Brad walked over to me — and punched me in the arm! Hard!

I punched him back! Just as hard!

"Jockhead!" I said, smiling.

"Geekhead!" he replied, smiling.

"You know, it's not too bad here on your farm when the animals are normal. I think I might get to like it — even the morning chores!" I said. "Just promise me one thing for the rest of my vacation, Brad."

"Sure, Winston. Anything for my favorite cousin! Just ask," Brad answered.

"Tell your father not to buy any weird computer games!" I said, snickering. "We don't need any more games coming to life!"

"Yeah, ok! Sure," Brad said, snickering along with me. "Unless maybe he can find one called, *Beautiful Teenage Girls Who Kiss Jockheads and Geekheads*!"

For some reason, we both thought that was

very funny and laughed together for a long time.

BE SURE TO READ THESE OTHER
COLD, CLAMMY SHIVERS BOOKS.

A GHASTLY SHADE
OF GREEN

JASON'S MOTHER TAKES HIM AND HIS
LITTLE BROTHER ON A VACATION TO
FLORIDA – BUT NOT TO THE BEACH. SHE
RENTS A LONELY CABIN ON THE EDGE
OF THE EVERGLADES, WHERE THE
ALLIGATORS BELLOW AND THE PLANTS
GROW SO THICK THEY ALMOST BLOT
OUT THE LIGHT. JASON DOES NOT LIKE
THIS PLACE AT ALL. AND STRANGE
THINGS START TO HAPPEN: KEEPSAKES
DISAPPEAR FROM HIS DRESSER. HIS
BEAGLE WINDS UP MISSING. AT FIRST
JASON SUSPECTS BURGLARS, BUT THE
TRUTH IS MORE FRIGHTENING. JASON
MUST MAKE A DESPERATE EFFORT TO
SAVE HIS FAMILY – AND HIMSELF.

Shivers™

GHOST WRITER

M. D. Spenser

Chapter One

Amber Elliston loved her life. But she hated a lot of things, too. Asparagus. The gross smell when her dad smoked his pipe. The dumb dress with a big bow on it that her mom made her wear to a wedding.

But so far in her twelve years, she had hated nothing more than this.

Her family was moving.

They were going to live in some lame small town in Georgia where nothing ever happened. So what if her mom, Carol, had grown up in Jackson? Big deal. That didn't mean she had to live there again.

This place didn't have a movie theater. There wasn't an FAO Schwarz. Or even a McDonald's!

Boring, boring, boring. Amber thought to herself. My life is over.

How was she supposed to know about the strange and scary secret that was waiting for her in Jackson? The one that would change her life forever?

It was August. The Elliston family sat crammed into their black Honda, driving away from Amber's home.

Ever since she was a baby, she, her older brother, David, and her parents had lived in an apartment in a tall building in New York City.

Amber loved it there. She loved the rows of skyscrapers out her window high above the busy street. She loved running to the elevator in the lobby, and pushing the button that said UP. She would miss the noise outside. She already missed playing in the crowded park. She missed her friends.

"You can write to them," her mother said, trying to make Amber feel better.

"Write them? Nobody writes letters anymore," Amber complained. She knew she would probably never see her home again.

Amber looked out the window of the back seat for a long time. She watched her city disappear. As the family drove south, the towns got smaller and smaller. Finally, they were in a hot, lonely part of the country where there were more trees and fields than houses.

David rode in the back seat, too. He spent most of the time reading a book. It was one of those adventure stories about dragons and castles that boys seemed to like. He was fourteen, and didn't talk much anymore. His legs had gotten so long he had to stick his knees up just to fit in the car.

Amber's mom sat in the front looking at a map. Her dad was driving.

Amber looked at the back of her dad's head and was angry. He was the reason they were doing this. It had all started when her dad was walking home from work late one night. That was when he had felt a cold, clammy hand on his shoulder.

And a gun pressed hard against his back.

Chapter Two

Amber's dad had decided to move the day he got mugged.

He had lived in New York all his life, but no one had ever tried to hurt him like that before. Thankfully, a police officer had walked by just as the big, scary man pulled the gun. The thief ran off into the night. And Amber's dad wasn't hurt.

But it changed his life forever.

Other than being her dad, he was Mark Elliston, Newspaper Editor. After years of working for The New York Times, he had suddenly decided to take a new job. He was going to own the newspaper in the small town where her mom was from.

Amber would never forget the day he told them.

"Guess what? I've got great news," her dad said with a smile that looked fake.

He ran his fingers through his long shaggy hair

like he always did when he was nervous. She and David sat on the sofa waiting for the worst.

"I'm tired of living in the city," Dad said. "We're moving to Georgia."

"Georgia!" Amber and David said in disbelief. "Where is that?"

Amber started crying. David went to his room and slammed the door.

"Oh come on," Dad said. "You're going to like it. Really. I promise. There's too much crime here in the city. This is a chance for us to spend more time together. Everything is going to be okay."

Sure, Amber thought. Everything's going to be okay. For *you*. It's always about you, she thought. What about us?

For days, Amber and David begged not to go. They had long talks with their mother.

"Why? Why do we have to do this?" Amber pleaded. "I'm not moving!"

"Honey, it will all be for the best. You'll see," her mom said. "I can still do my job, and I think your dad will be much happier."

Amber's mom was a graphic artist. That meant she drew pictures on a computer, which she could do anywhere. She sold them to people, who put them on things like brochures and greeting cards. One time she even made a picture that they used on MTV in between videos. That was pretty cool.

But Georgia? Way uncool.

Amber went on strike and refused to come out of her room for hours. Or at least until she got hungry. David put a note on his door that said "Parent Free Zone." He played Myst for a whole week.

But that didn't change a thing. Here they were on their way to Jackson, Georgia. Wherever that was.

The Elliston family had been in the car for fourteen hours. Amber curled up on her pillow, which was the last thing she took from her room before the movers came. She felt like someone was dragging her away. Or pulling her away. She closed her eyes and listened to the road hum underneath the tires.

A song came on the radio. It wasn't anything she usually listened to, like rap or rock. Or that boring public radio her mom always had on. It was a really old tune. There was a piano playing. It sounded like the music from one of those old films her mom watched all the time on cable. It reminded Amber of the movie with a pretty woman who sang into one of those standup microphones. A high, haunting voice began a song.

6

"Come to me, come to me, oh beautiful one. Come to me, or I shall come to you . . . "

The sad melody made Amber look out the window. It was night now, and very black. There were no lights anywhere. It was so dark all she could see was the faint outline of her own reflection in the window.

Amber stared at it like she was looking in a mirror. Slowly, something started to change in the glass. Her long straight brown hair drew up and became light and curly. There was a flower tucked in her hair over her ear. Her lips curled up into a big smile with bright red lipstick. She laughed.

But Amber had not moved her own face at all.

Then she saw it. The painted mouth slowly whispered.

"Come to me, come to me, oh beautiful one. Come to me, or I shall come to you."

Amber's eyes opened wide. She put her hand over her mouth.

Suddenly, the face in the window became very frightened. Its eyes got big, and started to cry. It screwed up into a horrifying ball of terror and pain.

Suddenly, there was a terrible scream.

Chapter Three

"Honey! Honey! Are you okay?"

It was Amber's mom. She was leaning over the back seat, shaking her daughter's leg.

"Jeez, you scared me to death," David said. "What's your problem? You sounded like you'd seen a ghost or something."

"I did! I did see something!" Amber insisted. "It was a face. And it was looking at me in the window!"

"Oh, Amber. You must have had a bad dream," Mom said.

"Or maybe something popped out at you. A Velociraptor maybe. Eeeek! Eeeek!" David teased. He leaned over and pretended to bite her arm.

"Stop it! Stop it!" Amber cried. She hated that dinosaur movie, especially the part where the girl had to hide in the kitchen. That's what she felt like now.

Trapped and afraid. Something weird had happened. Something unnatural. She had seen that face. It was real!

Or maybe she really had just fallen asleep.

"Honey, it's okay. It's been a long day and I'm sure you're tired," Mom said in her comforting voice. "Settle down. It's time to wake up now. We're getting close."

"Close to nothing," David grumbled.

Their car hummed along a narrow country road. Rain started falling. Amber's dad turned on the windshield wipers. The drops got bigger, so he made the wipers go even faster. Soon the rain got so hard that Amber couldn't see out the front window. Even the light from the car headlights could barely shine through the huge sheets of rain that pounded through the darkness. The downpour was so loud it sounded like water gushing from the fire hydrants on her street back in New York.

"Here," Mom said, pointing to the left. "I think we turn here."

Amber's dad slowed down the car, and turned onto a dark narrow road. Amber heard a ping-ping-ping noise under the car. Her mom explained that it was gravel. They didn't have paved streets out here.

The road went deep into the woods. Her dad drove very slowly now. Amber could tell he was nervous. He gripped the steering wheel tightly with both hands. Mom was leaning forward in her seat, trying to see through the pounding rain and the black night.

As they wound around curve after curve, the headlights hit things Amber had never seen before. A yellow sign blew wildly in the wind. It had a picture of a cow on it.

What was that all about, she wondered?

Around another curve, the headlights lit up a rusty old car half way down a ditch. She saw a big black mailbox. Then the car headed over a wooden, one lane bridge. The water underneath sounded like the roar of a subway train.

Suddenly lightning flashed, lighting up their faces as if they were having their picture taken. Bang! The thunder cracked right on top of their car!

"I'm scared!" Amber cried as the wind blew against the Honda.

Then Mom screamed.

"Mark! Look out! Someone's in the road!"

The last thing Amber remembered seeing was the flash of a young girl in the headlights. She was wearing an old white party dress and standing right in front of a giant tree next to the river bank.

Their Honda was heading straight for her, until Amber's dad swerved. She heard the sound of the tires skidding on the gravel. Amber clutched her seat belt right before she heard the loud *BOOM!* followed by the tinkling of broken glass.

She felt something wrap itself around her neck.

Chapter Four

Amber looked up from the back seat of the car. A giant tree limb had crashed through the front windshield. Its branches stuck into their car like legs from a giant wooden spider. Sticks and twigs were strewn all over the place — in her hair, all over her clothes. A vine was wrapped around her neck.

She looked over at David, who was brushing leaves off his wet shirt.

"Oh my gosh! Oh my gosh! Is everyone all right?"

It was her dad's voice.

"Yes, yes, I'm okay," Amber's mom answered. "Kids! Are you all right?"

"Yeah, I'm okay," David said.

Amber couldn't speak. She just cried.

"Boy, that was a scare," Dad said. "Let's not panic. First, everyone make sure they're not hurt in any way. Can you move? Do you hurt anywhere?"

The family sat in silence for several minutes. All of a sudden, the rain stopped. They heard the sound of a car up ahead. Amber could see the headlights coming towards them.

"Hey, is anybody in there?" a man's voice shouted. They heard the slam of a car door.

Amber's dad managed to open the door on his side of the Honda. He got out, shaky, but okay.

"Hello! Yes, I think we're all fine here," he said to the man. "Couldn't see in all this rain, and I guess we got too far off the road."

"Well, you're really lucky. You almost hit that big tree there," the man said. "Good thing you swerved in time to run into nothing but that branch. I'm Bill Johnson. I'm the sheriff around these parts. What are you doing out here this time of night?"

"We're the Ellistons," Amber's dad said. "We're moving here. I guess that makes us your new neighbors."

"Oh yeah," the man said, running his hand over his gray beard. "I know about you. You're the ones who bought the old McAfee place. You're from New York, aren't you?"

"Yes," Amber's mom said. By this time she

had gotten out of the car too. "I'm Carol Elliston. Actually, I used to be Carol McAfee. That's my grandmother's old house. It's been empty for years, but we decided to buy it and fix it up. I lived in Jackson when I was a little girl, but we moved to the city a long time ago. I haven't been back here since then. Mark's going to be the new editor down at the paper."

Amber's dad suddenly asked, "What was that young girl doing out here in the middle of the night? She was standing in front of that tree. We nearly hit her!"

Mr. Johnson stared at them for a long time. When he spoke again, he did not mention the girl.

Chapter Five

"Well, tell you what," Sheriff Johnson said finally. "Doesn't look like your car is going to be getting anywhere for a while. What do you say we get everybody in my patrol car and let's get you home."

Their parents turned and looked at Amber and David and motioned for them to get out of the car. It wasn't easy, but Amber crawled over the mess and climbed out on David's side.

Everyone piled into Sheriff Johnson's big yellow and black Ford. It had a radio in the front, pieces of paper all over the floor and Coke cans scattered about.

"Wait a minute!" Amber called out.

She hopped out of the car, ran back to the Honda and grabbed her pillow.

"Guess you'll need that tonight, honey," her mom said. "We all could use some sleep."

Sheriff Johnson drove up the road, around a

curve, and started up a hill. They saw a small farm-house. They passed a wide open space, then another house. Then a barn, then one more house. All the buildings looked very old, and were made out of wood.

The patrol car turned left and headed up a steep hill. Amber figured this must be a driveway.

"Well, here you are," Sheriff Johnson said, pulling the car to a stop.

Everyone got out and stood and stared at their new home. The house was much bigger than Amber had expected. Although it was night, a full moon had popped from behind the clouds so Amber could see clearly.

The house was three stories high, with big pointed windows sticking up on top. There was a long porch that wrapped all the way around the front. An empty rocking chair creaked back and forth.

Must be the wind, Amber thought.

"Wow, you weren't kidding when you said this place needed fixing up," Dad said to Amber's mom.

"Well, honey, no one has lived here in fifty years," Mom said sheepishly. She had only shown Dad pictures of the place, taken when she was a kid. "I think a little paint and elbow grease will do the job."

Sheriff Johnson was very quiet.

"Nope," he said. "I don't think anybody has lived here since the accident."

Chapter Six

The accident? Amber thought.

Her mom and dad stared silently at each other.

"I think it's about time we got in out of this weather and got some sleep," Dad said finally, changing the subject. "Amber, why don't you be the first to walk through the door of our new home?"

He tried to make it sound as if it was a big honor.

"The real estate lady told me there's no lock on the door," Mom said. "You can probably walk right in."

Amber climbed slowly up the front steps. Her sandals made creaky noises as she walked across the wooden boards of the porch.

She came to a giant door, with all kinds of fancy swirls around the edges. A big M was carved in the middle. A metal door knocker dangled from a single nail, and looked as if it was about to fall off.

Amber reached out and touched the door knob. It was funny looking — made of some kind of white glass that was very cold when she touched it.

Slowly, she turned the knob. Just as she was about to push the door inward, something pulled hard on the other side. It jerked her so quickly she fell face down inside, onto a very cold, hard floor.

A creepy glowing light hit her straight in the face.

Chapter Seven

"Gotcha!"

Amber heard a scary — but very familiar — laugh.

"David! I hate you!" she cried.

She looked up to see her brother standing inside the house in front of her, holding a flashlight.

"Oooooo. Ooooooo-oooo! I'm the ghost of the old house! I'm the face you saw through the car window," he said. "I'm coming to get you."

He held the flashlight up under his chin, making his face glow like a monster's.

"David, you come out here this instant," Mom said in her I'm-really-angry-now voice. "That was a really mean trick to play on your sister."

"Oh, Mom. I was just kidding," he said, hoping he wouldn't get into trouble.

"How did you get in there?" Dad asked.

"While you were talking, I went around to the back. The door there was wide open, so I just came on in," he said. "Boy, this place is a mess!"

Mom had had enough.

"Look, we've been through a lot tonight," she said. "It's getting really late. Let's all go inside and let Sheriff Johnson go home."

David pointed the flashlight into the big living room. A huge fireplace was built into one wall. Paint peeled from the ceiling.

Amber's dad took the flashlight from David and shone it around the room. It finally lit up a long string hanging down from a light bulb.

"Here, this should do the trick," he said, pulling on the cord.

A bare light flashed on. Now they could see the room around them.

It was completely empty.

"Drat!" Mom said. "The furniture isn't here yet! The moving company told me they were going to deliver everything today!"

"Oh, honey. Don't worry," Amber's dad said. "They probably got stuck in all this rain."

"I've got some blankets and sleeping bags out in the patrol car," Sheriff Johnson said. "You can use

21

those tonight."

Amber's dad followed him outside.

David started walking through the old house, turning on lights like he had seen his father do. There was a big bedroom off to one side.

"This is where your dad and I are going to sleep," Mom said.

As Amber and her mom looked at the big, dusty room, they heard a loud crash.

"Mom! Mom!" David shouted from the next room. "Something's got a hold of my foot!"

Chapter Eight

Amber and her mom ran to where David was screaming.

He was lying on a big, winding staircase. It led up to a dark hallway on the second floor of the house. His foot was sticking down inside one of the steps.

The old wood had cracked underneath David's big tennis shoes. His foot had gone straight through the step.

"David, David," Mom said reassuringly. "Nothing's got your foot except that old step. Look down and you'll see. You've fallen in through a hole in the wood."

David looked down and pulled his foot out of the broken step. He looked embarrassed that the accident had scared him so much.

"Guess we'll have to get some carpenters in to fix that as soon as possible," Mom said. "Especially since your bedrooms are upstairs. Let's go up and take a look."

The three of them climbed the rickety steps to the second floor. Another bedroom opened to their right. On their left, they found a smaller room with a big window.

"This is where you're going to sleep, Amber," Mom said. "This is your new room."

Amber wasn't sure she liked it very much. It was musty, and smelled like the closed-up section of the library at her old school. But the window was really neat. It was taller than any she had ever seen before in someone's house. And there was a seat built right into it!

I could sit there and read my books, she thought. Or talk on the phone to my friends.

Then she got sad. She remembered that she didn't have any friends to talk to here. But she was too tired to think too much about that now.

She yawned.

Dad and Sheriff Johnson walked into the room with a bundle of sleeping bags.

"Here you go," Dad said. "This should get us through the night."

Amber's mom helped her spread the soft blankets over the hard floor. Amber still clutched her pillow. She plopped down on her makeshift bed, holding the pillow close to her chest.

"Goodnight," Mom said, rubbing Amber's hair softly. It made her feel safe, like when she was a little girl back in New York. "Everything will be better in the morning," Mom added. "You'll see."

Amber lay on the floor a long time, but could not go to sleep. The moon was bright. She almost felt as if she was back in the city, where the lights outside never went out.

She could see her room clearly now. There were big flowers on the wallpaper. An empty bookshelf was built into a closet. Someone had left an old picture of the ocean on the wall.

I'll have to get rid of that, Amber thought. Right then she decided one of the first things she would do when the movers came would be to put up her posters.

And I could hang my crystals in this big window, she thought excitedly.

She jumped up and ran over to see just where they could go.

Looking outside, she noticed that her house sat at the top of a big hill. The moon lit up the yard, which rolled steeply down toward a house next door.

Funny, she hadn't noticed it when they drove in.

It was much smaller than Amber's home. She could barely see what it looked like, except for a light in a window upstairs.

Wow! Someone must live there! Amber thought. Maybe it was a family. A family with kids! Maybe there was a girl she could play with. That would be great!

Amber pressed her face to the glass to get a better look. Suddenly, she saw a shadow behind the curtains of the other house. It was the outline of a person, but Amber could not tell whether it was a boy or girl.

She wiped the dust off her window and stared harder.

Suddenly, the curtains moved. Someone was standing in the other window!

It was not a kid. It was an old lady with long white hair that hung to her waist. She had very white skin, and coal black eyes that shone in the dark.

And they were staring straight at Amber!

Chapter Nine

The next thing Amber knew, it was morning. The sun was filtering down on her face. It was hot and sticky.

Then she remembered. She wasn't in her bed in New York. She was on the floor of a spooky old house that was going to be her home now. No bed. No friends. Not even any air conditioning.

Amber lay on the strange blankets and looked at the ceiling. Then she sat straight up.

That lady! That lady was staring at me from the window last night! She remembered. Suddenly she was afraid.

Amber jumped up off the floor, and ran into the hall and down the stairs.

"Mom! Mom!" she cried.

She heard the sounds of someone cooking. The smell of bacon hung in the air. But where was the kitchen in this old house? Where was her family?

"Honey, I'm in here. In the back of the house," Mom's familiar voice said. "Just keep going straight ahead of you."

Amber walked toward the back of the house and into the huge, old kitchen. Her mom stood over a big, white stove. She was poking at something in a big black skillet.

"Feel like some breakfast?" Mom asked with a smile.

"Sure, I guess so," Amber said. "But where did you get any food? Or stuff to cook with? Have the movers come?"

"No, not yet. But Sheriff Johnson came over first thing this morning and brought up a whole box of supplies. And some pots and pans to make things in. His wife sent over bacon, eggs and even some home-made biscuits. Come on over here and get yourself a plate. You're about to sample some real country cooking."

Suddenly, Amber didn't feel like eating.

"Mom," she said. "I saw something really scary last night."

"We all saw some pretty scary things last night, honey," Mom said. "But Sheriff Johnson, Daddy and David have gone to get the Honda. They think it will be okay as soon as we get the windshield fixed. And the movers will probably show up today with all our things. I promise — it's going to start feeling just like home, real soon."

"But that's not what I'm talking about," Amber said. "I saw something outside my window last night."

"What?" Mom asked.

"Well, after I went to bed I couldn't sleep. So I got up and looked outside," Amber said. "Did you know there's a house just down that hill?"

"Yes," Mom nodded. "It's been there for a very long time."

"But Mom," Amber continued. "When I looked over at it last night, there was someone in the window. It was an old lady. And she looked just like a witch!"

Chapter Ten

Amber's mom turned off the stove and set the food aside.

"Sit down," she said. "I want to tell you something."

The two of them sat cross-legged in the middle of the empty floor.

"That was not a witch you saw," Mom explained. "That's old Miss McAfee. She's lived here all her life. In fact, she used to live in this house when she was a little girl. And she's related to you. She's your great aunt. That means she was your grandmother's sister."

This was all very confusing. Amber had never known her grandmother. She had died before Amber was born. In fact, she didn't know any of her mother's family. They had never been to New York. And Amber's family had never been here.

Before now.

"Remember last night when Sheriff Johnson said no one had lived in this house since the accident?" Mom asked.

"Yes," Amber said. "But I didn't know what he was talking about."

"Well, many years ago, the whole McAfee family lived in this house. There were three sisters — Helen, Hannah and Harriet. Harriet was my mother — your grandmother. Helen and Hannah were my aunts. That would make them your great aunts. The woman you saw in the window last night is Hannah. She's old now, and the only one left. She's lived by herself for fifty years. She hardly ever comes out of her house. I haven't ever even met her myself."

"But why? Why would someone want to be alone like that?" Amber asked.

"Fifty years ago, there was a terrible accident. Helen was killed," Mom said sadly. "They found her on a rock in the middle of that river we crossed over last night. She was only sixteen years old. Hannah was the one who found her. The sheriff said it was an accident. But soon everyone started rumors that Hannah had pushed Helen in. They had been angry at each other. They were both in love with the same boy.

Hannah heard people whispering about her at Helen's funeral. She ran away for a long time. Then she moved into that house next door, and hasn't spoken to anyone since."

Amber could not believe what she was hearing. A murder mystery! Right in her own family!

"But you don't need to worry about any of that," Mom said. "It happened a very long time ago. And old Miss McAfee keeps to herself. She's harmless. She'll never bother you. They say all she does is tend her garden. And play an old piano."

Amber and her mom got up, went over to the stove and fixed their plates.

It was very quiet out here in the country. Too quiet.

But all at once, Amber heard a very strange noise.

A loud roar came up their driveway. Amber could tell it was not a car. Suddenly it stopped with a loud screech.

Then a noise louder than anything Amber had ever heard shook the room.

BLAM!

Although she had never heard one, except on TV, Amber knew it was a gun.

Chapter Eleven

Amber and her mom dropped their plates and ran outside. Sheriff Johnson stood in the back yard holding a long shotgun. He leaned over and reached for something on the ground in front of him.

Amber gasped. He picked up a big, black snake.

"That fellow was heading straight for the house," he said, tossing the snake into the woods. "But you're lucky. It was just a chicken snake. Not anything that would hurt you. But I like to get rid of 'em anytime I see 'em."

Amber heard someone giggle. A chubby little girl stood next to Sheriff Johnson. She wore shorts, a T-shirt and a pair of flip flops. A pair of glasses sat on her nose. She looked like she might be just Amber's age.

"Hey!" she said, with an accent Amber had

never heard before. "My name's Kelly."

"This is my daughter," Sheriff Johnson said. "She heard you were here, Amber, and she wanted to come up and meet you."

Kelly had not ridden up to the house in a car. She'd ridden a strange-looking motorbike that now sat in the driveway. It wasn't a motorcycle, exactly. It had four wheels, not two. And it was kind of small.

Amber stared at the strange vehicle. What was really weird is that Kelly had obviously been driving it. And she sure didn't look old enough to drive!

Kelly noticed Amber's confusion.

"That's my four-wheeler," she said. "Don't you have one?"

Amber shook her head.

"Oh, wow! All the kids here have four-wheelers," Kelly said. "That's how we get around. Want to take a ride?"

Before Amber could say "No way," her mom jumped in.

"I think maybe Amber's had enough excitement," Mom said. "Why don't you girls come inside and get to know each other?"

Kelly looked up at her dad, who nodded that it was okay.

"I'll be heading back on into town now," he told Amber's mom. "But Kelly can stay here and play a while."

"Sure," Amber's mom said. "That would be great!"

Amber could tell Mom was trying hard to make her feel better. But she was not sure she wanted this Kelly girl forced on her. She didn't look like the friends Amber had had in New York. She didn't sound like them either.

She bet Kelly had never even been to Central Park. She probably didn't like to read, and never even painted her fingernails pink. Amber thought Kelly looked like a real tomboy.

But, Amber thought to herself, I'll give it a try.

Sheriff Johnson hopped in his patrol car. Just as he was about to drive away, he stopped.

"Oh, by the way," he said to Amber's mom. "I forgot to tell you. When I took Mark and David into town this morning to see about getting the car fixed, I got this strange message."

Chapter Twelve

Sheriff Johnson reached into his shirt pocket and pulled out a note.

"Somebody named Don called my office looking for you," he said. "He left a message that said, 'We're coming now.' What does that mean?"

"Oh, thank goodness!" Amber's mom sighed. "Don is the guy from the moving company. That means our furniture will get here today!"

Sheriff Johnson shook his head as if he didn't quite understand.

"Well, we don't have moving vans come into these parts much," he said. "I didn't know what the guy was talking about."

He pulled out of the driveway, leaving Amber and Kelly standing there staring at each other. Amber figured she needed to be nice.

"Uh, want to come in and see my room?" she

36

asked.

"Sure," Kelly said.

The girls headed into the house and climbed the old stairs to Amber's new room.

"Watch out," Amber said. "Don't step on that third step. There's a big hole there. David nearly killed himself last night when his foot went right through it."

Kelly climbed over the broken step, and held on tight to the old wooden railing. It wobbled back and forth in her hand.

"Looks like that step isn't the only thing that's going to need fixing," she mumbled.

The girls reached the top of the stairs, and Amber took Kelly down to her new room.

"Wow!" Kelly exclaimed, looking around the big, empty space. "This is downright spooky!"

Even though Amber felt the same way, it kind of made her mad to hear someone else say it.

"Well, it's going to look great in here once my bed's up and I put my posters on the wall. And see?" she said, walking over to the big window. "I'm going to hang my crystals right here. . . . Ouch!"

Pain shot up through Amber's leg like she had been cut by a knife. She sat down on the floor, about to cry. She grabbed her foot and looked at the bottom.

Kelly gasped.

"Blood! There's blood all over your foot!"

Chapter Thirteen

Amber looked down and saw blood pouring from just below her big toe. She was cut. Something sharp had ripped open her skin. It really hurt.

"Mrs. Elliston! Mrs. Elliston!" Kelly yelled down the stairs.

Soon Amber heard her mother's footsteps pounding up to her room.

"What is it? What's going on?" Mom gasped.

"Amber's cut her foot! And it's bleeding real bad," Kelly said.

"Let's take a look at that," Mom said, cupping Amber's foot in her hands. "Kelly. Go downstairs and bring me a wet paper towel."

Kelly rushed off. She returned in a minute holding a wet paper towel. Amber's mom wiped it gently over the cut, sopping up the blood.

"Oh, honey, this isn't so bad," she said.

"Looks like you just stubbed your foot on a splinter or something. These floors are so old. I bet that's what happened."

"I've got a first aid kit on my four-wheeler," Kelly said. "My dad makes us all carry one. That's the only way he'll let us drive 'em. I'll go get it."

As Kelly raced outside, Amber's mom hugged her hard. They rocked back and forth gently as Amber started to cry.

"I hate this place! I hate this place!" she whimpered. "I wish we had never come here! I want to go home!"

Kelly showed up with a red plastic box. She sat on the floor and popped open the top.

"See," she said. "Here's a band aid. And a bottle of Methiolade."

Amber's mom opened the bottle and swabbed the red stuff over the cut.

"Ouch!" Amber cried. "That stings!"

"Oh, it only lasts just a second," Kelly jumped in. "We have to use it all the time. You get lots of cuts and scrapes out here in the country. A lot of times I put it on spider bites or when a thorn gets me good in the leg."

Amber's mom could see that her daughter

wasn't happy. She peeled the plastic stickers off the band aid and placed it on the bottom of Amber's foot.

"See, that's helped already, hasn't it?" Mom asked.

Amber sniffled. But she had to admit her big accident was not that bad after all.

Suddenly there was a loud roar outside. People slammed car doors, and shouted to one another.

"Oh, my," Amber's mom gasped. "It's the movers! Sorry, honey. I've got to go downstairs and show them where to put everything. Will you be okay?"

Amber nodded. Mom raced out the door.

The two girls sat on the big seat underneath the tall window. Amber nursed her foot. Kelly started chatting.

"I'm going to be in the seventh grade next year. My dad says you will be, too," Kelly said. "We'll be in the same class, because there's only one class for each grade here. Won't that be fun? Maybe we can sit next to each other. I'll introduce you to everybody. And I'll teach you how to ride my four-wheeler. I bet they don't have those in New York City. That's where you're from, isn't it? My dad said you lived in New York."

Amber wasn't listening much. She kept staring at the spot on the floor where she had cut her foot.

How could that have happened, she wondered. No splinters poked up. The old wooden floor was worn completely smooth.

She looked more closely. She saw one board that seemed to be a bit higher than the others. Its edges stuck up about an inch above everything else.

"That's what did it!" she cried. "I dragged my foot across that old floorboard."

Kelly stopped talking.

"Why is it sticking out like that?" she asked.

The girls got very quiet. Amber got up and walked over to the funny spot in the floor. She pushed her other foot against the strange board.

Whoosh!

It popped open.

Chapter Fourteen

Two girls peered down into a small, secret hole hidden underneath the floor.

They stared into the secret compartment. A piece of paper lay there, tied up in a faded pink ribbon. It looked very old.

"What is that?" Kelly asked.

"Shush," Amber said. "Be quiet."

She screwed up her courage, reached her hand into the dark hole, and pulled the paper out.

"A letter!" Kelly gasped. "It's an old letter!"

Amber held the crumbling note in her hand. She turned it over several times, examining the treasure she had just found.

"Should we open it?" Kelly asked. "I wonder what it says? Or who wrote it? Or how long it has been here?"

"Well, Mom said no one has lived in this house

in fifty years," Amber said. "So it must be really old."

Amber walked back to the window seat and held the old note up to the light. It was written on paper that had once been pale blue. It had nearly faded to white.

Eerie, ancient-looking handwriting adorned the front. It didn't look like the loopy cursive Amber had learned in the third grade. The words looked more like something off an old map. Or like those signatures she had seen at the bottom of the Constitution the summer her family had visited Washington, D.C.

"Look at that stamp," Kelly whispered. "I've never seen any like that before!"

Amber didn't recognize the picture on the old stamp. She did notice it only cost two cents. She looked closely at the handwriting on the front. The letter was addressed to Helen McAfee.

"It's from 1945," she told Kelly. "That would have been around the time of the accident."

Amber decided to hold the letter up to the light that streamed in through the big window. She saw a black spot right in the middle.

The spot started to move.

All of sudden, the black spot jumped out of the old letter and landed on Amber's face!

<u>Chapter Fifteen</u>

"Eeeeek!" Amber screamed, brushing her face wildly with her hands.

Kelly jumped up and stamped her foot hard on the floor.

"A Palmetto bug," she said. "It was a Palmetto bug."

Amber stared at her new friend.

"They're all over the place here," Kelly explained. "They're really big, and they look really scary. But they won't hurt you. The grossest thing about them is the way they look after they've been squashed."

Amber looked down at the greasy, yellow guts on the floor.

"Yuck!" she said. "That's worse than the roaches we had back in New York."

She picked up one of the paper towels her

mom had used to nurse her foot and wiped the bug guts off the floor.

"Amber, there's something I want to ask you," Kelly said.

"Sure," Amber said, tossing the dead bug in the corner.

"So, you know about the accident, huh?" Kelly asked.

"Not much," Amber said. "Just what my mom told me last night."

"Well," Kelly continued. "I wasn't going to say anything to you. But everyone has always said this house is haunted. They say the ghost of Helen McAfee walks here at night. Some kids say they have seen her out on the hill, wearing a white dress. Sometimes she picks flowers. She puts them in her hair. But she disappears before anyone can get close. She was killed, you know. Down by that big tree your family almost hit last night by the river. Her crazy sister, Old Miss McAfee, lives right there. Right next door to you."

Amber got very quiet.

"What? What is it?" Kelly asked.

"We saw a girl down by that tree last night," Amber said. "That's why we had the accident. My dad was trying to keep from hitting her. She was standing all alone in the rain. And you know what's weird? She had on a white party dress. And a flower in her hair."

Kelly stared at Amber. Suddenly, she grabbed the letter and pulled on the pink ribbon. The note unfolded, and the girls stared at the first lines written on the paper.

"Come to me, come to me, oh beautiful one. Come to me, or I shall come to you."

Before the girls could read the rest of the letter, a gust of wind blew through the window. It swept the letter out of their hands and sent it fluttering to the floor.

Amber jumped down to retrieve her treasure. Another blast of wind blew the letter back into the secret hole in the floor. Without thinking, Amber stuck her hand down inside to pull it out.

Then she froze. Something touched her fingers.

Something alive!

Chapter Sixteen

Amber screamed. She yanked her hand back from the black hole.

"What was that?" she shrieked.

Kelly rushed over and peeked in.

"Oooooh!" she yelled. "It's a rat!"

This was too much for Amber. Rats were supposed to live in New York City, not out here in the country. Her dad had promised it would be safe here. He said they were coming to Jackson because of all the crime and trouble in the big city.

Well, Amber had never touched a rat in New York City. And certainly not in her own house!

"Hey, don't get so upset," Kelly said. "I was just teasing you. It's not a rat. It's just a mouse. You find them out in the country all the time. We've got 'em in our house, too. My dad just sets traps, and that takes care of them. It won't hurt you."

Amber did not think Kelly's joke was funny at all. But before she could get too mad, she heard her mother calling from downstairs.

"Girls! Girls!" her mom hollered. "Come down here. I need you to run an errand for me."

Amber stared straight into Kelly's freckled, round face.

"Don't tell anyone about this," Amber said holding up the letter.

"Okay," Kelly said. "I won't."

Amber certainly didn't want to put her hand back into that hole. So she grabbed the faded blue letter and stuffed it into her pocket.

I'll finish reading it later, she thought.

The girls ran down the stairs into the kitchen. Amber's mom was busy telling the movers where to put all the boxes. They had already brought in the kitchen table, and some chairs.

"Yeah!" Amber shouted. "It's our stuff! Our table! Our chairs! They're finally here!"

Amber's mom motioned for her to quiet down.

"Listen," she said. "It's just crazy around here. It's going to take hours for the movers to unload everything, so why don't you girls do me a favor?"

Amber and Kelly listened.

"I want you to walk down to the mailbox. It's right at the foot of the hill," Mom said. "You know — right next to Old Miss McAfee's house."

Chapter Seventeen

Amber's mom reached into her purse and pulled out several letters.

Actually, Amber realized, they were bills. One was to the gas company. Another to the phone company. And one to the electricity people.

"I've got to get these in the mail today or we'll be in trouble," Amber's mom laughed. "We don't want them to shut off the lights before we even get moved in! Take these down to the mailbox, and put them in. Amber, you don't know this, but you've got to raise up the red flag to let the mailman know there's something waiting for him."

They didn't have to do things like that to mail bills in New York. At Amber's old home, they'd had a post office box down in the lobby of her building. Not one of these big black mailboxes that sat by the side of the road.

"Oh, don't worry Mrs. Elliston," Kelly piped up. "I know all about how to get your bills on their way."

Amber's mom handed the bills to her daughter just as the movers headed through the door with the living room sofa.

"Run along now," Mom said. "I'll see you later."

Amber stuffed the bills into her pocket and headed out the door with Kelly. They started walking down the long hill when, suddenly, Kelly stopped.

"This is stupid," she said. "Let's ride my four-wheeler!"

"I don't think we should," Amber said, knowing her mom would not approve one bit.

"Oh, it's okay," Kelly urged. "I ride it all the time. There's room for you on the back. That way we can get there in half the time."

Amber got a sick feeling in the pit of her stomach. She knew her mother would not want her on that strange bike. Then again, Amber didn't feel like taking a long hike into a place she had never been before. It *would* be a lot faster.

And maybe, Amber thought secretly, it might be kind of fun.

The girls headed back up the driveway. Kelly climbed on the four-wheeler, and motioned Amber to hop on behind her. With the flip of a switch, the machine fired up.

"Hold on!" Kelly said with a laugh.

Then something happened that made Amber feel more afraid than she had ever felt in her life.

Chapter Eighteen

She felt like she was going to die.

Forget the car accident the night before. Or the time she had fallen down the stairs in her old apartment building. Or even when they'd had to give her that big shot in her mouth to pull her teeth.

Amber felt as if her body was totally out of control, going so fast that she was sure to be killed.

Here she was, with a girl she hardly even knew, hurtling down the hill at breakneck speed. Amber was terrified. They went faster than she had expected, dizzyingly fast — faster than she had ever gone on the bike path in the park. Trees whizzed by. She held onto Kelly tightly as they zipped around corners and bounced over bumps in the gravel road.

It seemed like forever, but soon Kelly slowed the four-wheeler to a stop. The girls were sitting in front of two mailboxes.

"Here it is," Kelly said with a grin. "Stick your stuff inside. Then let's *really* do some riding."

Amber was relieved. She hadn't died. She hadn't even fallen off!

With a sigh of relief, she reached into her pocket, pulled out the bills, and placed them in the mailbox. She even remembered to put up the red flag her mom had told her about.

Without warning, Kelly started up the four-wheeler. In seconds, the girls were zipping down a rough trail off the main road. It wound through the woods, by a creek, and past an old barn. Amber could see someone's garden up ahead. It was filled with rows of corn, marigolds and other green things.

"Oh my gosh!" Amber yelled suddenly. "Kelly! Kelly! Stop this thing!"

Kelly slowed to a stop.

"You know what I did?" Amber said in a panic. "I put that old letter in the mailbox with Mom's bills! We've got to go back and get it!"

Without a word, Kelly turned the four-wheeler around and headed back to the road. Just as they approached the mailbox, she pulled behind a bush and turned off the engine.

"Oh no!" she said. "There's the mailman!"

A man with a baseball hat was driving a big, old green car down the shoulder of the road. He was sitting on the passenger's side, with his hand stretched way over to the steering wheel.

How could he drive a car like that, Amber wondered.

He leaned over to the mailbox and pulled out the stack of bills — and the old letter. He put them all in his big mail pouch. Amber and Kelly sat silently as he drove away.

"Well, I guess we'll never get to know what was in that letter," Kelly said with a sigh. "Maybe it was from Old Miss McAfee. Maybe she was threatening to murder her sister! Maybe she had written that she was going to kill her, and *we* would have solved the crime!"

Just as Amber was going to tell Kelly to shut up, she froze.

Someone put a hand on her shoulder. Someone with bony fingers and long chipped fingernails.

Someone whose hand looked like that of a witch!

Chapter Nineteen

Amber looked up at the person who held her shoulder so tightly.

It was an old woman. Amber had seen her somewhere before. Now she remembered — it was that white hair that hung down below the woman's waist. And those coal black eyes.

It was the woman she had seen in the window the night before!

Just as Amber was about to shriek, Kelly gunned the four-wheeler.

The girls zoomed out from behind the bushes. Kelly wheeled the bike as fast as it could go down the dirt path. Soon, they were back out on the main road. They zipped past the mailboxes, back up the road toward Amber's house.

Suddenly, Kelly pulled over and stopped.

"Oh my gosh," she said. "That was old Miss

McAfee!"

"Wow. I thought it was a witch," Amber sighed. "I thought we were done for."

"No, she's never hurt anybody. She's just kind of strange and creepy," Kelly said. "Funny, though. She *never* comes out to talk to anyone. Much less touch them. She must have been really mad at us."

Kelly and Amber sat on the bike at the side of the road for what seemed like a very long time. They didn't say anything to each other.

But that was okay. Although they had just met, somehow they knew they were going to be great friends. Being great friends means that sometimes you don't have to talk at all.

The sun was high above the fields. Amber heard the chirping of birds all around her. That was something she hadn't heard a lot in New York City.

Kelly leaned back and let the sun shine on her face. Amber did the same thing, trying to rest from her scare.

"I think I'd better go home now," Amber said.

Just as Kelly reached down to fire up the four-wheeler, the girls heard something strange.

It was piano music.

It began very softly. Then it got louder and

louder, as if someone was pounding on the keys. The music was old and sad.

"Gosh, that's creepy," Kelly said, starting to go.

"No. Wait!" Amber gasped. "I've heard that somewhere before."

A high, wailing voice began to sing.

"Come to me, come to me, oh beautiful one. Come to me, or I shall come to you."

Chapter Twenty

Kelly pulled the four-wheeler back onto the main road as fast as she could.

The girls sped up the hill. They were so frightened they didn't even try to hide that Amber had been on the bike without her mom's permission.

Amber's mom was standing on the front porch with her arms folded.

"Amber Elliston!" she said. She always called Amber by both names when she was mad. "Who told you you could ride on that bike with Kelly? Those things are really dangerous if you don't know what you're doing. And you weren't even wearing a helmet!"

Amber looked down and said nothing.

"It's my fault, Mrs. Elliston," Kelly said. "I talked Amber into riding with me. It's really not as bad as you think. All the kids out here ride four-wheelers."

Wow, Amber thought. Kelly is a good friend to stick up for me like that.

"Well, I don't care what all the other kids do," Mom said. "Do not *ever* get on that thing again until your dad or Sheriff Johnson can give you a safety lesson. Kelly, I think it's time for you to go home now."

Amber climbed off the bike and waved at Kelly as she drove down the drive. Just as Kelly reached the main road to town, Amber saw a familiar car turn into the driveway.

It was Dad and David. And the Honda!

They pulled up to the house and parked behind the moving van. David hopped out excitedly.

"Look! We got our car fixed!" he said.

"We were really lucky," Dad said, shutting the car door. "No major damage. They just had to replace the windshield."

"And guess what?" David added. "I've been bitten by a shark!"

Chapter Twenty-One

As Amber stared at her brother, he started laughing.

"Oh, David, quit teasing your sister," Dad said. "What David is trying to tell you is that he's *become* a shark. A Jackson Shark. David's now a member of the Jackson Swim Team!"

As the family went into the house, David told them how he had walked around town while the car was being repaired.

"There's a big pool right near Dad's new office," he said. "They were signing people up for the summer swim team. We start practice tomorrow."

David had been swimming since he was a baby. He had been on the swim team at his old school in New York. In fact, one of the things he had hated most about moving was leaving his swim team.

Even though he drove her crazy most of the

time, Amber couldn't help being happy that David was going to make some new friends, too.

Amber looked around the house. It was starting to feel like home. All their living room furniture was arranged neatly around the old fireplace.

Amber raced up the stairs to her room. There it was! Her bed! Her stuffed animals! Her books and posters!

She lay down on her bedspread with the pink flowers, curled up and fell asleep.

Hours later, when she woke, it was night. She went downstairs, and made herself a peanut butter and jelly sandwich. David was already asleep in his room. So was her dad.

Amber found her mom in a small room at the back of the house, hunched over her computer.

"Hi honey," Mom said. "Guess you can tell this is going to be my office."

She was drawing the illustrations for a new children's book.

"Were you able to get some sleep?" Mom asked, stifling a yawn.

"Yeah, I guess so," Amber said. "But I feel wide awake now."

"Tell you what," Mom said. "I think I'm going

to head to bed myself. But if you want to, why don't you play around on the computer for a while? It's okay. And guess what? We've even got our E-mail up and running — way out here in the country!"

Amber sat down. Her mom bent over and kissed her goodnight.

Amber stared at the menu on the screen. She clicked on the E-mail program and heard the familiar sound of the modem hooking into the phone line. She entered her password, and watched the color picture of a mail box flash on.

She was surprised when the flat computer voice said, "You've Got Mail."

Who would this be from, Amber thought. None of my friends in New York know my E-mail address.

For some reason, her girlfriends had just never gotten into computers. Usually, Amber just sent computer messages to fan clubs of her favorite music artists. None of them ever messaged back.

Amber clicked on the mailbox, and a message appeared.

Suddenly, Amber could not move. She felt frozen in place. A shiver ran down her spine as she read the words:

"Come to me, come to me, oh beautiful one. Come to me, or I shall come to you."

A photograph started to materialize on the screen. It was very old. First Amber saw blonde, curly hair. Then the face of a young girl emerged, with bright, painted lips.

She had a flower in her hair!

Just as Amber was about to run from the room, the picture moved. The girl in the photo turned her head slowly, looked straight into Amber's eyes and said:

"Help me. Help me. Help me help her."

Chapter Twenty-Two

Amber switched off the computer and ran straight to her bedroom.

She snuggled between her pink sheets. Soon, she was sleeping like a baby. She didn't stir until she heard the *clunk-clunk-clunk* of David's big tennis shoes on the stairs the next morning.

"Amber! Amber!" David shouted. "Get up and get down here for breakfast!"

Still in her nightgown, Amber trotted down the stairs to the kitchen.

Mom had a big breakfast spread all over the table. It was Amber's favorite — French toast, with lots of syrup and butter. She sat down at the table with her mom, dad and David. It had been a long time since the family had been able to do this.

"What time did you finally get to sleep last night?" Mom asked.

"Oh, I went to bed right after you did," Amber said.

"Didn't you get the computer to work?" Mom asked. "It was doing fine when I was on it."

"Yeah, it worked okay," Amber said nervously. "Uh, I just didn't feel like messing with it very long."

Amber sat quietly, thinking.

Should she tell her mom what she had seen on the screen?

No, she decided. She would just say I was dreaming, like she did when I saw that face in the car.

The family finished breakfast, and cleaned up together. It was great to have all their things on the shelves and in the cabinets. Even David seemed happy and talkative.

"Hey, Sis!" he said.

He must be in a really good mood, Amber thought. He hadn't called her "Sis" in years.

"Want to go exploring?" he asked.

Amber wasn't sure why David was being chummy all of a sudden. He usually didn't want to have anything to do with her. But she said, "Sure."

She ran upstairs, changed into her shorts, and found David out on the front porch. They started walking down the hill.

"Hey, kids!" Mom yelled as they were about to turn onto the main road. "Would you check the mail for me? I'm hoping my magazines will show up today."

They walked to the mailbox by Old Miss McAfee's house.

Amber peeked inside, but saw nothing that looked like a magazine. She stuck her hand deep into the back, just to be sure.

She felt a small piece of paper and pulled it out. It was a letter, on pale blue stationery. It looked very old. There was no return address.

Then Amber felt a lump in her throat. She stared at the front of the letter. The handwriting was the same as she had seen on the note in her room the day before. So was the stamp!

And the letter was addressed to Amber Elliston.

Chapter Twenty-Three

David stared at his sister. He knew something was very wrong.

"What is it?" he asked. "What's that old letter? And why is it addressed to you?"

Amber tore open the envelope and read the short message inside. It said: *"Go with your brother today. Help me. Help me. Help her."*

David and Amber stood in front of the mailbox in silence. They stared at the letter for a long time.

Finally. David put his hand on Amber's shoulder.

"Listen, Sis," he said. "There's something I've got to tell you. Some really weird things have been happening to me ever since we got here. I've heard that message before."

Amber looked up at her brother, wanting to hear more.

"Remember that night in the car when you saw that face in the window?" he said.

"Yes," Amber nodded.

"Well, I saw it, too," he said. "And the girl by the tree just before we had the accident? I saw her, too. Then last night, after I went to bed, I heard someone crying. I got up to see what it was, and looked out my window. I saw that same girl walking on the hill down from our house. She looked up at me and said: *"Help me. Help me. Help her."*

David paused.

"Amber, I don't want to scare you," he said. "But I think it's a ghost."

Amber felt more relieved than scared. She had someone who would believe her, who would not think she was nuts.

She poured out her whole story to David. She told him about the computer message, and the photograph that had talked to her. She told him about the letter she had found in the floor of her room. And the strange song she kept hearing.

"And David, what's even creepier is the story behind all this," she said.

Just as she was about to tell him the tale of Helen McAfee and how she died, he interrupted.

70

"I know all about it," he said. "When I was down at the swimming pool yesterday, I met some guys who are going to be in my class next year. I told them where I was living, and they got really funny looks on their faces. They said our house is haunted! They told me how Helen McAfee was found dead on a rock in the river a long time ago. And how everyone blamed her sister Hannah. And that's why Old Miss McAfee lives here alone. And has for fifty years."

"I saw her!" Amber cried. "I saw her yesterday! She grabbed me when Kelly and I were down here on the four-wheeler. It nearly scared me to death! She looks just like a witch!"

David kicked his shoe into the dirt, and thought a minute.

"Listen, the reason I wanted to go exploring today was I know where it all happened," he said. "Remember that tree by the river where we had the wreck? Well, the guys in town told me that, years ago, that used to be the old swimming hole. There used to be an old rope swing tied to that tree. Everyone would swing on it and jump into the river. That's where Helen McAfee fell — or was pushed. No one has gone swimming there since. I want to go down there and check it out."

"Well, someone is trying to tell us something," Amber said. "Maybe it's a ghost — the ghost of Helen McAfee. And maybe we'd better start listening to her."

Chapter Twenty-Four

Amber and David started walking down the gravel road toward the river.

It was a long hike — maybe two miles. They said nothing to each other along the way. The sun overhead got hotter and hotter.

Gosh, Amber thought. I thought New York was hot in the summer. That's nothing compared to this.

David swatted a mosquito. Beads of sweat dripped down his face.

They passed a few farmhouses, and several old barns that had fallen down. Cows grazed in the fields. A skunk ran across the road.

After half an hour, they rounded a corner. The road sloped down into open country, with huge fields of corn. In the distance, they saw the one-lane bridge over the river. The metal across the top of it zigzagged like something made out of Legos.

"Look!" David said. "That's it! That's the tree!"

Next to the bridge, an enormous oak stood tall against the sky. It hung over the river like a big green claw. The trunk was huge.

"Oh my gosh!" Amber gasped. "What if we had hit that thing when we swerved?"

"We'd all be dead," David said softly. Suddenly, he started running.

"Wait! Wait for me!" Amber cried, racing along behind him.

It only took a minute to reach the bridge. David and Amber walked slowly onto the old wooden planks, and looked at the water swirling furiously beneath them.

"I can't believe kids used to swim in there," Amber said. "Wouldn't it be really dangerous?"

"I guess that's why they don't do it anymore," David answered. "And why Helen McAfee got killed."

Just as they were about to head over to look at the tree, they heard the sound of a four-wheeler. It was Kelly.

"Hey! What are y'all doing?" she called as she drove over the bridge.

"Come here," Amber said. "I want to show you something."

She pulled the ghost letter out of her pocket and handed it to Kelly.

"Wow!" Kelly gasped. "Where did you get this?"

"It came in the mail," Amber said. "Today."

Kelly looked up at David, as if she were not sure it was OK to talk in front of him.

"It's okay," Amber said. "He knows all about it. And guess what? He's seen the ghost, too!"

"We came down here to look at the spot where Helen McAfee died," David said.

Kelly pointed to a big rock sitting in the middle of the water. The river bubbled around it furiously on either side.

"It was right down there," Kelly said. "Let's get a closer look."

Before David and Amber could say no, Kelly parked her four-wheeler and headed across the river bank to the old tree. Without thinking, David and Amber followed.

The three of them crawled over the huge roots, which curled up like fat snakes sticking out of the ground. They walked around to the side of the tree facing the river, and looked down.

There it was. The spot where Helen McAfee died!

Chapter Twenty-Five

The big, flat rock stuck up through the green water like a small island. The water around it was very fast and deep.

There was a steep drop from the tree down to the river below. There was no sign of life anywhere.

Suddenly, David whispered "Get down!"

The three of them crouched behind the bushes around the tree roots.

"What?" Kelly asked. "What is it?"

"Look. Over there," David said. He pointed to the woods on the other side.

At first Amber saw nothing. But as her eyes focused, she saw a thin stream of smoke rising above the trees.

"Maybe it's some guys fishing," Kelly said. "Maybe they've made a campfire or something."

A man stepped out of the woods. And he

wasn't carrying a fishing pole.

He was very big, with long gray hair that looked as if it had not been combed in years. He had a scraggly beard. His clothes were dirty.

Right behind him was the meanest looking dog Amber had ever seen. It barked and growled, and chewed on an old tin can.

"A pit bull," Kelly whispered. "That's a pit bulldog!"

As the three of them watched in silence, their hearts pounding, the man reached into his shirt pocket and pulled out a pale blue piece of paper.

It was a letter. He stared at it for a moment, then ripped it into tiny pieces.

He threw them into the water, and let out a bloodcurdling scream.

Chapter Twenty-Six

Without a word, the kids jumped from their hiding place and ran back to the road as fast as they could.

David and Amber kept going, racing toward their house. Kelly hopped on the four-wheeler, and soon caught up with them.

"Who was that?" Amber asked, out of breath.

"I have no idea," Kelly said. "And I've lived here all my life. I've never seen that guy before. I didn't think anyone lived down here by the river."

"Listen," David said, very seriously. "I think that guy is dangerous. And I think he might have seen us."

The three kids stared at each other, wondering what to do.

Then David said he had a plan.

"Amber, we need to get home as fast as possible," he said. "But we've also got to get to the bottom of this. I've got an idea. My dad works at the newspaper. Maybe we could go down to his office and look up the newspapers from fifty years ago. Those old stories might help us find out what really happened to Helen McAfee. And maybe someone there can tell us who that man is. And how he's connected to all this."

Amber and Kelly nodded.

"I've got to eat lunch with my grandma today," Kelly said. "But I could meet you later this afternoon. Maybe around three?"

"That would work," David answered. "I've got swim team practice, but it gets out about that time. Amber, that leaves you. You've got to figure out a way to get Mom to drive you into town. Then you can meet us at Dad's office."

"Mom promised she'd take me to the Wal-Mart to buy some new curtains for my room," Amber said. "I'll get her to drop me off at the paper."

All three of them looked at the river one last time. They didn't see anything. All they heard was water rushing under the bridge. A hawk flew overhead.

Kelly turned her four-wheeler around and headed towards town. Amber and David started their long walk home. They stared at the ground, not saying a word.

They heard a dog bark.

It was not a friendly bark, like the yip-yip of the little poodle that used to live down the hall from them in New York. This bark sounded mean and wild.

Amber and David turned and looked back.

There it was, under the tree. It was the pit bull they had seen on the other side of the river. He barked furiously, as if he wanted to run at them but something was holding him back. He lurched and jumped uncontrollably.

"Do you see what I see?" David asked.

Amber squinted. Her eyes followed the taught rope that was around the dog's neck. It led back behind the old oak tree.

Suddenly, someone stepped out from behind the trunk.

It was the crazy man. He jerked the dog's collar back with a force so strong it made the dog whimper.

Then he looked straight at Amber and David.

Chapter Twenty-Seven

"Let's get out of here!" David cried.

Amber and David ran the nearly two miles home. They were sweating and panting by the time they reached the old mailboxes.

David stopped and squatted on the ground, out of breath.

"David, I'm really scared!" Amber whimpered. "I think maybe we're in big trouble."

"As crazy as he looks, that guy didn't follow us," David said. "He didn't turn his dog loose on us or anything. So I don't think he's going to hurt us. He doesn't even know who we are."

"Yeah, but did you see what he threw into the river?" Amber asked. "It was a letter! A letter that looked just like this one!"

Amber reached into her pocket and pulled out the mysterious note. She unfolded it and read it again.

"*Go with your brother today. Help me. Help me. Help her,*" she read. "What do you suppose that means?"

"Obviously, someone wanted us to see that guy," David answered. "But help her? Who is her?"

Just then, they heard something very creepy.

Piano music.

The same piano music Amber had heard when she was at Old Miss McAfee's place with Kelly.

David looked up and saw Amber staring at him.

"I know," he said. "It's that song that was on the car radio the night we got here. I've been hearing her play it every night. Let's get home, and get into town as fast as we can."

They walked up the hill to their house. They were too tired to run any more. Their mom was on the front porch, planting red flowers in big ceramic pots. She looked up at them and smiled.

"Did you get to see some of this beautiful country?" she asked.

Amber and David just nodded.

"You got back just in time," Mom said. "David, I've got to drive you into town for your swimming lesson. Run upstairs and get your swim trunks. There are some towels in the bathroom. And don't forget the sunscreen!"

Amber knew this was her chance.

"Mom? Can I go with you?" she asked. "You said you'd take me to Wal-Mart to get some curtains for that big window in my room. Could we maybe do that today?"

Amber's mom seemed irritated. Then she looked at her hot and tired daughter, and changed her mind.

"Sure, honey. Sure," she said. "I've got to pick up some computer supplies anyway. I'll drop you off at the store and you can look around."

The Ellistons piled into the black Honda. Except for a few scratches on the hood, it seemed as good as new, in spite of the accident. They drove away from their house, back onto a paved road and into the small town of Jackson.

Amber had seen small towns before, but mainly on TV. This one was actually smaller than she had even imagined. A few stores formed a square around an old courthouse. Most of the stores were empty and closed.

Amber's mom drove a few blocks farther, and pulled the car into a huge parking lot. There stood a giant Wal-Mart. Next to it was the community swimming pool.

David hopped out of the car.

"See you later," he yelled as he walked toward the pool. "Wish me luck!"

"Amber, you go on into the store. Ask someone where you can find the curtains, and see if there is anything you like," Mom said. "I've got to drive over to the next town for my things. There's no computer store in Jackson. It will probably take me a couple of hours, but you can browse. Or if you get tired of that, why don't you walk down to Daddy's new office? It's just across from the courthouse. You'll recognize it. It's an old building that says 'Jackson County News' on the front door."

Wow, Amber thought. This couldn't have worked out more perfectly.

Chapter Twenty-Eight

Amber walked through the sprawling Wal-Mart for a few minutes.

She didn't even go to where the curtains were displayed. Instead, she walked up and down the aisles where the toys were. She thought about buying a new board game. Or an outfit for her Barbie. But, somehow, she couldn't keep her mind on toys.

I've got to get down to the newspaper office, she thought.

She looked at her watch. An hour had gone by. She headed out the door of the store.

Just as she started walking down the street, she heard a familiar voice.

"Hey!" It was Kelly.

Amber hardly recognized her here in town. It occurred to her that this was the first time she had seen Kelly without her four-wheeler.

"Where's your bike?" Amber asked.

"I just use that for riding out in the country," Kelly said. "My dad won't let me ride it in town. Too many cars. You on your way to the newspaper?"

"Yeah," Amber said. "David should be getting out of swim practice any minute. I'm dying to get a look at the old stories about Helen McAfee, and how she died."

The girls headed off together.

The newspaper office occupied a very old building. Amber thought it looked run down. It didn't seem anything like the big office of the New York Times, where her dad used to work. It made Amber kind of sad.

Kelly pushed the door and walked in.

A middle-aged woman with big blond hair sat behind the counter. She had very long red fingernails. She was smoking a cigarette.

Yuck! Amber thought. Most of the offices in New York didn't allow people to smoke at work.

"Hey Kelly. How are you doing?" the woman said, smiling.

"Just fine," Kelly said. "Joanne, this is Amber. Her dad is the new editor here."

"Well, sugar, how nice to meet you!" Joanne

said, standing up. She leaned over the counter and gave Amber a big hug.

"We just love your daddy," she went on. "He's going to do great things for this town. He's right back there in his office if you want to go see him."

Amber and Kelly didn't say anything. Amber didn't know what to say. How was she supposed to tell this Joanne woman with the big hair what they really wanted? Just as she was about to screw up the courage to ask to see the stories on Helen McAfee, David burst in the door.

"Hi!" he said confidently.

Even though he didn't talk very much, David always seemed to know how to get along with people.

"I'm David Elliston."

"Then you're Amber's brother!" Joanne gushed. "Glad to meet you. Guess you kids want to see Mr. Elliston. Let me go get him for you."

"Actually, there's something else we'd like to see," David said.

"Oh, really? What's that?" Joanne asked.

"Do you keep copies of old newspapers here? Ones from a really long time ago?" he asked.

"Yes. They're all in the back. We keep them in big books. And they go back a long time. This news-big books. And they go back a long time. This news-paper has been around since 1922," Joanne bragged. "Whatcha looking for?"

"Do you have the ones from 1945?" David asked.

"You bet!" Joanne said. "Let's go see what we can find."

Joanne led the kids behind the counter, down a narrow hall, and past their dad's office. They could see him working at a big desk. He was talking to someone on the phone, and didn't notice them. They ended up in a tiny storage room lined from floor to ceiling with huge leather books filled with yellowing newspapers.

Joanne ran her fingers down the spines. The side of each book was stamped in gold with a date.

"Let's see," she said, going down the stack. "1949, 1948, 1947, 1946. Oh! Here it is. 1945!"

David helped Joanne pull the big book from its place on the shelf. They plopped it on a big table in the center of the room. It smelled very old. David opened it up and started thumbing carefully through the pages.

These old newspapers did not look anything like the ones published today. They were mostly words — very few pictures, and no colors.

The news back then was all about World War

II. Amber remembered that her grandfather had fought in World War II. Like her grandmother, he had died before she was even born.

David turned the pages through the months. April. May. June. July. Nothing. Absolutely nothing about Helen McAfee.

Just as the kids were reaching the end of the book, David flipped the page over to August 26, 1945.

Amber gasped.

On the front page of the paper, the headline said "Local Girl Killed in River Accident."

Underneath it was something Amber could not believe.

A photograph showed a young girl with curly blond hair. There was a flower in her hair. The caption said "Helen McAfee."

It was the same photograph Amber had seen on her computer screen.

Chapter Twenty-Nine

Amber, David and Kelly stared at the old photo.

"Wow," Kelly said. "She was really pretty!"

David started reading aloud.

"Helen McAfee, 16, was found dead in the Jackson River yesterday morning. She was lying on a rock near the Jackson County Bridge. The cause of death was apparently a head injury. Authorities said the young woman did not drown.

"McAfee, a sophomore at Jackson County High, had been missing for nearly 24 hours. She was discovered by a group of boys. Her sister, Hannah McAfee, who had also been missing, came forward shortly after workers removed the body from the river. She said she didn't know anything about her sister's accident, or what had happened.

"The sheriff's office has ruled this an acci-

dental death. Services will be held at the Smith-Austin funeral home on Saturday."

"Well, that doesn't tell us much," David said.

"But what about that part about Hannah being missing too?" Amber wondered out loud. "That's kind of strange. Why would she have disappeared?"

A sharp, raspy voice cut in.

"Cause she did it."

Chapter Thirty

It was Joanne, the receptionist.

She had overheard the conversation. She looked at the old paper with the kids.

"No one ever got to the bottom of it," Joanne said. "But pretty soon after this happened, pieces of the story started coming out. Everybody around here thinks Hannah pushed Helen into the river. She was mad at her. They were both in love with an orphan boy named Jim who had come here for the summer to stay with some relatives. Both of those McAfee girls just went crazy for him. They say he was very good looking."

"But why would people think Hannah would actually kill her own sister?" Amber asked.

"Jealousy," Joanne said, flicking another cigarette. "See, this Jim played the guitar. And Helen wanted to be a singer. They hit it off right away. They would sit down by the river singing songs and holding hands. Hannah was furious. She liked music, too. I think she played the piano. They say she even wrote a song for Jim. And that's when it really got bad."

"What do you mean?" asked Kelly.

"The night Helen McAfee disappeared, there was a talent show down at the high school. My mother was there, and she told me all about it. Hannah McAfee was going to play the piano. Helen was the singer. She was really pretty, you know. Always wore a white flower in her hair.

"Well, right before they started, Hannah got up and said she was dedicating the song to a boy named Jim," Joanne continued. "Helen was furious. She was so mad she couldn't even sing the song. She ran from the stage. Hannah followed her. They had a huge fight out in front of the school. People say Hannah screamed at Helen that she hated her so much she could kill her! That was the last time anyone ever saw Helen alive."

"What was the song?" David asked.

"Oh, gosh," Joanne said. "I don't remember."

Then she thought a moment.

"Here, let's look," she said, flipping back to the paper from the week before. She thumbed through the old pages, then stopped at the bottom of page six.

"See, here's a story about the upcoming talent show."

She ran her fingers down the names of the students who would be performing. There she was — Helen McAfee. The story also listed the song she would be singing.

It was "Come to Me My Beautiful One."

The lights in the tiny room suddenly went out. It was so dark Amber couldn't even see her hand in front of her face.

It seemed as black as death.

Chapter Thirty-One

No one moved.

Suddenly, Amber saw the glow of Joanne's cigarette.

"Darn!" the receptionist blurted. "Those stupid lights! They go out every time Ed runs the presses."

Amber, David and Kelly watched the glow of Joanne's cigarette travel to the far corner of the room. She opened the door. The rest of the office was dark too, except for a beam of light heading down the hall towards them.

"Joanne? Joanne?"

It was their dad's voice. He was carrying a flashlight. The beam hit Amber and David right in the face.

"Kids! What are you doing here?" he asked.

"We were just in that back room looking at some old newspapers," David said.

"Yeah, and then the lights went out!" Amber

piped up.

"Well, I guess this is kind of a bad time for your visit," Amber's dad said. "Seems like every time they start running the presses in the back, it cuts the power. Too bad. I'd really like to show you my new office."

They heard a click down the hall. Joanne had flipped a big switch in an old box in the wall. At once, light filled the office again.

"I was just about to close up for the day," Dad said. "Where's your mom? Do you kids need a ride home?"

Right then, Carol Elliston walked through the front door.

"So, what do you think of your dad's new place?" she asked, a big smile on her face.

The kids stood silently. Amber was still disappointed that the office was so much smaller than the one at The New York Times.

"Mom, is it okay if Kelly spends the night?" Amber asked, changing the subject.

"As long as it's all right with her parents," Mom replied.

"I'll call and ask," Kelly said. "I'm sure my dad won't mind."

Kelly phoned her house, and got the go ahead to spend the night with Amber. She headed out the door with the Ellistons, and they all piled into the Honda.

"I'll lock up Mr. Elliston," Joanne called out the door. Then she added, "Did you kids find what you were looking for?"

Amber and David nodded.

As they drove through town, they passed the Wal-Mart, the swimming pool and Jackson County High School.

"Look," Mom said. "That's where David will go to school this fall."

It was a very old building, surrounded by huge trees and covered in ivy. A sign out front had black, plastic letters that could be moved around to spell different things. The message today said, "Back to School August 30."

Darn, Amber thought. That's so soon. Summer's almost over.

As the Honda passed the school, Amber turned around and looked at the other side of the sign. There was a different message on that side of the sign.

It said, "Talent Show Tonight. Starring Helen McAfee."

Chapter Thirty-Two

"David, Kelly, look!" Amber whispered.

The kids turned around in the back seat and stared at the sign. Then they stared at each other.

It was nightfall by the time they got back to the house. Amber's dad made pizza while her mom worked on the computer.

After dinner, David went to his room and closed the door. The girls settled down in Amber's bedroom. Kelly looked through all of Amber's toys and books. They talked a little, then decided to go to sleep.

As they lay in the darkened bedroom, Kelly finally spoke.

"Amber, this is just about the creepiest stuff I've ever seen," she said. "I've always heard about the ghost out here, but I wasn't sure I believed it. Do you think your *house* is really haunted?"

"I don't know what to believe," Amber said. "But I got those letters. And I saw that picture of Helen McAfee on Mom's computer. And there was that message today at the school."

"What do you suppose it meant?" Kelly asked.

A cool breeze blew in through Amber's big window. Amber heard the soft chirping of crickets outside. She looked over and saw a full moon outside.

Then she heard the music.

It was the piano again. The music floated up the hill from Old Miss McAfee's house. This time it was some kind of classical piece, maybe Beethoven or Bach. It sounded soft, even kind of soothing.

"Does she play every night?" Kelly asked.

"Seems like it," Amber said.

The tune changed. It was that song again. The one Amber had heard in the car. The one the girls had heard on their ride down by Old Miss McAfee's garden.

"Come to me. Come to me, oh beautiful one."

Kelly started crying.

"I'm scared, Amber. I want to go home."

Amber climbed out of bed and walked to the window. She stared down into the moonlit yard.

And someone stared back up at her.

Chapter Thirty-Three

It was David.

He was standing in the yard all alone. He put his hand over his mouth, signaling Amber to be quiet. He waved for her to come down.

"Come on, Kelly," Amber said, stepping into her sandals. "David's down there. He wants to show us something."

"I'm not going out there, Amber," Kelly whimpered. "I'm scared. I want to go home."

"All right," Amber said. "You can stay here. But I'm going down to check it out."

Amber tiptoed down the stairs and sneaked past the room where her mom was still working. She went out the back door and closed it quietly.

David was still in the yard. He put his hand on her shoulder and pointed to the light in Old Miss McAfee's window.

"Look," he said.

Amber squinted. At first she did not see anything. The piano music had stopped. The wind began to blow a little harder.

Then she saw Old Miss McAfee standing in her yard. Her white hair blew wildly in the wind. She carried an old purse and walked toward an old garage behind her house.

David started walking down the hill.

"What do you think you're doing?" Amber asked, racing to catch up.

"Sssssh," he whispered sharply. "I'm going to see what she's up to."

The kids walked down through the dark woods to the house.

They heard a car engine start. It popped and roared, startling them. They were down on the old dirt trail, close to the spot where Old Miss McAfee had grabbed Amber.

"Duck down!" David said.

A set of headlights pulled out of the garage and headed towards them. They belonged to an ancient pickup truck, and Old Miss McAfee was behind the wheel. She drove slowly past Amber and David, who were hiding in the bushes.

"Thank goodness," David said. "She didn't see us."

Suddenly, they heard a loud *BLAM*. The old truck had backfired, and stalled.

Rrrrrrrr. Rrrrrrr. Rrrrrr.

Old Miss McAfee was turning the key, trying to get it started again. David grabbed Amber's hand and tugged on it.

"Let's go see," he said, hopping up from their hiding spot.

Amber was terrified, but she followed her brother.

He crawled along the ground on his hands and knees, right up to the back of the truck.

To Amber's shock, he hopped onto the back! He motioned for her to join him. She froze, wide-eyed, and shook her head.

The truck started up again.

Screwing up all her courage, Amber hopped onto the back. The truck took off and turned onto the main road. Amber could tell that Old Miss McAfee had turned right.

She was heading for the river.

Chapter Thirty-Four

The old truck popped and jerked.

David and Amber lay down in the back. Apparently Old Miss McAfee had not noticed them. She drove very slowly. The truck weaved back and forth. Amber was afraid it was going to run off the road.

Guess she hasn't driven in a long time, Amber thought to herself.

She lay next to David, keeping as still as possible. She looked up at the big yellow moon, and watched the tree limbs pass overhead. David reached over and held her hand.

The truck rounded the bend, and headed down a hill. All of a sudden, Amber heard the sound of rushing water.

They were going over the old bridge!

The old planks popped and creaked as the truck drove over them. Amber looked back and saw the giant oak tree — the one her family had nearly hit the night they moved to Jackson.

An old rope hung from one of the branches. It had been broken, and it whipped wildly in the wind.

The truck turned sharply to the left, headed down a steep gravel road, and began rolling slowly through the woods.

David stared at Amber. She smelled smoke.

Then she heard a dog bark.

Chapter Thirty-Five

Slam!

The truck had stopped. It shook as Old Miss McAfee slammed the door. The kids heard her walking away.

After a few minutes, David peeked over the side of the truck bed.

"Look!" he whispered.

Amber sat up. They were parked in front of an old log cabin. It was very small, and pieces of the roof had caved in. The cabin was hidden by trees and vines. Tied to a rope in the yard, Amber and David saw the pit bulldog.

It was not barking any longer. Old Miss McAfee was nowhere in sight.

A faint light came from under the door of the place. Then the kids heard two voices shouting inside. The voices were muffled. Amber and David could not make out what the people were saying.

"I'm going to get closer," David said.

He hopped out of the truck and walked slowly up to the old cabin.

Amber was terrified. She did not want to be here. She certainly did not want to go any closer to this creepy place.

But she did not want to be left alone either, so she followed David.

They stopped in front of the rotting door. David pressed his ear to the wood. Amber did too.

They heard two voices. One belonged to a woman — Old Miss McAfee. The other belonged to a man. They were shouting at each other.

"You did this! You did this to me!" the man yelled. "What do you think you're doing? Are you trying to scare me or something? Why don't you just leave me alone!"

"I didn't do anything to you," Old Miss McAfee yelled back. "Look! I got one too!"

The pit bull began to growl. It stared at the kids huddled in front of the door, then began barking wildly.

With a jerk, someone threw open the door.

<u>Chapter Thirty-Six</u>

Amber and David stared into the face of a wild man.

His eyes were wide with rage. His hair was tousled. His clothes were dirty. He smelled bad.

The air in the whole place stank. The inside of the cabin was a mess. There was very little furniture. An old cot stood in one corner of the room. Empty soup cans and potato chip bags were piled on the floor.

Old Miss McAfee stood in the corner.

"Who are you?" the man screamed at the kids. "What are you doing here?"

Before either could answer, the man grabbed David by the neck and pulled him into the room. Then he reached for Amber.

The kids found themselves huddled on the floor. The wild man stood on one side of them. Old

Miss McAfee stood on the other.

"Don't hurt them!" she cried. "They're my grand-niece and grand-nephew. They're Carol's kids. She's just moved her family into the old house."

Amber and David stared in silence.

"You kids shouldn't be snooping around here," the man said in a low, mean voice. "You should mind your own business."

Then Amber spotted it. The wild man was holding a piece of paper. It was a faded, blue letter.

It looked just like the one she had gotten in the mail.

"I know what that is!" Amber blurted out. "It's a letter. And it's from Helen McAfee, isn't it?"

The wild man glared at her. He thrust the letter in front of her face.

"That's it, isn't it?" he said. "You kids are playing tricks on us, aren't you? Well, I'll show you what happens to kids who play tricks."

"No! No, Jim!" Old Miss McAfee cried out. "I got one too. And I don't see how these kids could have done it. It was in Helen's handwriting."

David grabbed Amber's hand and jumped up. He started to run out the door, but bumped into a table. An old record player sat on it, like one of those old phonographs the kids had seen in museums.

As David jumped back, a piece of metal with a needle on the end of it dropped down with a plunk and landed on an old record.

A scratchy tune began to play. A woman's voice sang sweetly.

"Come to me, come to me, my beautiful one. I am coming to you."

A faint ball of light began to materialize in the middle of the room. Amber could make out the shape of a woman. She was young. And very pretty.

And she had a white flower in her hair.

Chapter Thirty-Seven

The room was deadly quiet except for the soft sound of the music. Then Old Miss McAfee began to cry.

"Helen! Oh, Helen!" she sobbed. "It *is* you!"

The ghost looked over at her sister and smiled. Then she spoke.

"Amber, David," she said. "Don't be afraid. No one is going to hurt you. I've brought you all here for a reason."

Amber could not believe what was happening. Her heart pounded, and her throat felt so tight she had trouble breathing. David stared at the ghost with his mouth open.

"Something terrible has happened. Something more terrible than my death," the ghost continued. "Hannah, you stopped living the night I died. You know you had nothing to do with it. It was an accident. Jim, you've lied to everyone all these years. You let Hannah take the blame. It's time for it to stop."

The wild man began to cry.

"I'm sorry! I'm so sorry, Helen!" he wept. "I didn't mean for it to happen. You were angry and upset after the talent show. When I asked you to meet me out here by the tree, I didn't know what had happened. You thought I was seeing Hannah. You were hysterical. I was only trying to grab you to calm you down. I didn't mean to push you in the river!"

Amber and David stared in shock. The ghost spoke again.

"Jim, I know it was an accident. But you should have come forward and told what happened. You didn't. And my sister has had to live her whole life in shame and sadness. It's *your* fault. *You* need to make it right."

The ghost of Helen McAfee began to float across the room. It reached down and turned off the record player. Then it traveled in the air and stopped over Amber and David's heads.

"You children are my family," it said. "You need to help heal her. You've put me at peace."

The ghost floated over to Old Miss McAfee. They stared into one another's eyes, and looked very much alike. But one was old. The other was still a young girl.

The ghost paused over her sister, then leaned down and kissed her.

"I'm sorry," it said. "I love you. Be at peace."

In an instant, it was gone.

Amber heard the sound of breaking glass.

Chapter Thirty-Eight

The wild man — Jim — started smashing everything in the cabin.

He grabbed an iron poker from the side of the fireplace. He pounded the record player to pieces.

Then he turned toward Old Miss McAfee, and raised the poker over his head, ready to smash it down on her.

David jumped up and grabbed the poker. He and Jim wrestled wildly as Jim continued to flail with the poker.

Amber heard the sound of a siren. Car doors slammed. She heard footsteps running up to the cabin.

The door flew open. Sheriff Johnson burst in, pointing a gun.

"Stop right now!" he shouted. "Put down that poker."

Jim stared at the sheriff for what seemed like

114

several minutes. Then he hung his greasy head down, and let the poker drop to the floor.

Amber heard another car. Her mom, dad and Kelly rushed into the cabin.

"Oh, my gosh!" Amber's mom cried, running over to her son and daughter. "Are you all right? Are you all right?"

Amber started crying. David started shaking badly.

"I think we'd all better calm down and figure out what's going on here," Sheriff Johnson said. "Miss McAfee, can you tell us what happened?"

Old Miss McAfee was still crying. She walked over to a wooden stool and sat down. She didn't say a word.

David finally spoke.

"Mom, Dad, Sheriff Johnson," he said. "This is the man who killed Helen McAfee."

As the grown-ups stared in disbelief, David told them the whole story. Kelly stood by her dad, her eyes wide open as she listened.

Sheriff Johnson was quiet for a very long time.

"Jim. Is it true?" he asked, putting his gun back in his holster.

The wild man nodded his head.

"I'm not really sure what happened here tonight," Sheriff Johnson said. "I can't say that I believe that stuff about the ghost. But I do know that two kids were out in the night where they weren't supposed to be. David, Amber — your parents were worried sick about you."

Kelly piped up.

"I called Daddy to come take me home," she said. "But then we couldn't find you. I told them I had seen you two out the window going down to Old Miss McAfee's. Then I saw her truck head down here. So when Daddy got to the house, we figured that's where you must be."

"And a good thing, too," Amber's dad said. He sounded frightened and worried. "Sheriff Johnson, what are you going to do?"

"It doesn't look like anyone was hurt here," the sheriff said slowly, as if he were thinking out loud. "And I'm not sure we can do anything about something that happened fifty years ago. And Helen McAfee's death was officially ruled an accident. Let's just leave it at that.

"But Jim," the sheriff continued. "I don't want to ever see you around these children again. Or near Miss McAfee. You seem to like keeping to yourself.

Keep it that way."

Amber and David walked out to the Honda. Their dad walked with them, an arm around each of them. Their mom went over to Miss McAfee and hugged her tightly.

"Why don't we get you home now," she said softly. "And let's get to know each other. I believe your story. It happened long ago. It's time to get on with your life now."

Carol walked Miss McAfee out to the truck. Kelly hopped in the patrol car with her dad, and waved good-bye to Amber.

Jim sat alone in the cabin, holding his head in his hands.

As the Ellistons drove home, Amber turned to look back at the big oak tree. Floating just underneath the branches, she saw the ghost one last time. It smiled at her.

Then Helen McAfee blew Amber a kiss.

Chapter Thirty-Nine

Everyone in the Elliston household slept late the next morning. By the time Amber made it downstairs to the kitchen, she noticed there was an extra plate on the breakfast table. Her dad sat down to eat. So did David and her mom.

Then in walked an old woman who looked kind of familiar, yet somehow different. Her white hair was tied in a neat bun. She wore a new dress, and smelled of perfume.

Oh my gosh! Amber realized. It's Old Miss McAfee!

But Amber's great aunt didn't look like a witch anymore. She was very pretty for an old woman. She smiled broadly and carried a pot of flowers.

"Here, Amber," she said. "These are for you."

She patted Amber on the head.

The family ate breakfast. Amber's dad dashed off to work. David went out in the back yard to shoot baskets.

"Amber," her mom said. "We all went through a horrible experience last night. But I've had a long talk with your great-aunt Hannah this morning. I think you've helped her a lot."

Then Miss McAfee spoke.

"I've lived my whole life alone, bitter and afraid," she said. "I didn't mean to scare you that day when you were down near my garden. But you looked so much like my sister when she was a little girl, I wanted to talk to you. I think maybe your coming here caused all these things to happen. I know some of them were very scary. I can't really explain it myself. But I've learned something very valuable. Love is important. And people are important. I want to get them back into my life."

Amber's mother spoke up.

"Honey, your great-aunt Hannah wants to give you piano lessons. Would you be interested?"

Amber had always wanted to play the piano. But she wasn't sure about going back down into Old Miss McAfee's house.

Her great-aunt sensed her fear.

"Come. Come with me," she said. "I think you're going to be surprised."

Chapter Forty

Amber got up from the table and followed Miss McAfee down the hill to her small, frame house.

It didn't look so spooky in the daytime. Someone had put big pots of fresh flowers all over the rickety front porch.

They went inside. The downstairs was just one big room. A beautiful old grand piano sat right in the middle.

Miss McAfee took her place on the piano bench, and motioned for Amber to sit next to her. The old woman pulled out some sheet music.

"This is a good one for us to start on," she said. "And a good way for us to get to know each other too."

As Miss McAfee began playing the simple tune, Amber looked around the room. Old family pictures covered the walls. There was a man in a soldier's uniform. A woman who looked like she might have lived during the Civil War. A family posed on a front porch. Amber recognized it as the house she now lived in.

Her eyes traveled to a neat round table standing next to the piano. It was covered with a beautiful, white embroidered cloth. An old picture in a gold frame stood on top of it.

It was a photograph of two young girls, sitting side by side. They both wore white party dresses. They both had blond, curly hair.

And each wore a white flower in her hair.

Miss McAfee stopped playing the piano for a moment.

"Yes," she said. "That's me and Helen."

Amber gasped. Twins! They were identical twins!

As Miss McAfee put her hands back on the keyboards and began the tune again, Amber took one long last look at the picture. She wasn't sure, but she could have sworn the girl who was Helen blinked her eyes and smiled.

Under the piano music, Amber heard a voice whispering faintly.

"Thank you," it whispered. *"Thank you."*

BE SURE TO READ THESE OTHER COLD, CLAMMY SHIVERS BOOKS.

THE CURSE OF THE NEW KID

LUCAS LYTLE IS USED TO BEING THE NEW KID IN SCHOOL. HE'S TWELVE YEARS OLD – AND HE'S ALREADY BEEN IN EIGHT DIFFERENT SCHOOLS. WHEN EVERYBODY FROM THE SCHOOL BULLIES TO THE CLASS NERDS PICK ON HIM, HE FEELS LIKE HE IS CURSED. BUT THEN STRANGE AND HORRIBLE THINGS START TO HAPPEN TO HIS ENEMIES. AT FIRST LUCAS IS CONFUSED BY WHAT IS HAPPENING. BUT THEN HE STARTS TO ENJOY IT – UNTIL IT BECOMES TOO FRIGHTENING FOR HIM TO HANDLE.

Shivers™

THE HAUNTING HOUSE

M. D. Spenser

Chapter One

Caitlin was afraid.

After all, moving to a new house is never easy.

Moving means saying good-bye to old friends. Moving means going to a new school where everyone is unfamiliar. Moving means settling into a strange home in a strange city when you liked the old home and the old city just fine.

Caitlin had never moved before and it did not sound like fun to her. So what if her father had a new job as a scientist in the next city over? Why couldn't he just drive a little further to work every day?

At least she wouldn't have to share a bedroom anymore with her dorky younger sister, Lynne! That was one good thing about the move.

Each girl now would have her own bedroom, with a bathroom attached.

To Caitlin, Lynne was a big pain in the neck.

Lynne was only nine years old and didn't know nearly as much about anything as Caitlin, who was almost thirteen.

But Lynne liked to pretend she was just as smart. That annoyed Caitlin.

Actually, Caitlin did not mind that as much as she minded the way Lynne always caused trouble. Lynne liked getting into everything she was not supposed to get into. And she always managed to blame Caitlin when things went wrong.

Caitlin ended up in trouble for things she hadn't done. It just wasn't fair!

But in the new home, Caitlin could lock the door to her big bedroom and be all by herself.

As her father drove the family toward their new home thirty miles away, Caitlin smiled when she thought about having a private bedroom and bathroom for the first time in her life.

Maybe her parents would even let her have her own phone! And her own TV and her own computer!

Well . . . maybe not.

Caitlin decided she had better wait a while to ask for anything new. She knew her parents were spending a lot of money to repair the old house they had just bought in the suburbs outside Detroit.

They had always wanted to buy a home that was almost a hundred years old, like this one, and then fix it up. It was an abandoned house on the end of a dark dirt road, far from the busy center of the city.

No one had lived in the house for ten years! And the people who lived there last had left in a hurry — without even selling the place.

That seemed very weird to Caitlin.

She had only seen the house once and it looked like a creaky old dump to her. But her parents thought the place was "cool" — that was the exact word they had used.

Caitlin just rolled her eyes when they said this.

Why did parents always try to use words like that, anyway?

Besides, what could be cool about this house? It looked like something out of an old black-and-white horror movie!

She was sure the place was haunted or something.

Caitlin didn't get scared easily, like some kids.

3

And she didn't really believe in ghosts, even though she had a book about them.

But everything about the house seemed frightening to her.

It was a large two-story wooden house with wide, white shutters beside every window and a huge, dark basement. The home had old thick-paned windows and old wood floors and old heavy doors in every room. And it was topped with a steep old roof with some of the shingles missing.

When you walked around inside, the house looked old and smelled old. And it sounded old as you stepped across the floorboards. They groaned.

The broad lawn around the house was surrounded by woods, though the trees had no leaves at this time of year. It was already past Thanksgiving, nearly winter.

Caitlin thought the trees looked exactly like an attacking army of stick people, with long, sharp claws on the end of their limbs, ready to tear apart anything that got in their way.

Maybe the army of trees was the reason the last family had left the house so quickly. Maybe the trees had tried to kill everyone who lived there. Maybe the tree-claws had strangled someone in the middle of the night.

Caitlin laughed under her breath in the car, and told herself not to believe such silly things. Things that don't move can't attack people, she thought. Trees couldn't hurt anyone.

They were planted in the ground as firmly as the house. And everyone knew that a house could never do anything to hurt someone!

But, for some reason she could not put her finger on, Caitlin felt like something bad was going to happen at the new house.

She did not know what exactly. And she hoped she was wrong.

Now, out of the woods, the house loomed up in front of them. Their father pulled into the driveway. Caitlin and Lynne shoved each other to get out of the car first.

"Last one to the back yard has to do the dishes tonight!" Lynne yelled, pushing out the door ahead of her sister.

"No way!" Caitlin shouted.

"Way!" Lynne bellowed, running toward the back yard.

"You kids be very careful out back!" their father hollered. "And stay away from the hole!"

Behind the house, a wide hole gaped in the middle of the lawn. Just a big, empty hole in the ground. No one knew why it was there.

Caitlin's parents said the old owners must have been building a swimming pool when they'd had to move out in a hurry. Caitlin's father had said he might finish building the pool in the springtime.

Caitlin and Lynne thought having their own swimming pool would be excellent! Maybe the new house would not be so bad after it was all fixed up, Caitlin thought as she chased her sister to the back yard.

"Beat ya! Beat ya!" Lynne yelled. "You do dishes tonight!"

"No *way!*" Caitlin answered firmly. "I didn't agree we were racing! Besides you cheated to get a head start. You're such a little kid!"

"Am *not!* I'm almost as tall as you are!" Lynne said, pouting like a little kid.

The two sisters walked around the back lawn for a few minutes, looking at the shrubs outside the house and the trees at the edge of the brown grass.

Suddenly, Lynne was gone!

"Lynne! Lynne!" Caitlin called. *"Lynne! Where are you?"*

Caitlin looked around — toward the woods, toward the house, toward the hole. Everywhere!

Lynne was nowhere in sight.

"Lynne! This isn't funny!" Caitlin cried. She was becoming frantic. *"Lynne,* where *are* you?"

She saw no sign of her sister. And she heard no sound except the rattling and clacking of tree limbs in the cold autumn winds.

What was going on here? Caitlin wondered desperately. How could anything have gone wrong so fast?

Her family had only been at the new house ten minutes and something bad already had happened.

Something very bad!

Something much worse than she had ever imagined!

Her younger sister, Lynne, had simply disappeared — vanished from the back yard without a trace!

Chapter Two

Where had Lynne gone?

What could have happened to her? Was she dead?

Maybe the trees really *had* attacked somehow, grabbing Lynne in their claws and passing her from limb to limb until she was deep in the woods.

Caitlin felt terrible about all the mean things she had ever said to her sister. She promised herself that she would never utter another nasty word to her — if only something could bring her dear sister back!

"Lynne, oh no! *Oh no, oh no, oh no,*" Caitlin repeated again and again.

Then she felt a small stone hit her in the back!

Caitlin turned — and ducked as another small stone arched slowly toward her.

"Lynne!" Caitlin said angrily. "I'm going to kill you!"

She could hear giggling. Now, she understood what was happening.

She walked over to the edge of the hole in the ground and looked down.

Lynne was hiding inside the hole, tossing pebbles at her sister.

"You think you're funny!" Caitlin snapped. "This isn't funny at all, Lynne! I thought you were hurt or something had happened to you! Next time, you might be hurt and I won't come looking for you! That's not smart!"

"Oh yes it is! Smarter than you are! It fooled *you*," Lynne crowed.

Lynne really did act much younger than her sister, you see. She had not yet learned that it's always a mistake to pretend that something is the matter when everything is really OK.

Even though Lynne was only nine, she looked older. She was tall and slim, with pretty brown hair that fell over her shoulders. She had large, round eyes and even, white teeth and a beautiful smile.

Caitlin was not as pretty as her sister. But it didn't matter.

Not to Lynne. Not to their mother. Not to their father.

Not even to Caitlin herself.

Everyone in the family understood that what's inside a person means more than the way someone looks. They all knew that it's much more important to be smart and kind and considerate and loving than it is to look pretty.

"There's nothing wrong with looking beautiful, of course," their father told them. "As long as you understand you can't judge someone by beauty alone."

Caitlin was short for her age, and a little heavy. She wore braces to straighten her crooked teeth. Her hair was blond but on the stringy side, and cut close to her head. She had to wear contact lenses so she could see clearly.

Both sisters were very bright — even if Lynne still had some lessons to learn about staying out of trouble. And both had been popular in their old school.

Lynne was something of a tomboy who liked to hang out with the guys her age, playing baseball and football. She was strong and athletic.

Not Caitlin. She was a talented musician who performed on both the piano and the guitar during school concerts. And she loved to sit around the house, even when it was sunny and warm outside, reading novels and poetry or talking with good friends on the phone.

Of course, Caitlin was by far the more mature of the two. And she tried to play the protective big sister now.

"Lynne, get out of that hole right away!" she said. "It's dangerous in there! And if Dad catches you, you'll be in trouble."

"Nah, nah-nah, nah-nah, nah!" Lynne taunted. She loved to drive her sister crazy. "I'm staying in here as long as I want. And you can't *make* me get out if I don't want to!"

"Listen, Lynne, if you don't get out of there right now, I'm going to go tell Dad," Caitlin said.

"Go ahead! Tattletale!" Lynne said. She knew Caitlin almost never tattled to their parents about anything she did.

"OK, I'm coming down there to get you!" Caitlin said. "It's not safe down there!"

As her sister giggled mischievously, Caitlin knelt down at the side of the great hole and lowered herself in.

She grabbed her sister by the coat and started pulling her toward the edge of the hole. Lynne laughed and half-tried to get away.

"Come on, get out!" Caitlin shouted. "Right now, Lynne!"

"Uh-uh, no way!" Lynne teased, struggling to get free. "I didn't want to move here anyway. I hate this house! I'm going to live in this hole!"

The two sisters wrestled and grabbed at each other in the hole, with Lynne laughing and Caitlin getting angry.

Neither one noticed the danger right over their heads.

Directly above them was a monstrous pile of dirt and sand and rocks, everything that had been dug from the ground to make the hole. It was packed into one enormous mound, where the earth and stone had rested undisturbed beside the edge of the hole for a decade.

Until now.

As Caitlin and Lynne wrestled, a few grains of sand spilled from the top of the pile into the hole. They dropped right next to the girls' feet.

But they didn't notice.

Several more grains of sand and dirt, along with a few pebbles, dribbled down beside the girls. Still, Caitlin and Lynne saw nothing.

"I hate this house! I'm going to stay right in this hole," Lynne repeated, laughing.

And then dozens and dozens of grains of dirt and sand spilled into the pit, along with clumps of clay and rock. Some of the sand fell into Lynne's hair and across Caitlin's shoulder.

The girls stopped wrestling and looked up — and were horrified by what they saw.

The entire mass of dirt and rock was quivering, teetering on the edge of the great hole. The mound was starting to crumble, right over their heads!

"Aaaaaaaaaaaaaahhhhhhhhh!" Lynne screamed.

"Avalanche!" Caitlin shouted.

This old house is going to kill my sister and me, Caitlin thought, in a panic. We're going to be buried alive! There is nothing we can do to get away!

Slowly at first, and then faster and faster, the pile of earth and stones started to tumble into the hole on top of them.

Chapter Three

Caitlin was sure it was too late!

The mass of dirt and rocks began to topple over like a stack of cans someone had bumped into in the supermarket. Everything rained into the hole at once. Enough soil and stones to bury two girls.

Both girls screamed in fright.

Lynne leapt desperately to one side, away from the falling pile of earth. As she jumped, she grabbed Caitlin by the neck and pulled hard.

The girls tumbled across the hole, just out of the way of the collapsing dirt.

They looked back to see a cloud of dust rise into the air from the fallen mountain of soil.

"Wow, that was close!" Lynne said, breathing heavily from fear.

"I thought we were going to die for sure,"

Caitlin said, her voice quivering. She could feel her whole body shaking. "I've never seen so much dirt fall in one place. It was awful! But you saved us, Lynne! If you hadn't pulled me away, we'd be buried under all that dirt right now! We were really lucky!"

But then the parents of these two lucky girls came racing around the corner. And the parents' faces looked very afraid.

"Lynne! Caitlin!" their father called. "Girls! Are you all right?"

"Girls! Girls!" their mother cried. "What happened? What happened? Are you safe?"

"Hi, we're down here," Caitlin said sheepishly. "Uh, we had a little accident."

"Hi, Mom!" Lynne said, as if nothing had happened. "No biggie. We're OK. Just some dirt fell into the hole. No problem."

"No problem? Do you know what could have happened if all that dirt fell on top of you?" their father said angrily. "Look at you two! You're a mess. Now get out of there! I told you to stay away from the hole!"

"But, Dad . . . " Caitlin started to say, trying to

explain.

"Don't you 'but Dad' me, young lady! You're old enough to know better than to play near some place that's so dangerous," her father interrupted. "You should have made sure neither of you were even near that hole!"

He helped pull his two daughters out of the pit. Caitlin's pants were smeared with mud. The sleeve of Lynne's jacket was torn.

"But, Dad, I didn't . . . " Caitlin began to explain again. But it was no use.

"Now, I don't want to hear any excuses," their father said. "You both could have been killed! I want you two to go inside and stay there the rest of the day. And I want you to stay away from this hole from now on! Do you understand me this time?"

"Yes, sir," Caitlin said quietly, looking down.

"Yes, sir," Lynne said, fidgeting with her torn jacket.

The sisters walked slowly toward the house. Caitlin was getting angry.

Lynne had done it again, she thought. Her sister had gotten her in trouble — and Lynne was the one who had disobeyed and gone into the hole.

It just wasn't fair!

But she had to admit, her sister *had* saved her life! She couldn't get too mad at her this time.

"You wouldn't listen to me when I said it was dangerous in that hole!" she said to Lynne. "You're such a little kid!"

When the girls got inside, each went into her own bathroom and took a long, hot shower, washing the dirt from her face and hands and hair. Then each started unpacking the boxes filled with her belongings.

Moving is such a pain, Caitlin thought. Already she missed her old house and her old city and her old friends.

This new place is so weird, she thought.

Something about the house just did not seem right. For reasons she could not explain, she simply did not like it.

She decided that maybe she should walk around and take a better look at everything. Her parents were working outside, trying to fix some of the things that were cracked or broken. And there were many.

Maybe her home would not seem so weird once she got to know all the old rooms and hallways better.

So she went exploring.

From one dark room to another, Caitlin wandered.

Down the narrow hallways, opening the heavy, moaning doors that sealed off each room in the house. But somehow, in every room she entered, she felt like an intruder.

It was as if she were an unwelcome stranger, disturbing the peace of the silent old home.

First, she opened the door to the dining room.

Mmmmmwwwwaaaaaaahhhhhnnnn!

There was nothing there, except the dining room furniture and boxes the movers had brought from their old house.

And the odd feeling of being watched by unfriendly walls.

Then, she opened the thick door to her father's study.

Kkkkkrrrraaaaaaaaaggggg!

Nothing there either, except more furniture

and more boxes. And more sensations of being observed — even though no one was around.

And then, she opened the door to the living room.

Wwwwwwwwwooooorrrrrr!

Nothing but the sofas and chairs and tables. And the same strange feelings.

And some footprints . . .

Footprints!

These were like no other footprints Caitlin ever had seen. They were very large prints, left in the thin layer of dust that coated the floor.

They were the footprints of a big man. A *very* big man!

The man who made these footprints would have to be at least seven feet tall, Caitlin figured. And if he was seven feet tall, he probably would weigh three hundred pounds!

Caitlin knew that her father was nowhere near seven feet tall or three hundred pounds. And none of the movers was that large, either.

Someone else was in the house!

Maybe this was why she felt as if somebody

was watching her every move. Maybe somebody was!

Some massive man was hiding in their home, skulking from room to room.

Watching.

Waiting.

Plotting and planning.

He could be a robber. He could be a kidnapper.

He could be a killer!

Whatever he was, he was up to no good.

Caitlin felt she had to find out what it was. She did not want her father to surprise the man and get hurt.

She decided to track the footprints through the dust by herself. She planned to sneak up on the man without letting him spot her.

Then she would tell her father where the man was hidden, and her father could call the police!

But for now, she had to be quiet! *Very* quiet!

She had to follow the dusty footprints of a very large, very bad man.

And she had to pray that he wouldn't find her before she found him!

Chapter Four

The footprints of the monster man trailed off through the living room, circled around the main sofa, and headed into the back hallway.

Filled with dread, Caitlin tiptoed down the hall, following the path.

At any moment, the enormous, powerful *thing* might reach out and grab her!

Trying to be as brave as possible, Caitlin bent low to the floor, looking at the faint prints in the dust.

They led down the narrow dark hallway — directly into the kitchen.

A thick, creaky door separated the kitchen from the hall. Caitlin stood in the shadows, holding her breath, trying to get up enough nerve to push it open.

"Don't chicken out now," she told herself. "You have to do this to help Dad!"

After a few deep breaths — in and out and in and out — she started a countdown to make herself look inside the kitchen.

"Ready?" she asked herself. "OK. One, two, three. . . .Go!"

Gently, inch by inch, she pushed the door open. Little by little, she could see more of the kitchen. And then more. And then more.

She saw no monster man.

But he might be hiding right behind the door, waiting to grab her arm when she reached in far enough. Or he might be tucked inside the kitchen closet, ready to pounce if she walked inside.

Desperately, Caitlin tried to be even quieter, hoping to make absolutely no sound at all.

Then it happened: The door squeaked.

Ccccccrrrrrraaaawwwwwmm!

Caitlin wanted to turn and run. The monster man was probably reaching around the door to grab her by the throat.

Before she could flee, she heard a familiar voice.

"What are you doing, dipbrain?" said Lynne,

with a laugh. "Why are you sneaking around the kitchen?"

"Ohhhhh, nooooo!" Caitlin groaned.

Now she understood what had been happening.

Lynne was sitting on a kitchen chair, happily munching on a peanut butter-and-jelly sandwich. Her feet were resting on top of the kitchen table.

And on her feet were huge, fuzzy pink slippers.

Slippers the size of a monster man's feet!

Lynne was smiling. Caitlin was not.

"It was *you!*" Caitlin said. "I should have known! It's *always* you!"

"What are you talking about, Caitlin? I didn't do anything this time," Lynne answered, biting into her sandwich again.

"You do something wrong even when you're not trying to do something wrong," Caitlin snapped. "Where did you get those slippers? I've never seen them before!"

"Mom bought them for me when she took me to that dollar store at the mall last week," Lynne said. "This is the first time I've worn them. So what? What *about* my slippers?"

"Oh, never mind! Why should I even bother explaining anything to you? You wouldn't understand anyway," Caitlin replied. "Just leave me alone. I don't know why I take anything seriously around this family. I should just understand that when anything goes wrong, you're always the reason."

Lynne got up from her chair and slid her pink slippers along the tile floor, as if she were ice skating. She skated over to the kitchen cabinets and opened a drawer to get out a knife.

"I'm still hungry. I think I'm going to make another sandwich," she said. "Do you want one? I'll make it for you — though I don't know why I should be nice to *you!* You always say such mean things to me. I think you're even worse since we moved. I don't like living in this house at all!"

"Why do you have to be such a kid all the time? Can't you grow up?" Caitlin asked. "No, I don't want a sandwich. I'm going up to my room to unpack. Just don't come in my room! You're such a jerk!"

Caitlin turned to walk out of the kitchen. A sudden scream stopped her.

"Ooooooooowwwww!" Lynne hollered. "My finger!"

Caitlin turned angrily.

"Stop playing stupid games, Lynne!" Caitlin said. "I told you before, it's not smart!"

"My finger! Oooowwww!" Lynne whimpered. "The drawer closed on it. I'm hurt, Caitlin."

"Yeah, right," Caitlin said. "Good try! But I'm not falling for any more of your stupid pranks!"

"It's not a prank!" Lynne said, a tear running down her right cheek. "It *hurt!* The drawer just closed on my finger. Come here and see for yourself."

Caitlin walked over and examined her sister's finger. It *was* hurt — already swollen and bruised.

"How could you possibly have done that?" Caitlin asked.

"*I* didn't do it! That's what I'm trying to tell you," Lynne whined. "The *drawer* did it! All by itself, Caitlin. It closed on my finger without me touching it! As if it *wanted* to catch my finger in there. As if the drawer was trying to hurt me real bad!"

Chapter Five

"That's just silly!" Caitlin said. "Drawers don't move all by themselves!"

But in her heart, she was not so sure.

This was a strange house. Somehow, she realized that right away.

Maybe the house was even stranger than she had imagined.

"Tell me what happened, right now," she said firmly. "I don't want to play around with your kids' games anymore. You must have bumped the drawer somehow, Lynne."

"Honest! I'm telling you the truth, Caitlin," Lynne answered. "I just reached in the drawer for a knife. And the drawer started to slam shut on my fingers — fast! I tried to pull my hand out in time but the drawer caught my finger really hard."

28

The proof that Lynne wasn't lying about the injury was right there — in one very black-and-blue finger. And her voice sounded as if she was not lying about anything else, either.

Still, this was too much to believe. Drawers could not move without someone touching them.

Could they?

And even if it was true, what could she do about it? What could anyone do about it?

There was no use telling her parents — they would *never* believe a ridiculous story like that. No one would.

So Caitlin tried to pretend nothing was wrong. She told Lynne that she must have bumped the drawer somehow, maybe with an arm or a hip.

And she told herself the same thing. As she walked up the stairs alone to her room, she tried hard to make herself believe it. Lynne had bumped the drawer into her own finger. That was all that had happened.

Nothing was wrong with her family's new house. Nothing whatsoever.

But, deep inside herself, Caitlin knew the truth was something else. Something too frightening to even think about.

Chapter Six

Caitlin was surprised when she got back upstairs. Surprised — and troubled.

The door to her room was wide open.

"That's strange," she said to herself. "I *know* I closed that door! And Lynne was downstairs. And Mom and Dad are still outside working. Hmmmm."

But she shrugged her shoulders and shook her head and again pretended to herself that nothing was wrong. Doors don't open by themselves, she thought.

And she tried hard to believe it.

Until she noticed that her window was open, too. Even though it was almost winter outside and the cold late-autumn air was filling her room.

She *knew* no one in her family would have opened the window, wasting expensive heat.

But if not her family, then who *had* opened it?

Then Caitlin saw that clothes she had un-packed from three boxes and hung up in her closet also had been moved.

But moved in a very strange way.

The clothes were all back in the boxes, which were neatly sealed with heavy packing tape.

Caitlin shuddered with fear.

"How could this possibly happen?" she asked. "My door is left open. The window is letting in cold air. And my boxes are packed up again! It's just not possible!"

Then Caitlin snapped her fingers, realizing what must have happened. Her expression changed from fear to irritation.

"Lynne!" she said out loud.

It *had* to be Lynne, pulling some stunt again. It was *always* Lynne.

So Caitlin marched downstairs toward the kitchen to scold her little sister. But when she reached the bottom of the stairs, Lynne was already there, looking at her with puzzled eyes.

"Hey, Cait, why is it so cold in here?" Lynne asked. "Did you turn down the heat?"

"*You* should know! You left my window wide open with the freezing air coming inside," Caitlin snapped.

"Huh? You're crazy. I didn't open your window. I haven't been in your room once since we got here," Lynne said.

"Don't lie to me, Lynne! It had to be you," Caitlin said.

"I'm *not* lying, Cait! Why don't you ever believe me? I have not been in your room. I *swear*!" Lynne said.

She sure sounded as if she was telling the truth.

Caitlin did not know what to believe. Then she noticed the goose bumps on her arms.

"You know, you're right about something. It *is* cold in this house. Too cold to be caused by just one open window," she said, scratching her head. "I turned the heat up when we came inside. It should be nice and warm in here. But it seems to be getting colder instead of warmer."

She walked over to the thermostat and found something very peculiar.

The heat was turned off.

Not just turned down, but completely off. As if there were not a house full of people that needed heat.

As if no one were going to live in the house at all.

Who would turn off the heat when it was so cold and windy outside?

Lynne would never do that, even if she had been playing some stupid kid's trick in Caitlin's room. Lynne complained more than anybody else in the family about feeling cold. She always wanted the heat turned up high whenever it was the least bit chilly.

And her parents certainly would not turn off the heat. And Caitlin knew she hadn't done it.

But someone had. Or some*thing* had!

"Lynne, this just weirds me out!" Caitlin said, trying to hide her fears from her little sister. "Very strange things are happening in this house. I can't explain any of them. You *swear* you haven't been in my room? You're not fooling around with me? This is serious, Lynne!"

"No, honest, Cait. I swear!" Lynne said emphatically.

"Then this really is very, very weird, Lynne. The drawer, the door, the window, the heat," Caitlin said, thinking about everything that had happened. "And my clothes! That was the most bizarre thing of all! How could they have been packed back in their boxes?"

"Huh? What door? What clothes? What do you mean they were packed back in their boxes?" Lynne asked.

"Never mind, Lynne. I'll tell you everything later. But we have to decide how to break this to Mom and Dad. We have to find some way to make them believe what's happening here," Caitlin said quickly. "Our lives might be in danger!"

She paused to think again.

"What do you mean, Cait? What *is* happening in our new house? How are we in so much danger?" Lynne said.

Her voice sounded very worried.

"There is only one explanation, Lynne," Caitlin explained. "There's only one answer for all the weird things that are going on everywhere around here. I always knew something was strange about this place.

But now I know what it is — for sure!"

But even though the answer was in her mind, Caitlin was afraid to say it. Afraid that if she spoke the words, that would make them come true.

"What? What? What do you *mean?*" Lynne asked, almost frantic.

"It's the worst thing that could happen. Nothing worse can ever happen to a house! Our new home is haunted, Lynne," Caitlin said, reluctantly.

"The whole place is filled with ghosts!"

Chapter Seven

"*Ghosts?* You're *crazy*, Caitlin!" Lynne exclaimed. "I'm only nine years old and even I know there's no such thing as ghosts!"

"Oh, yeah? I didn't believe in them either. But come with me and I'll prove it to you," Caitlin answered, in that know-it-all voice girls sometimes use with younger sisters.

Caitlin turned the heat back on and walked upstairs with Lynne, explaining about the opened door and the opened window and the clothes packed back in their boxes.

"I can *feel* something in this house, Lynne. I just know it. I've always known it, since the first moment I set foot in this place," Caitlin said, opening the door to her room. "There's a bad presence, like something or someone doesn't want us here. Come over to my desk and I'll show you what I mean about ghosts."

Caitlin pulled out one of the books she had unpacked from a moving company box earlier that day — a book all about the supernatural. It was called, *Ghosts, Goblins and Ghouls: The Real Story Behind House Hauntings.*

"When we were downstairs talking about everything that happened in our house, I remembered reading this book a couple years ago," Caitlin said, thumbing through the pages. "And that's when I knew for sure we had ghosts in our house. I'll show you, as soon as I find this one chapter about — Yeah, here it is."

She began to read to her frightened little sister from the ghost book. As she read, she became frightened, too:

"Ghosts are the spirits of people who died with some terrible conflict unresolved, or in some terrible pain. Often they died violently, by murder or suicide," the chapter about ghosts began.

"They can inhabit any building but especially are fond of older structures. Commonly, ghosts are

discovered haunting abandoned buildings such as houses, businesses and railroad stations. They create disturbances in the environment and can cause fear and misery — but never injury or death — for any living person who enters their habitat."

"Just because we live in an old abandoned house doesn't mean we have ghosts, you big jerk," Lynne said. "That stuff in the book doesn't mean anything."

"Let me finish reading this page to you, Lynne," Caitlin said. "I'm just getting to the part that proves we have ghosts."

She continued to read:

"Ghosts are looking for some way to resolve the pain or conflict that caused them to remain among the living after their bodies died. Sometimes these spirits do this through terrorizing human beings they come in contact with. Poltergeists are the most common form of terror employed by ghosts: Objects move around on their own. Doors, cabinets and drawers may open and close. Windows may shut so tight no one can pry them loose or open so far no one can close them again. Household items like furniture

and clothing sometimes disappear from one place, turning up somewhere unexpected."

"You see what I mean," Caitlin said nervously. "It sounds almost exactly like what happened to us. We have ghosts — and they're creating a poltergeist. We're living in a haunted house, Lynne!"

"But Cait, remember what the book said about ghosts not hurting people?" Lynne recalled. "It said ghosts 'can cause misery — but never injury or death — for any living person.' I was injured by that drawer. Look at how swollen and sore my finger is."

Lynne's index finger looked like a long blue thumb now, thick and bruised from being slammed in the drawer.

"It *can't* be ghosts, Caitlin. Whatever it is in the house, it hurt my finger pretty bad," Lynne said.

"Maybe the book is wrong about ghosts not ever injuring people. Or maybe we've got a really mean ghost!" Caitlin said. "There's just no other explanation. Our home is haunted, Lynne. We might as well face it and get Mom and Dad to believe it, too. And then they'll sell this house so we can move away!"

"But there was something else that happened to us, Cait. Remember how we almost got buried under all that dirt in the hole out back?" Lynne said. "Maybe that wasn't an accident, like we thought it was. Maybe something was trying to *murder* us!"

This made Caitlin stop to think. The huge mound of dirt certainly had fallen into the pit, nearly killing them both. And the drawer had seemed to close by itself right onto Lynne's finger, Caitlin had to admit.

But if not ghosts — what? What could be causing so much weirdness in one old home?

And, whatever it was, why was it trying to hurt her family?

This house was a terrible place to live!

Just then, the girls heard a tremendous crash and clatter, as if pieces of metal had splattered across the tile floor downstairs. The sound made both of them jump.

"Wha — uh, what was that?" Lynne asked, dreading the answer. "Was — uh, was it, uh — *ghosts*, do you think?"

"It sounded like something fell in the kitchen.

Probably the ghosts knocked something over to scare us again," Caitlin said. "Let's go see what happened."

Caitlin actually felt relieved as she hurried down the staircase with her sister. Now she was really sure there was at least one ghost, maybe more.

It seemed a lot better to imagine their house was haunted by a ghost that meant no harm, rather than by something else that really wanted to hurt people.

Probably the ghost had not wanted to catch Lynne's finger in the drawer. And probably the ghost had never really intended to bury the two sisters under the pile of dirt.

Ghosts were spooky but they were harmless. The book said so!

Lynne and Caitlin pushed open the squeaky kitchen door and found the silverware drawer on the floor, with knives and forks and spoons scattered everywhere. It was the same drawer that had closed so hard on Lynne's finger.

Then the girls heard another noise — like water running somewhere behind them.

They whirled around and saw their father at

the kitchen sink, behind the door. He was washing his hands.

"Dad, what happened here?" Caitlin asked. "Were you in the kitchen when the drawer came out? Did it just fly out of the cabinet on to the floor, or what?"

"Fly out? What the heck are you talking about, Caitlin?" their father said. "I cut myself on a knife when I reached into the drawer. And when I pulled my hand away quickly, this stupid old drawer came out and dropped on the floor."

"So *you* did this? You mean, the drawer just fell out by accident?" Caitlin asked, even more relieved now.

Maybe there wasn't a ghost or anything else in the house, after all. Not even one.

"How else would it fall out? As I said, I reached in the drawer and cut myself on a knife," the father said, wrapping a paper towel around his bleeding finger. "But one thing does seem kind of strange, I guess. Because I don't know exactly *how* I got cut. I hadn't even really touched the knife when I felt it slice through my skin."

"You hadn't touched it?" Lynne asked, looking uncomfortably at her sister.

"No, I really was only starting to reach in for the knife," their father replied, his eyebrows twisted in confusion. "It was almost like the knife jumped right out at my finger. I know that sounds silly but it all happened really fast. It just seemed like the knife came out of the drawer after me — as if it was trying to cut my finger right off!"

Chapter Eight

Caitlin and Lynne were startled.

"Dad, are you sure the knife jumped out at your finger?" Caitlin asked. Her voice wavered with tension. "Maybe it was just your imagination, huh?"

"Yeah, maybe everything happened so fast you really just cut yourself before you knew it," Lynne said.

The father looked at his daughters with a bewildered expression, then smiled.

"Listen, don't let your imaginations run wild, girls," he said. "Of *course* I cut myself on the knife. What else do you think happened? Knives don't jump out and cut people. I was only saying that's what it *seemed* like. It's great to have a vivid imagination — but don't let it carry you away."

"But, Dad — well, see, things have been hap-

45

pening," Lynne blurted out. "It's really scary. Something is weird in this house, Dad."

Caitlin felt annoyed with her sister. She was not sure this was the time or place to tell their father about the ghosts.

But Lynne had already opened her big mouth, Caitlin thought. There was no choice now.

"Dad, Lynne's right," she said. "All kinds of things have been happening. Doors have been opening by themselves and clothes I've hung in the closet have been getting packed back in boxes."

Caitlin realized how ridiculous this sounded, but there was no turning back now. She pressed ahead with her explanation.

"And the heat was shut off by itself and — "

"Wait, wait, wait. Hold on here, girls," their father replied. "This all sounds like something you saw on TV or read in one of those *Shivers* books. Now just stop and think about it. How could these things really happen?"

"But, Dad — you said yourself that the knife seemed to jump out of the drawer and cut you," Caitlin answered.

46

"And Dad, remember the dirt that almost fell on top of Caitlin and I? How did that happen?" Lynne said.

"Caitlin and *me*," their father corrected.

"Whatever. But Dad, you don't get it! This is serious," Lynne answered.

"It's true, Dad. For once, Lynne is right. There is something really wrong with this house," Caitlin said, trying to get up the nerve to say the word to her father.

The same word she did not want to say out loud to her sister. The scary "G" word.

"Ghosts, Dad!" she said, finally. "Ghosts! We have a house haunted by ghosts!"

Their father laughed.

"Look, girls. If you want to scare yourselves, that's fine," he said. "But you're being silly and I think you're both old enough to know it. Now I have some things to finish outside before it gets dark. We can talk about all this later — at dinner."

"But, *Daaaaad* — " Caitlin whined.

"But, *Daaaaad* — " Lynne whined at the same time.

Their father laughed again, waving his hand at them as he walked out the door.

"Good-bye, girls," he said with an amused snort. "Do me a favor and wash all that silverware before you put it in the drawer again, will you? I swear, I don't know where you two get your imaginations. I think you're both going to grow up to be writers or something. You can tell me more ghost stories later if you want to!"

And, still grinning, he closed the door behind him.

"You stupid little kid!" Caitlin said, slapping Lynne's arm. "Why did you have to say something about the ghosts when Dad was busy? Now he'll never believe us! He's going to have to see the strange things happen for himself!"

"Don't call me stupid! Dad told you never to say that to me," Lynne responded. "Besides, what's the difference when we told him? He would never believe some dumb story like this anyway! He's a scientist. Scientists don't believe in ghosts!"

"Well come on, let's pick up all this stuff on the floor and — "

But Caitlin stopped in the middle of her sentence.

Her mouth fell open in shock. And fear.

Lynne's mouth hung wide open, too.

Because when the girls stopped arguing and turned around to face the spilled silverware, the silverware was gone.

A single cardboard box on the floor had taken the place of the knives and forks and spoons.

The small box was closed. It was sealed with heavy packing tape.

And a sticker on top of it said, "Silverware."

In the few moments the sisters had turned their backs, the family's silverware had been packed back inside a moving company box.

As if some ghost or some monster or some troll who lived in the basement — as if *something,* at any rate — wanted the family to pack all their boxes and leave this old house forever.

Chapter Nine

During dinner, Caitlin's mother and father had a good laugh about the ghosts.

"You really do have quite the gift for fantasy, my dear," her mother told her.

"It's great that your mind is so creative, honey," her father said. "But as I told you earlier, don't let your thoughts get so carried away that you scare yourself with them. And you're scaring your little sister, too. That's not right."

"Dad, Cait isn't imagining things. That box of silverware got all packed up on its own," Lynne replied, trying to defend her sister.

"Well, I wish those ghosts would *unpack* our boxes instead of packing them up," their mother said with a laugh. "Now *that* would be useful!"

"Mom, Dad — please! Try to listen to me for a

change," Caitlin begged. "I know I'm just a twelve-year-old kid and everything, but I am not imagining this stuff! This is not something I've made up or read in a book or seen on TV. It is real! Our house is haunted!"

"Then why haven't your mother and I seen any evidence of these so-called ghosts, Caitlin? In science, we learn that you do not believe in anything until you can prove its existence," their father answered. "Not one strange thing has happened to us. Nothing unusual has taken place in our presence. I think you're just worked up because of the move — and your mind is playing tricks on you."

"I mean, really, darling," their mother said casually. "We wouldn't be going out tonight if we thought this place was truly haunted."

"Going *out*?" Caitlin asked.

"Going *out*?" Lynne asked, at the same time.

"Yes. Going out," their father said. "We have been invited over to one of our new neighbor's homes for the evening. It's just several houses away from here. But we will be out rather late, I think. So you girls will have to get yourselves to bed on time."

"But, *Daaad*! What about the *ghosts?*" Lynne whined.

"Dad, please! I know I said I'm too old for a baby-sitter, but I do not want to be alone with Lynne in this house tonight," Caitlin said. "I'm really scared, Dad! There *are* ghosts in this house!"

"For the last time, girls. There are *no* ghosts in this house — or anywhere else for that matter," their father said firmly. "Now I expect you both to behave as grown-ups tonight and take care of each other. Have fun, watch some TV in your new home. And stop worrying about ghosts!"

"And get to bed by ten at the latest. Both of you," their mother added. "We need you to help clean up and unpack around the house tomorrow. You'll need your rest."

There was no point in arguing any more, Caitlin understood. Her parents were going to visit neighbors for the whole evening — and there was nothing anyone could do to stop them. She and Lynne would be alone in the house.

Alone.
With the ghosts.

Caitlin and Lynne got together before their parents left. The girls made a sacred pact as sisters: They agreed to stick together through the night, no matter what happened.

They would not try to scare each other as a joke. They would not leave each other alone for more than a few moments.

And if they had to, they would fight the ghosts together.

When it was almost eight, and their parents were walking out the front door, Caitlin and Lynne kissed them both on the cheek. They told their parents to have fun. And they stood in the door, waving good-bye.

They hoped it would not be the last good-bye they ever waved to their parents.

Caitlin closed the door and looked at her sister. Neither said a word.

They walked toward the kitchen to make popcorn.

They had decided to watch a Disney video to distract themselves, and make them feel better. Maybe popcorn and Mary Poppins would make the ghosts stay away.

"Shouldn't we lock the door first, Cait?" Lynne asked. She glanced at the deadbolt.

"*No! No!*" Caitlin said. "I'm not worried about locking anything out tonight. I'm worried about being locked *in* with ghosts!"

At that exact moment, a blood-chilling howl echoed up from the basement.

Mmmmmwwwwwwooooooooooaaaaaaaaaaahh hhhhhhhhhhhh!

Terrified, the sisters stared at each other. Their eyes were as wide as saucers. Lynne shook with fear. Caitlin could not move at all.

And then they heard another sound. And this one was even more frightening.

It was the sound of the doors locking — all by themselves!

One by one, the heavy metal locks slammed shut.

First the front door: *Gggwwaaccckk!*

Then the back door: *Gggwwaaccckk!*

Then the door to the garage: *Gggwwaaccckk!*

Then every window locked itself, one after another after another, all around the old home: *Ppphhheewwwtt! Ppphhheewwwtt! Ppphhheewwwtt! Ppphhheewwwtt! Ppphhheewwwtt!*

Caitlin ran to the front door, hoping to force it open before it was too late.

It was already locked!

She grabbed and twisted the deadbolt lock — but she could not budge it.

She wrestled frantically with the door handle, yanking and jiggling it with all her strength.

No use!

Caitlin and Lynne were locked inside this strange, horrifying, haunted house!

With no one to help them!

And no place to hide!

And no way out!

Chapter Ten

"We can't panic, Lynn!" Caitlin said, but the quaver in her voice betrayed her own fear. "Let's use our heads. We've got think how to deal with this!"

"Cait, I'm scared," Lynne cried. Tears streamed down her cheeks. "What is going to happen to us?"

"Nothing! Remember what the book said? Ghosts don't injure or kill people. They only cause fear and misery," Caitlin said. "All we have to do is *not* be afraid, no matter what happens. And just wait for Mom and Dad to get home. Let's go call them. They left the number for us, remember?"

"I wish they were here now," Lynne whined. "I really do not like this house."

They tried the telephone in the front hallway.

The phone was dead. It was as if the line to the

house had been cut.

Caitlin and Lynne walked nervously, hand in hand, through the living room, down the hallway toward the kitchen.

The ghosts were only trying to frighten them, Caitlin kept reminding her sister. She was trying to convince herself at the same time. If she said it over and over and over, in a firm enough voice, maybe she would find a way to believe it.

"The only thing we need is courage," she said. "Just don't be afraid and nothing can happen. Ghosts cannot hurt us!"

And so together, still holding hands tightly, the two girls pushed open the heavy door and walked into the kitchen.

But this time, there was no squeak from the door.

Instead, there was a long, low, whining wail — spooky and shrill.

Eeeeeeeeeeeeeeeeeeeeeeaaaaaaaaaaaaaaaarrrrrr rrrr!

And when the wail began, the doorknob started to shake in Caitlin's hand until the whole door

57

rattled and vibrated wildly.

Caitlin tried to hold on to the knob, but couldn't.

The door pulled loose from her hand — and swung back toward the girls.

Lynne jumped away but the door slammed into Caitlin's forehead, knocking her to the floor.

"Caitlin! Caitlin! Are you OK?" Lynne shouted, rushing to her sister's side. "Cait! Talk to me!"

Caitlin tried to shake off the pain, rubbing her forehead and moaning.

"Ooowwww! Yeah, I'm OK. I *guess*," she complained. "But my head hurts. Just let me rest here for a minute before I get up."

But there was no time for resting — or anything else.

Because now all the cabinets and all the drawers in the kitchen began to open and close by themselves. Rapidly and loudly, each one opened and shut, opened and shut — without a human hand touching them!

Kkklaaacckk! went every cabinet.

Vhhhoooot! went every drawer.

Kkklaaacckk! Vhhhoooot! Kkklaaacckk! Vhhhoooot! Kkklaaacckk! Vhhhoooot!

It resembled a scene from a nightmare — loud and shocking!

Caitlin was too afraid to feel her bump on the head. Too afraid to do anything!

This, she knew, was no nightmare. This was a very dangerous reality.

Suddenly, a drawer blasted out of a kitchen counter, like a cannonball fired in a battle.

It hurled itself right at Caitlin and Lynne.

They watched, frozen in horror, as this kitchen missile sailed across the room toward them! Directly at their heads!

And as the drawer took dead aim at their skulls, the girls did the only thing they could think to do at that awful moment.

Together, in perfect unison, they screamed!

Aaaaaaaaaaaaaaaaaaaaaaaaaaahhhhhhhhhh!!!!

Chapter Eleven

The kitchen drawer was bearing down on their heads!

At the last moment, it seemed to get an extra boost of power from somewhere. It roared harmlessly over the sisters' heads!

They heard the drawer whistle past their ears and explode into a thousand splinters against the kitchen door behind them.

The splinters dropped around them like rain.

"Run, Lynne!" Caitlin shouted. "Run for your life!"

She grabbed Lynne's hand and dragged her out of the kitchen, through the long hall and up the stairs. They raced into Caitlin's room and shut the door behind them, locking it.

Lynne was crying. Tears streamed down her

cheeks. Her eyes were wide with fear, her nose was running, and she was shaking like a leaf.

"Caitlin, what can we do? What's happening?" she wailed, between sobs. "We were almost *killed* by that drawer!"

Caitlin fumbled around her desk for the book about ghosts, goblins and ghouls. There *must* be some explanation for what was going on inside their house!

Horrible things were happening! Dangerous things! Maybe even deadly things!

This did not seem like ghosts anymore . . .

"Cait, what are you *doing*!" Lynne shouted. "We have to get out of here right now! Why are you reading that stupid book?"

"I just need to find something, Lynne. Shhh! Be quiet a second! Let me read," Caitlin snapped.

Scanning the book as quickly as she could, Caitlin flipped through page after page after page. The pages shook and rustled as she turned them with her trembling fingers.

If these were not ghosts in the house, what were they?

Maybe once the sisters knew what was attacking them they could find a way to fight back.

Caitlin poured through the frightening ghost book, scanning pages and pages and pages, reading as rapidly as possible.

She saw nothing that could explain anything that had happened to them.

Until she got to the very last page.

She read the words slowly, carefully. As she read, her heart beat faster and faster. A cold shudder of fear made her hands shake so hard she could barely finish reading.

Caitlin looked up at her sister. Their eyes met. Both of them dreaded facing the truth.

"Wh-what? What is it?" Lynne asked.

"I know what's wrong with the house, Lynne," Caitlin said quietly, as though she felt they were doomed. "It hardly ever happens anywhere. But when it does happen, it's even worse than having ghosts! *A lot* worse!"

"Wh-what do, uh, you mean — uh, worse?" Lynne stammered, almost unable to speak.

"There are no ghosts out to hurt us, Lynne. It's the *house* that's trying to get rid of us," Caitlin said. "Our family moved into a house that hates people. It despises anyone living inside its walls. The house wants to force us to leave."

"The house hates people?" Lynne asked, starting to cry again. "What does that mean, Cait? What does that mean?"

"It means this house fights a war against anyone who tries to live here," Caitlin answered. "And it will do anything it has to do. Our own home would kill our whole family just to make us go away!"

Chapter Twelve

"Caitlin, that doesn't make any sense!" Lynne bawled. "How can a house attack anybody all by itself?"

"The book says houses have personalities, just like people, Lynne. And sometimes, a house gets mean," Caitlin said. "Here, listen. I'll read part of it to you."

*"There is an important distinction between a haunted house and a **haunting** house. The haunted house is troubled only by ghosts, which may frighten the human occupants but never will harm them. However, in a haunting house, anyone who lives in the dwelling is in grave danger,"* Caitlin read to her sister.

"Hauntings are very rare. They come only to homes that are old and unwanted. It helps to think of haunting houses as similar to old angry men who

want no one living nearby. The buildings become like hermits, resenting the human race for ignoring them. When humans attempt to move in, a haunting house comes alive. The wood and brick and glass and metal take on a life of their own, suddenly possessed by a violent force. (However, a haunting house has only very limited power over objects owned by the residents — these objects cannot be used for violence.)

"Instead, the house itself wages a war. It produces strange sounds from furnaces or door hinges or anything else that may frighten people. And the house will use doors or windows or any other weapons at its disposal to physically attack the residents, harming or killing the unfortunate occupants."

"I hate this house!" Lynne yelled. "I hate it! I hate it!"

"I hate it, too!" Caitlin said. "But we've got to figure some way to get out of here right now or we'll never live through this night! I don't think we have much time to waste!"

"Does the book say how to make the house stop attacking us, Caitlin?" Lynne asked. "Or maybe it tells us how to get out? Then we can run down the road and get Mom and Dad!"

Caitlin glanced sadly at her sister, shaking her head. Then she looked down at the book and read from it again:

"*There is no known way to rid a haunting house of its violent forces. The only way to survive is for the residents to leave quickly,*" the book said. "*Only a fortunate few have ever escaped a haunting house once the building has launched a full-fledged attack. Typically, the house will lock all the doors and windows. After that, the house will destroy any living thing left inside!*"

"What are we going to do?" Lynne said, starting to cry again. "We're going to be killed by our own house!"

"No, we're not!" Caitlin answered. "Come on, Lynne. Hurry up! I have an idea! And stop crying, will you? We have to be calm if we're going to find a way to get out of here!"

Holding Lynne's hand, she hurried downstairs and stood in front of a living room window.

Then she looked around for something heavy. She spotted a large lamp on an end table. It was her mother's favorite lamp but that didn't matter now.

If she didn't do something, her mother might never see either of her daughters alive again!

Without hesitating, Caitlin picked up the lamp and threw it through the window. The window glass shattered, falling on to the front lawn.

Now there was a big hole in the window — easily big enough for two young girls to crawl through.

It was their only possible way out of the house.

"Hurry, Lynne!" Caitlin shouted. "Get outside! I'll be right behind you! Just watch out for those sharp pieces of glass still hanging from the window!"

Caitlin watched as her sister scampered to the window and put one leg through the opening to the ledge outside. The ledge was littered with dirt and small pebbles, and Lynne tried to kick them aside to find a firm foothold.

All she had to do now was squeeze her body around the sharp glass and she would be safe.

But escape was not going to be so simple. Not with the deadly house watching every move!

Just as Lynne was about to crawl outside, the

window quickly unlocked itself — and suddenly began to open.

"Lynne, look out!" Caitlin screamed.

Huge shards of glass were pointed at Lynne. They were moving fast — very fast — toward her neck!

Caitlin felt helpless as the window flung itself open.

Her little sister was about to have her throat cut by a window full of jagged glass!

Chapter Thirteen

As the razor-sharp glass sliced toward Lynne's throat, her foot suddenly lost its grip on the window ledge.

She slipped on a small pebble, tumbling back inside the house as though she had stepped on a banana peel.

She flopped to the living room floor a split second before the window slammed all the way up. The sharp glass whooshed by her, cutting only air.

A tiny stone under her foot had saved Lynne from being carved into ribbons.

"Lynne! Are you hurt?" Caitlin asked, helping her sister off the floor. "I thought you were finished that time for sure!"

"Wow, another close one, huh? If I hadn't slipped on the ledge, I never could have moved out of the way in time," Lynne panted, looking at the window. "Hey, look, Caitlin! The window's open now. Come on! Let's jump outside and get out of here! Quick!"

But before they could get close, the window began to slide forcefully up and down, up and down, up and down. It would cut or crush anyone who tried to get through.

"There's no way, Lynne. We'll never make it outside!" Caitlin said.

The situation looked desperate. They were doomed if they stayed inside the house — and doomed if they tried to escape.

Caitlin tried to stay calm and think. Panicking would not help them now.

Suddenly, she brightened.

"I just thought of something else," she said. "The window's broken open! We can yell for help! Maybe someone will hear us!"

"The houses are all so far apart here, Cait. No one will hear anything! And besides, we're at the end of the road!" Lynne worried.

"We have to try! Come on!" Caitlin said

firmly. "Yell like your life depends on it. Because it does!"

And so the two girls stood peering out the broken window, which still rose and fell and rose and fell on its own. And they began to shout.

"Heeeelllpp!" Caitlin bellowed.

"Hhhheeeeeeeeellllllllpp!" Lynne yelled.

No sooner had the first sounds come from their lips than a pair of shutters slapped closed over the window.

Thhwwaaaaaaaappp! Thhhwwwaaaaaaaappp!

And then heavy wood shutters slammed tight over every other window in the house. Caitlin and Lynne could hear them banging shut everywhere, sealing the sisters even more tightly inside the killer house.

Thhwwaaapp! Thhwwaaapp! Thhwwaaapp! Thhwwaaapp! Thhwwaaapp!

"There's no way to get out now, Cait! There's nothing we can do," Lynne said.

She fought back her tears bravely, but fear still showed in her eyes.

"We're not going to give up, Lynne! We can't!

71

Mom and Dad wouldn't give up if they were here," Caitlin said. "We have to think of some way to beat this old, rotten, stinking house!"

"I hate this house!" Lynne said angrily.

"There must be *something* we can do!" Caitlin said.

She pressed her hands to her forehead, thinking as hard as she could.

At last, she got an idea . . .

But it was an idea that she did not like.

An idea that sent icy chills of terror up her spine.

They would have to go into the basement to look for a way out, Caitlin explained — into the dark, damp, cold, frightening basement.

In the best of times, walking into the basement felt like walking inside a large grave. And these were not the best of times.

But Caitlin insisted.

"Dad might have some tools down there we can use to break through the doors," she said. "Maybe he has an ax or something. *Anything!* We might be able to break out of here before the house murders us!"

"No way! *I'm* not going into that basement! Especially not now," Lynne said. "Nope, Caitlin! Sorry! Not me! No *way!*"

"Way!" Caitlin said. "We *have* to, Lynne!"

After several minutes of heavy convincing, Lynne finally agreed. The basement was their only hope.

With Caitlin leading the way, the girls opened the thick, squeaking door to the basement. They flicked on the switch. One dim bulb that hung on a wire from the ceiling spread a wavering and gloomy glow around the basement.

They took one step onto the wooden stairs that led down. The stair creaked loudly.

Rrrrrrrrrrrrrrrreeeeeeeeeeeeeaaaaaaaaa!

They took another slow step.

Rrrrrrrrrrrrrrrreeeeeeeeeeeeeaaaaaaaaa!

And another.

Rrrrrrrrrrrrrrrrrrrreeeeeeeeeeeeeeeeeeaaaa aaaaa!

The sisters were huddled together on the third of 13 steps into the basement when it happened.

The door behind them flung itself closed. At the same instant, the basement light went out.

It was completely black now, without even the faintest light shining under the basement door.

They felt as if they were shut inside a huge tomb.

"Aaaaaaahhh! We're trapped in the basement!" Lynne screamed. She began to sob uncontrollably. "We're going to die! We're going to be killed by something we can't even see!"

Chapter Fourteen

"Stop crying, Lynne! Stop it!" Caitlin ordered. "It doesn't help anything! And stop saying we're going to die! I know we can find a way out of here! Just wait. Stand right there!"

Caitlin carefully creaked back up the stairs, feeling her way through the darkness to the basement door. Neither girl could see anything at all.

The door squeaked as Caitlin pushed on it. But it opened. Now, however, the rest of the house was also shrouded in darkness.

"We're not locked in the basement, Lynne. The door's open. Come on back up here," Caitlin said. "There is no lock on this door. But it looks like all the lights are out in the whole house. We'll have to find Dad's flashlight."

Caitlin and Lynne stumbled their way into the

kitchen, where they found a box containing a long silver flashlight, a candle, and matches.

The house was pitch black. The heavy shutters prevented nearly all the pale moonlight from leaking in through the windows. It was almost impossible to see anything.

They turned on the flashlight, lit the candle and walked back to the basement steps. Caitlin held the flashlight. Lynne carried the candle.

They both knew what they had to do. They *had* to go back down those basement steps.

No matter how scared they were.

The tool they needed was in the basement — and it was their only chance to break out of the house and find their parents.

Step by creaky step, surrounded by darkness, the two girls walked down the old wooden staircase toward the basement.

Rrrrrrrrrrrrrreeeeeeeeeeeeeeaaaaaaaaaaa!

After every step or two, Caitlin and Lynne turned to look at each other, as if to make sure someone friendly was still standing close.

Rrrrrrrrrrrrrreeeeeeeeeeeeeeaaaaaaaaaaa!

Rrrrrrrrrrrrrrreeeeeeeeeeeeeaaaaaaaaaaa!

Finally, after thirteen frightening steps, they reached the basement floor.

"Uh, I — uh, well, I don't know — uh, if this was such a good idea," Lynne stammered.

"Yeah, I — I, uh, know what you mean," Caitlin stammered back.

The basement was the scariest place either girl had ever been.

There was something about the total blackness of the damp cellar, pierced only by a single flashlight and a single candle.

And there was something about the look of the room: Spider webs dangled from the wooden beams overhead. Water dripped from an old boiler. Black bugs crawled across the cold concrete walls.

And there was something about standing in the bottom of a house that was plotting to murder them!

This was a very dangerous place, and both sisters knew it.

"L-let's, uh, get out of here, Caitlin!" Lynne said nervously. "Something bad is going to happen if we stay in this basement!"

"Uh, yeah, OK, Lynne. B-but, let's find an ax or something first," Caitlin said just as nervously. "Dad must h-have something like that in his tools. We, uh, we have to find some way to knock down the door. Or we'll be stuck in this house forever!"

"I, uh — I don't, uh, know, Caitlin," Lynne answered. "But I guess you're, uh, right."

And then, from somewhere, came a loud, horrifying howl:

Mmmmmwwwwwwwooooooooooaaaaaaaahhhhhhhhhh!

It sounded like the wail of one very large, very angry bear!

Both girls screamed. They jumped back as far as they could jump, and grabbed each other.

Lynne dropped the candle. The flame went out.

Caitlin just managed to hang on to the flashlight as she hugged her sister.

Then Caitlin understood where the howl was coming from.

"Lynne, listen. It's just the boiler. Remember, like the book said — the house will make any sounds it can to scare people," Caitlin said. "It's the same thing we heard before, upstairs, only now we're standing right next to it. It's just that poor old boiler giving off a spooky sound to frighten us. That thing looks so old, I almost feel sorry for it. Come on, let's find Dad's tools and get out of here."

As Caitlin explained, the sound somehow abruptly stopped.

With only the flashlight to light their way, Caitlin and Lynne began to search the stacks of boxes.

Where was the box marked "Tools?" It had to be somewhere.

Caitlin had never paid much attention to her father's tools before. But he must own something that would break down a wooden door, she thought. And it must be inside one of these boxes.

The flashlight beam shone around the black basement as Caitlin searched for any sign of the tools.

"Oh, no!" she said. "Oh, no!"

"What? What is it, Cait?" Lynne asked.

"Look! Look where the tools are," Caitlin said. She pointed high overhead.

The cardboard box marked "Tools" was sitting

on the tallest shelf in the basement — far out of their reach.

"Dad would never have put that box up there," Lynne said.

"No, and he didn't! The *house* moved it up there," Caitlin said. "The book says a haunting house has limited power over our belongings, remember? The house can't hurt us with anything we own — but it can sure make our things move around a lot!"

The girls did not give up, though. They came up with a plan to get into the box of tools anyway.

Caitlin got on her hands and knees, ignoring the clammy feeling of the cold, wet basement floor. Lynne stepped on her sister's back, flailing at the box with the flashlight.

If Lynne hit the box with the flashlight hard enough, Caitlin said, the tools might fall to the ground.

Lynne swung at the box and missed. She swung again and hit it. The heavy box hardly budged.

"Hit it again! Hit it harder!" Caitlin urged.

"I *hate* this house!" Lynne said, swinging wildly at the box.

Just then, there was a noise.

A noise neither girl had heard before.

A noise like heavy wood bending and cracking and breaking.

"What's that?" Caitlin asked. "Shine your light around and see if you see anything, Lynne!"

Lynne did as she was told.

What she saw in the beam of light made her gasp in horror!

"Cait!" Lynne screamed. "Cait, *look*!"

One of the enormous wooden beams that held up the floor of the house was cracking in half — right above them.

The entire house was about to fall on top of the terrified sisters, crushing them under two tons of wood and brick and metal!

Chapter Fifteen

The crack in the beam was spreading.

The thick, square piece of wood began to sag in the middle.

Soon the entire house would plummet into the basement, killing anything under it.

Lynne froze with panic. She stood stock still, shining the flashlight on the beam. She could not even cry.

Despite the danger, Caitlin somehow stayed calm.

In an instant, she sized up how big the crack was, how fast it was spreading, and where, exactly, the beam lay under the floor.

She understood they still had a chance to survive.

But only if they moved together. *Now!*

"Jump, Lynne! Jump," Caitlin shouted.

She hoped her sister would react without thinking.

Lynne leaped off her sister's back, exactly as Caitlin had hoped.

"Now hold on to that flashlight!" Caitlin said.

Pulling her sister's arm, she bolted for the staircase. She could barely see because Lynne pointed the flashlight toward the floor.

But she could see just enough.

Spotting the outline of the staircase, she raced up the creaky stairs two at a time. She felt stronger than she had ever been before, almost as if she could lift her sister up the stairs.

The girls bounded up the steps until they reached the basement door.

It had closed itself again, but that was no problem, Caitlin remembered. The basement door had no lock.

If they got off the staircase before the beam broke, probably they would be safe. The kitchen floor would collapse into the basement, Caitlin understood — but the rest of the house should remain standing.

Caitlin pushed against the door.

It would not open. It had no lock but still it would not open. It seemed the house had found some way to lock the door anyway.

Maybe the killer house finally had discovered a foolproof plan for murder!

Caitlin pushed and shoved against the door. Desperately, she pounded it with her shoulder.

But the door was still shut tight.

The sound of the beam breaking grew louder and louder.

Remembering how strong her tomboy sister could be, Caitlin pulled Lynne up to the top step.

"Help me get the door open, Lynne! Push! Push! Push!" Caitlin screamed.

Together, they hammered against the heavy door.

"Push! Push!" Caitlin yelled.

Again and again, they pounded on the door.

At last the door popped open.

But it opened at the very moment the beam snapped in half with a deafening crack and crash.

Everything in the kitchen — the tables and

chairs and cabinets and drawers and boxes — exploded into the basement with a thunderous boom!

Dust and smoke billowed everywhere, as if a bomb had gone off.

As the kitchen tumbled into the basement, the staircase collapsed under the girls' feet!

Caitlin and Lynne grabbed on to the hallway floor and hung on with all their strength — their bodies half inside the open basement door, half outside.

Their shoulders and heads were on the first floor. Their legs and feet dangled toward the ruins of the basement.

Every other part of their bodies struggled to keep from falling.

Beneath them now was nothing but a long drop into a deep hole — into a pit filled with sharp debris from the kitchen.

"Hang on, Lynne!" Caitlin shouted. "Hang on with everything you've got!"

Caitlin could feel her own fingers beginning to slip, though. She reached for the doorway but it was no good.

She could not hold on to anything much longer!

Within seconds, Caitlin realized, she would fall helplessly to her death in the basement below!

Chapter Sixteen

Caitlin's fingers were sliding off the wooden door frame.

Slip — a quarter-inch.

Slip — a half-inch.

Slip — another half-inch.

Slip! — an inch.

Little by little, Caitlin was starting to fall.

At the same time, Lynne struggled to pull herself up, wriggling her legs and using all the muscles in her strong, tomboy arms.

With one last determined effort, she hoisted her body on to the hallway floor.

"*Aaaaaaaaagh!*" she said as her arms strained under the weight.

She lay on the floor, safe but panting from exhaustion.

Then she heard Caitlin's frightened little cry for help. She saw that her sister could not hold on more than a second or two longer.

"Ohhhhh," Caitlin said, her voice like a soft squeal. "Ohh, Lynnnne."

Lynne hopped to her feet and grabbed Caitlin's arms just as her fingers slipped off the door frame.

She caught Caitlin and pulled hard.

She braced her legs against the door frame for support, tugging and yanking on Caitlin's arms.

Caitlin was heavy, much heavier than Lynne. For a moment, it looked as if Lynne would not be able to save her sister, no matter how hard she tried.

Her arms shook. Her face turned red. Her legs wobbled.

But she held on tightly.

"*Aaaaaaaaaggghh*!" she grunted. "Don't give up, Cait! Hold on!"

The thought of Caitlin falling into the basement gave Lynne more strength than she had ever had before. She summoned all her effort for one last heave. She leaned back and pulled with all her might.

At last she dragged her sister into the hallway.

"Are you all right, Cait?" she asked, breathing even more heavily than before. "I was so afraid! I wasn't sure I could pull you up."

"You did it! You saved our lives!" Caitlin said. "You really were brave! You never quit trying! I will never call you a little kid again!"

They lay on the floor, tired and scared and confused.

What should they do now?

It seemed as if there was no hope.

Even though the kitchen floor had collapsed, the walls of the home had remained intact.

The tools, of course, were buried under tons of debris. The doors and windows were locked and sealed shut.

There still was no way out of the killer house.

The phones did not work. The lights were all off. Even the flashlight was gone — Lynne had dropped it when the staircase collapsed.

And their parents would not be home for hours.

The girls knew they could not wait for Mom and Dad to rescue them. By the time their parents came home, they would be dead.

"Cait, I just thought of something," Lynne said. "There's this thing in my room I didn't tell you about. Something cool I found. Maybe it's a way out."

"Huh? What do you mean, Lynne? What's so special about your room?" Caitlin asked.

"Well, I — I didn't tell you about this before because I thought you would try to make me switch bedrooms," Lynne explained. "See, there's this little passageway. It's almost like a small tunnel. I found the opening behind an old board in the back of my closet."

"A secret tunnel? In this house? Are you kidding me, Lynne?" Caitlin replied.

"No, honest! It's the truth, Caitlin!" Lynne said. "It's pretty small and I haven't tried to crawl through it yet to find out where it goes. I just hid some letters and, well, a diary in there behind the board."

"A diary! You keep a diary?" Caitlin said, surprised. "My little sister has a diary!"

"Oh, stop it, Cait! We don't have time to play around. Yes, I have a diary. So what? Just don't ever touch it!" Lynne said. "But I think we should find out where this passageway goes, Cait. It might take us outside the house. Who knows?"

The sisters' eyes had adjusted to the blackness around them. Just enough moonlight seeped in through the shutters to allow them to see dimly where they were going.

They hurried through the darkened house up the stairs to Lynne's room. They stood looking into the small secret tunnel hidden in the back of Lynne's closet.

"Wow," Caitlin said. "It really *is* a passageway. It's hard to see in this light — but it looks like it might be a tunnel that goes somewhere. We have to try."

"But, Cait — you're too big to fit through the tunnel. I have to go by myself. I'm the only one small enough to crawl through," Lynne said.

"You can't go crawling around through secret tunnels by yourself! You're my little sister. I have to make sure you don't hurt yourself," Caitlin said. "I'll just have to find some way to fit through there, too."

"No way, Cait! Look how small it is! I have to go alone. Please let me go! *Pleeeaase!*" Lynne pleaded. "It may be the last chance we have to get out of this horrible house!"

Reluctantly, *very* reluctantly, Caitlin agreed with her sister.

The tunnel at least offered some hope of escaping the deadly home.

Lynne kissed her on the cheek. For the first time this night, Caitlin allowed herself to cry.

"Bye, Cait!" Lynne said. "If I find some way out, I'll run for Mom and Dad. And we'll come back to smash down the doors and get you out, too!"

Caitlin brushed away her tears and held her breath as Lynne got down on hands and knees, and began crawling off into the blackness.

Caitlin thought that a small tunnel was probably a very bad place to be in a house that was trying to kill people.

She did not want to let Lynne go. But she *had* to.

As she watched the pair of small feet disappear into the dark, uncertain passageway, she began to cry again. She just could not make the tears stop.

"I may never see my sister again," she whispered to herself.

<u>Chapter Seventeen</u>

Caitlin could still hear the sound of hands and knees and feet shuffling across the floor inside the tunnel.

She wanted desperately to know that her little sister was all right. Since she could hear her shuffling, she figured she could keep talking to her, and reassure herself that way.

"Lynne, can you hear me?" she called into the tunnel. "Answer if you can hear me."

"Yeah, I can hear you," Lynne said, her words echoing through the small opening.

"Keep talking to me, Lynne! I want you to tell me what you're doing and seeing as you crawl through there! OK?" Caitlin said.

"Sure, but there's not much to tell you," Lynne answered. "I can't see *anything*! It's completely black inside here. And I just keep going and going. I don't know how far this tunnel will go. I just hope it takes me to the garage or someplace where I can get outside!"

"Just talk about anything! I only want to know that you're safe! You just keep talking to me!" Caitlin ordered.

"OK," Lynne said. "So far, this is just a long, empty tunnel. I'm starting to wonder if it goes anywhere. Maybe it just goes through the walls — you know, so repairmen can get to the electric wires or water pipes or something."

Lynne's voice sounded fainter now, and more wrapped in echo upon echo. She was getting farther and farther away.

"Lynne, talk louder! It's getting hard to hear you!" Caitlin said.

"Yeah, OK. The tunnel is turning now. It's going off to the right — toward your room, I think," Lynne said. Then her tone changed to disgust. "Aaaaaww, no!"

"What? What happened?" Caitlin called anxiously.

"Nothing. I'm OK. I just put my hand down and felt some dead bug. Yuck!" Lynne replied.

"Just keep moving, Lynne. Keep moving as fast as you can! I want you to get out of that tunnel as quickly as possible! It's too dangerous in there!" Caitlin said.

"I'm hurrying, Cait! Believe me, I'm hurrying!" Lynne said.

Lynne's voice grew still fainter. Caitlin thought her sister must be a long way off.

For a short time, Caitlin heard nothing. She began to worry.

"Lynne, keep talking to me! I don't care what you say. Just talk!" she said.

She heard only silence.

Suddenly, the silence was shattered by a loud yell from the tunnel.

"Eeeeeeeaaaaaaahhh! Oh, no! Cait! Oh, no!" Lynne shouted.

"Lynne, what's wrong? Talk to me? Where are you?" Caitlin hollered back.

"Oh, it's just — *Pew! Pah! Phhhhttth!* It's so gross!" Lynne cried out to her sister. "Cockroaches,

Cait! Hundreds of cockroaches! They're crawling all over me! Oh, noooo! *Phhhhttth! Pew! Pah!* Oh, gross! I hate this house!"

Caitlin hated bugs. But she knew Lynne hated bugs even more.

Lynne despised bugs.

Caitlin could imagine how frightened and upset her sister must feel, surrounded by swarms of little bug-legs inside a dark tunnel!

"Come back, Lynne! Come back! Get out of there right now!" Caitlin shouted.

"No, it's OK, Cait! It was pretty gross but I'm OK now. They're gone," Lynne said. "Besides, I *can't* come back! The tunnel's too small for me to turn around. And I don't think I can crawl backward that far. I have to keep going!"

"You sound really far away, Lynne! Talk louder! I can barely hear you," Caitlin called.

"What do you want me to say?" Lynne asked.

"I don't care! I told you — just say *anything*! Talk real loud and say anything! I want to hear your voice!" Caitlin answered.

"OK, OK! Then I'll just say I really hope I do

not run into any more bugs, Caitlin! That was awful! I hate bugs!" Lynne said loudly. "And I *hate this house*! I hate it! I hate it! I hate it!"

"Yeah, just keep talking!" Caitlin reminded her.

There was a brief silence.

"Lynne? Lynne, are you all right?"

"Uh, Ca-Caitlin? Caitlin! Uh, this is really going to sound weird bu-but I think — " Lynne stammered.

"What? What's wrong now? What's happening in there, Lynne?" Caitlin called fearfully.

Was it another dead bug, Caitlin wondered. Was it another gross attack of cockroaches? Was it something worse — a mouse maybe? Or a rat? Or something even worse than that?

"*Aaaaaaaaaaaaaaaaaaaaaaaaaaahhhhhhhhh*!"

The scream was so loud and so horrifying that it turned Caitlin's arms and legs into a mass of goose bumps. She wrapped her arms around herself and shivered.

"Lynne!" she hollered. "What's wrong? Is something in the tunnel with you?"

97

"Caitlin! Heeeeellllllpp! Heeeelllpp me, *please*!" Lynne screamed.

"Lynne, try to crawl back out to me! I can't come in!" Caitlin pleaded. "I'm too big!"

Lynne screamed again — this time even louder than before!

"*AAAAAAAaaaaaaaaaaaaaaaaaaaaaaaaahhhhh hhhh*!"

"Lynne! Lynne! Tell me what's going on in that tunnel!" Caitlin shouted.

"The tunnel is moving! It's squeezing down on me from the top and bottom, Caitlin!" Lynne answered. "I can hardly move now! It's getting smaller! It's going to squash me, Cait! It's going to smash me flat as a pancake!"

Chapter Eighteen

Caitlin felt completely, totally, utterly helpless.

Lynne was about to be squeezed like a human tube of toothpaste — and Caitlin could not do a thing to help her sister escape!

But she could at least yell!

"Crawl, Lynne! If you can move at all, crawl as fast as you can! Find some way out of there right now!" she shouted.

Maybe Lynne could hear her. Maybe Lynne could still move inside the tunnel. Maybe Lynne could find a passage out if she crawled fast enough.

Caitlin listened at the tunnel opening. She listened very hard. But she heard nothing.

Not a word.

Not a sound.

Nothing.

"Lynne? Lynne! Say something!" she shouted into the tunnel. "Speak to me! Please!"

Still not one word.

Not one sound.

Nothing.

Then, from somewhere inside the house, the voice of a small girl echoed.

"Caitlin!" the distant voice said. "I'm faaaaaaalllling!"

It was Lynne's voice, very faint, very weak.

Lynne was saying she was falling!

But how? How could that possibly be?

Caitlin thought for a moment and decided Lynne had found some way to squeeze through the contracting tunnel. She had not been squashed after all.

Her sister was still alive!

But Caitlin also understood the tunnel must empty into a chute of some kind — and Lynne had fallen down it!

"That tunnel must drop inside the house somewhere," Caitlin said to herself. "Lynne's probably laying someplace right now, all crumpled up from her fall. She could be hurt!"

Caitlin knew she had to find her sister — fast!

Hurrying through the darkness, she descended the stairs and began the search. She started checking out the area where the kitchen had collapsed into the basement. She looked and listened carefully from the edge of the open pit but saw nothing and heard nothing.

Lynne had not tumbled into that pile of sharp kitchen debris. Thank goodness!

So, Caitlin decided, her sister must have fallen into one of the rooms on the ground floor.

She ran down the shadowy hallway to continue the hunt for Lynne.

She soon discovered it was going to be tougher than she had imagined.

The haunting house opened the heavy wooden door to each room — until the moment Caitlin approached.

As she rushed toward the dining room, the dining room door slammed shut in her face!

As she rushed toward the living room, the living room door slammed shut in her face!

As she rushed toward her father's study, the study door slammed shut in her face!

No matter how hard she yanked on the knobs, the doors would not open.

She pounded on the doors, calling Lynne's name.

Still she heard no sound.

Caitlin was now locked out of every room on the ground floor. Only the hallway and stairs and bedrooms were open to her.

But Lynne was trapped inside one of the downstairs rooms somewhere, hurt or maybe worse.

The situation was getting more terrifying every moment.

She was all alone. Her sister was wounded. And the house was closing in for the kill!

Then Caitlin saw something that made her scream.

Under the staircase, crumpled in a heap, lay Lynne.

Even through the heavy blackness of the old home, Caitlin noticed some thick liquid dripping from Lynne's arm.

A thick liquid that looked like blood!

And Caitlin noticed something even more terrible: Lynne was not moving, not even a finger.

And she did not seem to be breathing, either.

As far as Caitlin could tell, her wonderful, brave, sweet nine-year-old sister was dead!

The killer house had killed already!

Chapter Nineteen

"Oooohh, ow!" came a sound from under the staircase.

It was Lynne's voice.

She was alive!

"Lynne, are you hurt? Tell me if you're all right," Caitlin said, running to her sister's side.

Caitlin could see now that the liquid on her sister's arm was only some greasy water. Lynne was not bleeding after all.

"Ow, Cait. I fell and must have bumped my head. It's kind of sore. But I'm OK," Lynne answered slowly.

Caitlin understood that Lynne accidentally had found the other end of the narrow tunnel.

The black passageway that began in Lynne's bedroom had turned into nothing more than a hole —

a chute that plunged from the second floor to the ground.

The hole emptied into a space under the stairs. No one had ever noticed that space before because it was covered by a small, secret door — a door that looked just like part of the wall.

Luckily, a lot of old rags and sheets were there to soften Lynne's landing. When Lynne had fallen, she had bumped her head, knocked the door open and rolled out on to the floor under the stairs.

"There's still something I can't figure out, Lynne. Why didn't you get squashed when the tunnel began squeezing down on you? How did you get away?" Caitlin asked.

"I heard your voice telling me to crawl as fast as I could. So I did! I got down flat on the bottom of the tunnel and pulled myself forward with just my arms. I pulled really hard!" Lynne said. "I was lucky I got to the hole really quick and fell. The tunnel was so small I could barely move."

Caitlin helped Lynne stand up and asked again if she was hurt anywhere. Lynne said she was OK. Except for a headache.

Caitlin told Lynne everything that had just happened — the desperate search and the locked doors and the killer house closing in around them.

"What can we do, Cait? We can't last much longer," Lynne said.

Her voice trembled with terror.

"I just remembered something in your room, Lynne!" Caitlin answered, snapping her fingers. "I saw it in your closet when you went into the tunnel. You have a big metal softball bat in there! Maybe we can use it to bash through the front door and get outside!"

"Yeah! And even if we can't break through, maybe someone would hear the noise when we hit the door," Lynne said. "Then they'll send the police to save us!"

"Come on, Lynne! Let's go!" Caitlin shouted.

She grabbed her sister's hand and raced to the staircase. Together, they ran up the dark stairs and down the shadowy hall.

The door to every room on the second floor was open now. The girls hurried to reach Lynne's bedroom before anything else happened.

Maybe they still had a chance, if only they

could get to that softball bat, Caitlin thought.

But they would never find out.

It already was too late!

Just as they were about to run into Lynne's room, the door slammed shut in their faces.

"Oh, Cait!" Lynne cried, pulling on the door handle. "We can't get in! It's locked."

"We have got to find somewhere to hide out and plan what to do next," Caitlin said. "Follow me!"

Terrified, they rushed down the hall toward Caitlin's room. At least it was better to sit in there than to stand stranded in the hallway, Caitlin thought.

But again, it was too late!

As they tried to hurry into the bedroom, Caitlin's door slammed shut in their faces.

Maybe their parents' room would be the safest place. It was the only bedroom with a door still open and unlocked.

They tore down the hallway and tried to jump through the door in time.

But they were too late once more!

Their parents' door slammed shut in their faces.

"We're trapped!" Lynne shouted. "We're trapped in the hall! We have no place to run any more! No place to hide! No way to get out of the house! I hate this house! I hate it!"

"I don't hate it, Lynne," Caitlin said softly. "I feel sorry for this house."

"Huh? Sorry for it? What are you talking about, Cait? Are you crazy?" Lynne asked.

"If a house as big and strong and old as this one has to pick on two little girls, it's just sad. That's all, it's just sad!" Caitlin replied. "I feel really sorry for anybody or anything that likes to hurt people! We haven't done anything to this house! The only thing we've done is move here and try to fix it up and make it pretty again."

"But, Cait! This house is trying to kill us! How can you feel sorry for something so mean?" Lynne wondered. "It tried to bury us under dirt. It tried to hit us with flying drawers! It tried to cut my throat with broken glass! And then it almost crushed us in the basement! And don't forget everything else it did to us! And now we're stuck in the hall with no way out. How can you say that you don't hate this house?"

"I mean it, Lynne! I don't hate this house. I never really did," Caitlin explained. "I just didn't want to leave our old house, that's all. But really, I did want to be happy here with our family and find new friends and get along in our new school. I don't hate this house. But now we'll never get to live here with Mom and Dad because the house is going to kill us. I wish this house didn't hate *us*!"

As Caitlin spoke, something strange began to happen.

It happened softly, slowly in the beginning — so softly and slowly that neither of the girls noticed for a minute.

First, the door to their parents' room gently popped open, just a little.

Then, Caitlin's door opened a crack.

Then, Lynne's bedroom door opened slightly, too.

"Hey, Lynne! Look! The bedroom doors are unlocked," Caitlin said.

She felt relieved but confused.

"I don't get it," she said. "Why is the house opening all the doors for us now?"

She paused to think about that. There *had* to be a good explanation. For some reason, the house seemed less menacing, less mean than it had just a few moments before.

But why?

"I think we should run into my room while there's time! The door's open. Let's get my bat right now!" Lynne said. "Then we can try to break through the front door. This place is trying to murder us! I don't care what you say about it. I still *hate this house!*"

Lynne stood at the top of the staircase, near the door to Caitlin's bedroom. Caitlin stood beside her, still thinking.

Caitlin thought very hard. She became so wrapped up in her thoughts that she did not see the danger Lynne suddenly faced.

Just as Lynne got through talking, a huge chunk of plaster broke off the ceiling over her head.

A chunk of heavy plaster, the size of a beach ball, was falling toward Lynne's brains!

By the time Lynne saw it dropping, the chunk was just inches from her head!

She did not even have time to scream.

Caitlin looked up. Her eyes grew wide with shock and fear.

She had absolutely no chance to pull Lynne away from the terrible, crushing weight that was about to smash into her skull!

Chapter Twenty

"I *love* this house!" Caitlin shouted. "I *love it*!"

It was the only thing she could do in time.

It seemed crazy!

It seemed just plain silly, when her sister was about to be bashed by falling plaster!

What good could come from yelling something nice about the old house?

But there was no chance to try anything else. So Caitlin just shouted at the house.

And it worked!

The large chunk of plaster instantly broke apart into dust that floated harmlessly down around Lynne's head and shoulders.

"*Puggggh! Kaaaaph!*" Lynne coughed. "Wha-what happened, Caitlin? You saved my head from being smashed. But how did you do that?"

"Lynne, I think I finally understand something about this house. I understand why this is a haunting house. There is a reason it hates us so much," Caitlin said. "It's such a nice old house, too. It really is when you take a good look at it. It's got beautiful wood on the floors and beautiful shingles on the roof. And everything is built so solid and strong."

"Caitlin, I'm getting worried about you. There you go again about this old house," Lynne said.

"I'm only telling you how much I love this place," Caitlin continued. "Because it has such nice old tile in the bathrooms. And I just love my room! I know you love your room too, don't you?"

Lynne still did not understand what her sister was doing.

"What? Love my room? *No*! I don't, Cait. I *ha* — " Lynne started to say.

"No, you really mean you *love* your room, Lynne!" Caitlin interrupted firmly. "Think about it, *please!* Think about how you really felt before any of this haunting began. I know you loved that room. It's bigger and you didn't have to sleep with me anymore. And you have your own bathroom!"

"Well, yeah. I guess if I think about it like that. It's true," Lynne admitted. "I did like my new room pretty much, I guess. But since then this house has been so terrible to us! And now I really *ha* — "

"No, you mean that you really *love* it just like you did before — *as long as* the house does not try to hurt us anymore," Caitlin interrupted again. "That's what you mean, right? Because I really could be very happy in this house with Dad and Mom. And I know I'll make new friends and I'll like my new school and teachers and everything. Our whole family is going to *love* this place!"

"Caitlin, you really are nuts, I think," Lynne answered. "Sure, I'd like this house fine if it wasn't a haunting house. I'd probably even love it, I guess. But it is a haunting house! Why are you saying all these things?"

"I'm only saying how much I really love this house, Lynne. And how happy we'll all be here — if the house just lets us live peacefully," Caitlin said.

At that moment, all the lights in the house came back on.

And all the locked doors unlocked.

And all the closed shutters snapped open.

The girls could hear things happening all around now.

"But Caitlin, how can such an awful, angry house turn into a good house so fast?" Lynne asked. "Why is it turning the lights on and unlocking the doors and opening the shutters after a whole night of doing horrible things?"

"It's simple, Lynne. The ghost book said there was no way to get rid of the violent forces in a haunting house. But then our bedroom doors opened after I told the house I felt sorry for it," Caitlin explained. "And I remembered how you were always saying you hated the house — right before something bad happened. And so it just made sense that the house was angry because we didn't like it. It was like a person whose feelings were hurt."

"Wow, cool," Lynne said. "Is my big sister smart or what?"

"It was just a lucky guess, Lynne. But when I saw that chunk of plaster break into dust over your head, I knew for sure I was right!" Caitlin said.

"I guess houses sometimes have feelings too,

huh?" Lynne said.

"Yeah, I guess so. We just have to show this house how much we love it. And then I think we'll all really like living here," Caitlin replied.

"It's pretty cool when you think about it. How many kids have a house with feelings?" Lynne said, laughing.

"Not many," Caitlin said. "I *hope!*"

When their parents finally got home, the house was a total mess.

The kitchen was gone. The upstairs ceiling was broken. A living room window was smashed. Their mother's favorite lamp was cracked to bits on the front lawn.

But the girls explained everything that had happened that night — and *why* it had happened. And even though it was hard for their parents to believe the story of a haunting house, they finally did believe it. They had no choice. There was no other logical, scientific explanation.

And they could plainly see the damage.

They made plans to start repairs the next morning — and to turn the old abandoned home into a more beautiful place than it had ever been before.

As Caitlin and Lynne walked upstairs together to get some sleep at last, they looked at each other and smiled.

"Wow, pretty freaky night, huh Cait?" Lynne said. "I'm glad it's over. But you know, I didn't mind it so much. You know why? It's because I — I really *love* this house now!"

"You're such a little kid!" Caitlin said, smiling.

They both laughed and kissed good night.

"Just one thing, though," Lynne said, stopping in the hall. "It's something really important."

"What's that?" Caitlin asked.

"Stay out of the tunnel in my room!" Lynne answered with a chuckle. "My diary is going back in there. Besides, it's way too cool for big sisters!"

They laughed again and went into their bedrooms without fear now.

And the two sisters slept quietly and pleasantly through this night and every other night they ever spent inside their new, old happy and well-loved home.

BE SURE TO READ THESE OTHER COLD, CLAMMY SHIVERS BOOKS.

THE ENCHANTED ATTIC

WHEN NICOLE AND HER LITTLE SISTER CASEY MOVE WITH THEIR FAMILY INTO AN OLD HOUSE IN MASSACHUSETTS, NICOLE THINKS THE NOISES SHE HEARS AT NIGHT ARE NOTHING MORE THAN THE SCURRYING OF MICE. BUT WHEN SHE STARTS TO HEAR EERIE MUSIC COMING FROM ABOVE HER CEILING, SHE REALIZES WITH A SHIVER THAT THE HOUSE MUST BE INHABITED BY SOMETHING FAR MORE TERRIFYING THAN MICE. AND IT IS UP TO HER TO FIND OUT WHAT IT IS.

Shivers™

TERROR ON TROLL MOUNTAIN

M. D. Spenser

Chapter One

Paul Alberti was *supposed* to be seeing the snow-capped mountains of Northern Italy, for the first time in his life.

Instead, he sat stuffed in the tiny back seat of his Uncle Freddy's car, staring at his beat-up red sneakers — and trying very hard not to lose his lunch.

"Come on, Paul!" called Mr. Alberti from the front seat. "You can stare at your sneakers back in Chicago. Look out the window. You're missing the best view!"

Paul's father knew all the best views. He had grown up in these mountains before he moved to the United States as a young man.

"Can't," Paul moaned.

He was trying to move as little as possible. And trying to speak as slowly as possible, too. Anything to avoid unnecessary motion.

"Still . . . car . . . sick," he croaked.

Mr. Alberti laughed loudly.

He had a thick mustache and an even thicker Italian accent. He loved to laugh and crack jokes — which sometimes embarrassed Paul, only because his dad was so *loud*.

"Maybe you should've stopped after just two sandwiches at the airport!" Mr. Alberti boomed, and laughed again. One of his favorite things to joke about was Paul's humongous appetite.

He laughed so loudly that Uncle Freddy started chuckling, too, even though he couldn't possibly understand what they were talking about.

Uncle Freddy was Mr. Alberti's younger brother. He still lived in Italy. The only English words Uncle Freddy knew were "cool" and "bye-bye."

After they finally stopped laughing, Mr. Alberti turned around in the front passenger seat to look at Paul.

"Don't worry, buddy," he said. "We're almost there."

"There" — the place they were headed — was Pinzolo, which is pronounced PEEN-so-low. Pinzolo was the mountain village where Paul's dad grew up, and where Uncle Freddy still lived.

Paul had just turned twelve years old, and Mr. Alberti had decided he was old enough to appreciate a three-week visit to Italy. Paul's mom couldn't come because she was a ballet dancer and would be touring all summer.

Paul was pretty tall for a twelve year old, almost as tall as his dad — who was actually pretty short for a forty-five year old. Some people thought Paul could stand to lose a few pounds, but he didn't agree. He just enjoyed food, that was all.

He had dark brown hair and wore thick, clunky glasses, which made him look like a nerd. But he wasn't, really.

The two most striking things about Paul, everyone agreed, were his feet. They were *huge*. Even though he was tall, they didn't fit his body quite right.

To put it bluntly, they were clodhoppers. If footballs were the size of Paul's feet, it would take a whole team to catch one. If Paul was on a sinking ship, a family of four could use one of his shoes for a raft.

Those were the kinds of jokes Paul had to put up with at school. Every day.

Now, he sat trapped in a tiny car, forced to stare at the same feet that gave him so much trouble. All so he wouldn't throw up all over the back seat of his Uncle Freddy's car.

Normally, Paul didn't get car sick. But he'd just spent eight long hours on a crowded, noisy airplane, flying all the way from Chicago to Milan, one of the bigger cities in Northern Italy. Now he had to ride three hours in a car from Milan to Pinzolo.

Uncle Freddy had picked them up at the airport.

Uncle Freddy's real name was Federico, which sort of translates to "Frederick." He was shorter than Paul's dad, and almost bald. A few wisps of hair made a messy ring around his head. Uncle Freddy was the type of guy who didn't believe in combs.

He was a great uncle. But he wasn't exactly the greatest *driver* in the world. He liked to shift gears a lot, so the car always lurched back and forth. He also liked to drive fast, even on windy mountain roads, which upset Paul's stomach even more.

4

Plus, it was a hot summer day. Cars in Italy use diesel gasoline, which smells really bad and gave Paul a headache.

OK, all right, Paul thought. Maybe he *shouldn't* have eaten that third sandwich at the airport. He just enjoyed food, that was all.

For all of those reasons, Paul was looking green at the moment.

His mom always told him, "If you ever feel carsick, stare straight ahead, right through the windshield, as far up the road as you can see. Then you'll be focused, and you won't feel as queasy."

The problem was that here, among the beautiful, snow-capped mountains of Northern Italy, the roads were so twisty and turny you couldn't stare more than ten feet in front of the car before another curve came along.

So Paul had fallen back on Plan B - staring at his shoes.

"How much longer till we get there?" he asked. His stomach was starting to feel better, but his neck was getting sore.

No one answered. Paul stared at his feet some

more.

"Did you hear me?" he asked.

Still, no one answered.

It felt like the car was going faster. Paul decided to risk it and look up.

The first thing he noticed was that Uncle Freddy wasn't smiling. Uncle Freddy *always* smiled.

Now he seemed almost . . . scared.

"What's the matter?" Paul asked his dad.

Mr. Alberti was talking to Uncle Freddy in Italian. Very quietly.

Another bad sign. When Paul's dad lowered his voice, it almost always meant trouble.

The car rocketed ahead even faster.

"Speak English!" Paul cried. "What's wrong? Why doesn't he slow down?"

They bore down on a curve in the road. Fast.

The car gained speed.

Uncle Freddy stomped on different pedals and moved the gear shift around. The car did not slow down.

"Why can't we stop?" Paul asked again.

He looked out his window and saw a steep

drop down the mountainside. A mountainside covered with sharp rocks and pointed trees.

Uncle Freddy shouted something in Italian. Paul didn't understand, but it didn't sound good.

Paul looked out the windshield again. They were barreling straight toward a flimsy wooden barrier that separated the road from the open space beyond.

"*Noooo!*" he shouted.

It was too late. The car crashed through the barrier at 90 miles per hour and went flying over the edge!

Chapter Two

"Paul! Wake up, Paul! Wake up!"

It sounded to Paul as if his dad's voice was coming from the bottom of a deep well.

Slowly, he opened his eyes.

The first thing he realized was that he had been having a bad dream. He was OK. His dad was OK. The car was OK.

The second thing he realized was that he had fallen asleep in a very uncomfortable position on Uncle Freddy's back seat. One of his arms was twisted behind his head and his knees were pushed up practically to his chest. He felt like one giant cramp.

The third thing Paul realized — the best thing of all — was that the car had finally stopped moving.

They had arrived. They were in Pinzolo.

Mr. Alberti shook one of Paul's big feet.

"Are you all right, buddy?"

Paul nodded. He felt kind of groggy.

"Well come on, then. Everyone wants to see you. We're here."

Paul stretched his sore legs and climbed slowly out of the car. They had parked on a street lined with old, gray houses. It was a sunny afternoon. Paul blinked, still dazed from his nap.

Before he had time to take in much of the street, he was overwhelmed by a single sound. The sound of lots of voices. All shouting at the same time. All shouting the same thing.

"PAULO!" they shouted.

In Italian, Paul becomes "Paulo." They pronounced it POW (like a superhero punching a bad guy) and LOW (like the score you'd get on a quiz you didn't study for). POW-low.

At first, Paul was confused from having been asleep for so long. Who were these strange people? Why were they shouting this strange word?

Then he realized they were shouting at him.

Soon he was being hugged. And kissed. On both cheeks. Someone mussed his hair. Someone else squeezed his arm. A third person gave him a playful punch in the stomach that kind of hurt.

Everyone talked at once. Very loudly. He heard the word "grande" a lot. He knew that meant big. He assumed they were using the word to describe him. It sure wasn't being used to describe his father.

Eventually, he started matching up the names and faces in the crowd.

Paul had lots of relatives in Italy. He'd never met most of them. He'd seen photographs, of course, but people looked different in person.

Whoever they were, they were all very excited to meet Paulo.

The one person Paul *had* met before was his grandmother, Bianca. That's pronounced BEE-yan-KA, and it means "white" in Italian. Paul's grand-mother was actually fairly pink, though, especially in her cheeks. She was short and round. Paul had to bend down to give her a hug.

She had been to Chicago several times to visit, and she hugged Paul longer than any of the others did.

Then there was Aunt Nat, Uncle Freddy's wife. Her real name in Italian was "Natalia," which translates to Natalie. Aunt Nat was tall and round. She was also a notorious cheek-pincher. She couldn't help herself. Every time she saw Paul, she reached over for a squeeze.

The rest of the crowd included cousins, friends of cousins, distant relatives and people who just happened to wander by.

Everyone had a great name. There was Carlo and Sergio, Pina and Nina, Maria Louisa Grazia and Pat. (Pat was short for something very complicated that Paul quickly forgot.)

After Paul's cheeks were red and sore from so many kisses and pinches, the party moved inside his grandmother's house. The house was big and roomy, and much, much older than most of the houses Paul had seen in Chicago.

Paul's grandmother, Bianca, yanked him into the kitchen. It seemed as if dozens of pots and pans were bubbling and steaming and sizzling all at once.

"You like?" she asked. She had learned some very basic English when she came to visit in Chicago.

Paul had no idea what was cooking, but it was food — and he liked food. Also, it smelled wonderful.

He nodded his head yes. His grandmother

smiled and gave him another big kiss, then shooed him back into the living room to relax.

"Put your feet up, buddy," Mr. Alberti shouted above the din. The crowd had moved inside. People sprawled on couches, tables and even the floor, still talking incredibly loudly.

"But I'm not tired, Dad," Paul protested. "I just took a nap in the car."

Paul stared out the window. It was still sunny and bright.

"It'll be a while before we eat," he said. "Can't I go exploring?"

Mr. Alberti frowned, but Paul could tell he was still in a good mood.

"Well, I suppose," Mr. Alberti said. "As long as you're careful. And as long as you come home in time for dinner."

"I promise," Paul called over his shoulder.

"Don't go too far," Mr. Alberti yelled over the dozen other voices that all chattered at once. "It's easy to get lost around here."

But Paul was already out the door.

<u>Chapter Three</u>

Paul enjoyed nothing more than exploring something new.

Sometimes, if his friends really liked a movie — like, say, "Dinosaur Island" or "The Big Tornado" — they'd want to go see it again and again.

Paul hated that. Once he'd seen something and knew what it was like and how it was going to turn out, he was ready for something new.

Sometimes, though, his curiosity got him into a fix.

Like the time he ate some dry cat food, to find out what it tasted like. The answer, he found out, is that it tastes just like dirt.

Or the time he walked around with his eyes closed, to see what it would be like to be blind, and he fell down the stairs. His mom had to take him to the emergency room, where the doctor put seven stitches in his knee.

Still, Paul remained as curious as ever. Now, he was really curious about Pinzolo.

The first thing he noticed, as he walked along, was how old everything was. Especially compared to Chicago, where everything was new and bright and big and flashy.

In Pinzolo, most of the buildings and houses were made of stone. They were only one or two stories tall. Sometimes, they were painted a faded yellow or brown. Mostly, though, they were left their natural gray.

Paul walked over to what looked like an apartment building and touched the wall. It was cold and damp, like what a dungeon must have felt like, back in the Dark Ages. Creepy.

Everything was old, like in one of those old black-and-white *Frankenstein* movies. But something else struck Paul as curious about Pinzolo. Everything was also *deserted*. Like a ghost town.

Paul had walked around for a good ten minutes and hadn't seen a soul.

All of the stores were closed. The butcher shop, the boot store, the magazine-and-candy stand — all locked up and dark.

Paul looked at his watch. It was two o'clock in the afternoon. Where *was* everybody?

Then he remembered something his dad had told him. In Italy, everybody takes *three hours* for a lunch break. The workers all go home and eat a huge lunch and rest and spend time with their families.

That's why the streets were empty and the stores were all closed.

Boring!

Since there was nothing going on in the town, Paul looked up at the mountains that surrounded it. Pinzolo was at the bottom of a valley. Wherever you looked, you could see the huge, tree-covered mountain ranges looming in the distance.

The mountains were so gigantic that they made Paul feel like an ant, or like a speck of lint under a bed. They made the Sears Tower in Chicago look the size of a stack of quarters.

He decided he had to check these mountains out. Up close.

Paul remembered his dad's warning to be careful. But there was *nothing* to do in town. Zero.

What could it hurt to poke around the bottom of one little mountain?

Well, OK, one *big* mountain. But it wasn't like he was going to try and climb all the way to the top on his first day.

Somewhere in the back of Paul's head, a voice of reason whispered.

"You'll see those mountains soon enough, with your dad," it said. "Why do you have to go right now, on your first day here?"

Paul ignored it.

A few minutes later, he was hiking along a dirt road. He headed straight for what looked like the closest mountain.

And he'd left Pinzolo far behind.

Chapter Four

After a few minutes of hiking, Paul came to a rickety old bridge.

His eyes lit up. This was exactly what he was looking for. Adventure! You'd never find an old bridge like this in Chicago. Some safety inspector would come and shut it down in a minute.

Paul pulled his plastic camera out of his pocket and snapped a picture. He kept a scrapbook of photos of odd places he'd been.

The bridge hung from a pair of cables. It ran across what used to be a decent-sized river.

At least, that's what Paul figured. Now the river was just a rock-filled gorge, with a tiny trickle of a stream running through it, as if someone had turned down the faucet.

Paul patted his belly for luck. Slowly, he began to make his way across the bridge. It wobbled and bounced, but the boards were solid.

He kept going.

He began to imagine what he would have to do if the flimsy thing collapsed. Probably grab hold of one of the cables, he thought, then swing to the opposite side, and climb to safety.

Then he remembered how hard it was to climb the rope in gym class. And that was with a mat underneath!

He gritted his teeth and kept going.

Soon enough, Paul was on the other side of the bridge. He couldn't help feeling a little disappointed.

Not that he wanted to fall into a gorge, of course. But he wouldn't have minded, say, a broken board. A *little* adventure.

Ahead of him, a narrow path wound its way into the foothills. Paul began to hike in that direction.

Soon, he was surrounded by trees. The mountains around Pinzolo were all very woodsy. There were also lots of rocks, most of them mossy and green.

The path was not a concrete sidewalk, like Paul had seen at some state parks in the United States.

This path was dirt. Old, gnarly tree roots crisscrossed it.

Parts of the path were very steep. Paul had trouble keeping his footing. But he kept going.

Finally, the path started to flatten out. Paul was glad. He wasn't exactly in the best shape, since he did like to eat so much. He couldn't wait to plop down on one of the mossy rocks and take a breather.

Between puffs and wheezes, he noticed the mushrooms.

They grew all along the side of the path, huge and brown, some of them as big as soup bowls. Paul remembered that, sometimes, Uncle Freddy sent dried-out mushrooms to Chicago. Paul's mom cooked them in stew. They were delicious.

Paul's stomach started to grumble, just from thinking about his mom's stew.

Then he came up with a brilliant plan. If he picked some fresh mushrooms and brought them back to his grandmother, she could cook them for dinner.

On his very first day in Pinzolo, he would be the hero of the feast!

There was only one problem. He didn't have

anything to put the mushrooms in.

He sat on his rock for a minute, thinking. Then he started getting hot. The sun was beating down on him from between the trees.

Suddenly, the solution hit him.

He slipped off his baggy button-down shirt and tied the ends together to create a bag. He still had on a white T-shirt.

He dropped to his hands and knees and began crawling around in the dirt and grass, looking for the fattest mushrooms.

He enjoyed himself thoroughly!

He spotted one giant mushroom growing behind a tree. He discovered another clump on a rock. Soon enough, his makeshift bag bulged with goodies.

He was enjoying himself too much to stop. He couldn't believe it. Here he was, picking mushrooms in the Italian Alps!

It wouldn't sound like much fun to his friends back in Chicago. They'd probably never seen a wild mushroom before. It wouldn't have sounded like much fun to *Paul* if someone else had told him about it.

But it was terrific. Spectacular.

A few feet ahead, he noticed the plumpest mushroom yet. He crawled to it like a hungry dog.

Just before he snatched his prize, he heard the ground crunch behind him. He felt a hot blast of breath on the back of his neck.

He whirled around.

And started to scream!

Chapter Five

The cow stared back at Paul, calmly chewing on a mouthful of grass.

Paul turned bright red and scrambled to his feet. His heart was still beating fast.

The *last* thing he'd expected to see when he turned around was a big, ugly cow face staring at him.

"You scared me!" Paul said angrily, shaking his finger in the cow's face.

He didn't shake his finger too closely at the cow, though. He had never met a live cow before, and he wasn't sure whether they liked to bite kids.

The cow went back to munching patches of grass near the path. Paul watched her eat.

Cows are really dumb-looking, he thought.

He was still embarrassed about having screamed so loudly, but it didn't look as if anyone else around. And the cow certainly didn't care.

"Where the heck did you come from?" Paul asked the cow. "What, are you lost?"

Then he really felt dumb. I am in the middle of the woods, he thought. Alone. Talking to a cow.

Lucky none of the kids from school could see him now!

The cow kept on grazing. She was brown, with big, sad eyes. Flies crawled all over her droopy eyes and wet nose. But she didn't seem to notice.

After a minute, Paul reached over carefully and patted her on the side. The cow ignored him. Her fur was matted and kind of rough.

"What should I call you? Bessie?" Paul asked. "Oh, wait, you're Italian. How about Sofia?"

The cow lifted her head and continued down the path.

"Hey, where are you going?" Paul called.

He decided to follow her. Cows move pretty slowly, so it wasn't hard to keep up.

The path curved. As they rounded the bend, the trees gave way to a large, grassy field. Dozens of other cows milled about, chewing grass or swatting flies with their tails.

Sofia slowly ambled over to her friends.

Paul looked around, but there didn't seem to be anyone tending the cows. He wondered what you would call someone who sat around and watched cows all day. A cow-herd?

He plucked a handful of grass and walked over to the nearest cow. This one was black. When she saw Paul, she looked up and stopped chewing.

Paul held out the grass with his palm open. The cow, without even sniffing to make sure it was good, leaned forward and swallowed the offering with a wet, slimy slurp! Then she went back to chewing at the ground.

"Gross!" Paul yelled. "Oh, man, why don't you show some manners?"

His hand was coated with cow spit.

Spying a fallen tree at the edge of the field, Paul sat down and furiously wiped his hand on a dry patch of grass. He had never been so disgusted in his entire life.

As he dried his hand on his shorts, Paul felt something fuzzy brush his shoulder.

Another stupid cow, he thought. But, glancing

back, he didn't see a cow.

He saw a hand. A hand covered with thick, brown fur.

A hand that wasn't human!

Chapter Six

"Aaaaaaaaaaaaah!"

The cows glanced up as Paul tore through the field. Then they returned to their never-ending meal.

Paul found the path and kept on running. Even when his big feet stumbled over a tree root and he fell and skinned his knee, he got right back up and kept on running.

Even when the rickety-rackety bridge felt like it was going to collapse under his pounding legs, he kept on running.

Even when the people walking around in the streets of Pinzolo stopped and stared at the muddy, shirtless, crazy-looking stranger, he kept on running.

Paul did not stop running until he reached his grandmother's house. By then, he was too out of breath to explain what happened.

His undershirt was ripped and dirty. He had

skinned his knee. Twigs poked out of his hair. Yet, somehow, he had never dropped his shirt-bag full of mushrooms.

He handed the mushrooms to his grandmother.

"I . . . " he puffed, "picked . . . these . . . for . . . you."

His grandmother looked confused.

"Never mind that," Mr. Alberti cried. "What happened to you, buddy? Did somebody hurt you?"

"Mountains," Paul gasped. "Mushrooms . . . Monster!"

He stood there gasping frantically for air, his chest heaving, his mouth open.

"Monster?" Mr. Alberti repeated. "Come on. Sit down. Let's take it from the top."

All the other relatives had gone home to change for dinner, so Paul's grandmother and his dad were the only ones around. Paul was glad not to have had such a huge audience for this particular scene.

He sat down in the kitchen and, while his grandmother made him some hot tea, he told the whole story of the path and the mushrooms and the cows.

Mr. Alberti translated the tale into Italian for Paul's grandmother. Paul could tell he was adding things like, "I *told* him not to go too far!"

Finally, Paul got to the part about the hand.

"I swear, Dad, it wasn't human," he insisted. "It was covered with thick, black fur! It tried to grab me, but I was too fast. My T-shirt got ripped, though."

Paul paused and pushed his glasses back up his nose. He waited to hear how brave he'd been. How he was such a great adventurer.

Instead, his dad turned red and let out a huge belly laugh!

"What's so funny?" Paul howled.

Mr. Alberti told Paul's grandmother something in Italian. Then *she* started cracking up, too.

"La Barba!" she cried, holding her sides as if they would burst.

"What barber?" Paul asked. "What are you guys talking about?" He was starting to get a little steamed.

Mr. Alberti wiped tears from his eyes. That's how hard he was laughing.

"La Barba is the old man who takes care of the cows," Mr. Alberti finally explained. "His real name is Italo. I remember him from when *I* was a kid, so that's how old he must be. Those were his cows you were playing with. He probably wanted to find out what you were up to."

"But the *fur*," Paul protested. "I saw it with my own eyes!"

Mr. Alberti chuckled and patted his son on the back.

"That's the funny thing about old Italo," he said. "Even when I was a kid, he was the *hairiest* guy we'd ever seen. I mean head to toe! He used to scare the younger kids. That's why we called him 'La Barba.' It means 'beard' in Italian."

Paul felt himself blush. He'd been humiliated by an old coot who needed a shave! Well, he told himself, at least my dad got such a kick out of the story that he forgot to punish me for wandering off in the first place.

Still, he vowed never to tell anyone else what had happened.

After all, he didn't want people here to get the wrong idea, and think he was just another silly American.

<u>Chapter Seven</u>

"So then he said, 'A monster grabbed me!' "

Everyone at the crowded dinner table howled with laughter as Mr. Alberti told the story of Paul's misadventure. In Italian, of course. But Paul didn't have much trouble figuring it out.

He managed to ignore most of the teasing. Mostly because he concentrated on something much more important.

Food!

Paul's grandmother had put together a Feast with a capital F. Paul was used to his dad saying, "We're having spaghetti for dinner tonight." And that would be all.

In Italy, spaghetti was only one course in the meal. After that came meat and vegetables and salad and cheese and fruit and dessert and, at the very end, strong Italian coffee served in tiny cups.

Paul skipped the coffee, but he had just about everything else — and massive amounts of it.

He also enjoyed the meal because he finally got to meet his cousin Anthony, Uncle Freddy's and Aunt Nat's son.

Anthony was Paul's age, and he seemed *tough*.

He was short and tan and wiry, with dark, mischievous eyes. He'd been at work earlier, painting houses, and his hands and arms were still freckled with white paint. Paul had never worked a job where he got his hands dirty. Once he'd had a paper route, but that was it.

Even better than meeting someone his own age, Paul thought, was meeting someone who spoke English. Anthony had taken English in school as a second language. He had an accent, of course. But he didn't have any trouble making himself understood.

The first thing he said to Paul was, "So. You like Chicago?"

"I like it OK," Paul replied. "But so far, I like it better here."

He wasn't trying to be polite. He really meant it.

To his surprise, a scowl crossed Anthony's face.

"Pinzolo?" he asked. "You like Pinzolo better than Chicago? What about all the big buildings in Chicago?"

"They're all right," he shrugged. "But you guys have these mountains."

Anthony snorted.

"Yes, the mountains are nice. But they were always here. Your Chicago buildings, they were made by humans."

Paul could tell his cousin was a real hot-head. He liked him immediately. Before they could continue the argument, though, yet another dinner course was served.

Mr. Alberti was just winding up his long, loud and entertaining account of Paul's run-in with La Barba. After he finished, Paul's grandmother said something in Italian. Mr. Alberti turned to Paul with a grin.

"Your Nonna wants to know if you've ever heard the legend of the Orco."

Anthony rolled his eyes from the other side of

the table.

"Don't believe these stories," he said. "They are only to scare little girls and boys." When he said "little," it sounded like "lee-tell."

"What's the Orco?" Paul asked.

Mr. Alberti smiled and translated Paul's question into Italian. The table erupted with voices — all talking at once, all talking very loud, and all talking to Paul about the Orco.

Mr. Alberti and Anthony attempted to translate.

"The Orco is a story they tell around here," Mr. Alberti began. "He's sort of like — hmm, what would you call it in English? A troll. An ugly troll that lives up in the mountains. He has great powers in the mountains, so he can find you wherever you go."

Cousin Sergio rubbed his curly hair and shouted something at Paul.

"Sergio says the Orco is hairy, like Italo," Mr. Alberti explained.

Uncle Freddy started yelling and waving his arms wildly. At first, Paul thought he might be having a fit.

"My dad says Orco has seven arms and seven legs," Anthony muttered, obviously not impressed. "But I tell you, don't believe their stories."

Aunt Nat shook her head.

"Your aunt disagrees with your uncle," Mr. Alberti translated. "She says the Orco looks just like a regular man. The only way you can tell he's the Orco is by checking his feet."

"His feet?" Paul asked.

"He has chicken's feet," Mr. Alberti explained. Paul laughed.

"See," Anthony cried. "I told you. It's silly."

"The Orco eats people," Mr. Alberti continued.

Sergio interrupted and pointed at Paul and Anthony.

"Oh, I'm sorry, I got it wrong," Mr. Alberti said, guffawing loudly. "He only eats *children*."

Paul looked at Anthony and rolled his eyes.

"Ooooh!" he said sarcastically, pretending to be afraid. Anthony giggled.

Paul's grandmother took over the story-telling. She removed her gold wedding band and held it up for everybody to see.

"Oh, this is the most important part to remember," Mr. Alberti warned. "If you ever run into the Orco, the only way to get rid of him is by throwing your wedding ring at him. The ring is a symbol of love and goodness, so the Orco will run away."

Paul flashed his dad a thumb's up sign.

"Got it," he said. "Now I'll know exactly what to do if I get into trouble."

Mr. Alberti laughed.

Anthony began explaining how, in Pinzolo, grown-ups treated kids like they were really stupid.

"I bet in Chicago, they show kids a lee-tell more respect," he grumbled.

Everyone else at the table continued talking and laughing and eating and drinking. Even though Paul had made a big show of joking around and acting brave, he couldn't help thinking about all of those Orco stories.

He didn't believe the stories, but still he tried to picture what the Orco would look like. Hairy. Ugly. With a man's body and chicken's feet.

Or even worse, with seven arms and seven

legs.

Seven hands. One to grab your left arm. One to grab your right arm.

One to grab your left leg. One to grab your right leg.

One to cover your mouth, so you couldn't scream.

And two left over to slowly wrap around your throat.

Chapter Eight

The next morning, Paul and his dad woke up before eight. Because of the time change, it felt like three in the afternoon to them.

"It's jet lag," Mr. Alberti explained. "It takes a couple of days to get used to."

Breakfast in Italy was nowhere near as elaborate as dinner. Basically, it was some crusty rolls and a big bowl of cafe latte, which is a little bit of Italian coffee and *lots* of hot milk.

Paul never drank coffee in Chicago. But his grandmother, like all grandmothers, knew exactly what he wanted. She filled his cafe latte with lots of extra sugar. It tasted great.

After breakfast, Mr. Alberti pushed away from the table and wiped his mouth.

"We'd better give your mother a call," he said.

Paul could barely hear his mother on the

phone. She sounded very far away. She was at a hotel in Pittsburgh.

"Are you having fun?" she asked.

"Uh-huh," Paul said. "I just drank a big bowl of coffee for breakfast."

Paul's mom laughed.

"I heard you ran into the Orco already," she said.

Paul felt his face redden. His dad had talked to his mom first and said a few things in Italian. He must have told her all about the whole meeting with La Barba.

"I wasn't scared," Paul lied. "I knew it was that hairy old coot."

Paul's mom could always tell when he was lying. It never failed.

"Now Paul, I know how they like to tease over there," she said. "And I know what an imagination you have. But don't go believing every story they tell you. They're just tall tales."

"I know!" Paul whined. "I'm not a baby, you know."

"Hey, take it easy," his mom said. "I know you

don't believe it. Just make sure you're careful, OK?"

"I will," Paul said.

"And promise you won't go wandering off again without your father."

Paul mumbled something into the phone. He didn't really say *anything*. But he hoped it sounded enough like "I promise" to fool his mom.

It didn't. She knew every trick.

"Paul," she ordered, more sternly. "Promise."

"All right, all right," Paul sighed. "I promise not to go off by myself and do anything stupid."

Paul's dad and his grandmother were sitting on the couch, looking through an old photo album. They didn't notice that one of Paul's hands had disappeared up into his baggy shirt sleeve.

Or that, just as he made his promise, two of his fingers happened to be crossed.

<u>Chapter Nine</u>

Since they were both still suffering from jetlag, Paul and his dad decided to put off any major sightseeing for a couple of days. The trips would be more fun if they were well rested.

"We need to start visiting relatives, anyway," Mr. Alberti said.

Paul groaned. It seemed as if *everyone* in Pinzolo was related to them somehow.

"Now, come on, buddy," Mr. Alberti said. "Aren't you interested in learning about your ancestors and finding out about your roots? It'll be like history class."

Paul kept his mouth clamped shut. He *hated* history class. His last history teacher, Mrs. Ludholz, had made them memorize the name of every single president. In order. Even Millard Fillmore!

For a moment, Mr. Alberti watched his son

squirm with unhappiness. Then the corners of his mouth started to turn upward. Finally, unable to contain himself any longer, he burst out into a long, loud laugh.

"Or," he said, catching his breath, "I suppose you could let Anthony show you around town."

Paul sighed with relief. His sore cheeks couldn't have stood another whole day of being pinched.

Twenty minutes later, Paul and Anthony were running down the front steps of their grandmother's house. Cries of "Be careful!" — in both Italian and English — echoed down the street after them.

It was still early, about 10:30 in the morning. The town was completely different from the first time Paul had seen it.

The streets were packed with people. All the shops were open. An outdoor market, teeming with people, took up several blocks. Vendors sold everything from live rabbits to fancy clothes to fresh tomatoes.

"The market comes every Wednesday," Anthony explained. "They travel to all of the towns in the valley."

Paul spotted a man selling toys and dashed over to the booth. He picked up a cool robot with seven different guns and a space chain saw.

"Sweet!" he cried. "I've never seen one of these before."

Anthony yawned.

"They're OK," he said. Then he lowered his voice, even though the vendor probably didn't speak English. "But the same people come here every week. They're nothing special. Nothing, I bet, compared to the shopping malls they have in Chicago."

Paul shrugged and put down the robot. He didn't have any money to buy it with, anyway.

"Well, malls are different, that's all, and ... "

"Tell me about America," Anthony interrupted, as they continued walking through the market. "There's nothing I want more than to travel to your country."

"Well, it's not bad," Paul offered. "The city is pretty crowded. And noisy. There are lots of cars. No mountains. It's really much better here."

Anthony looked at Paul as if he had just declared, "I am a giant, walking cheese." He raised his eyebrows and dropped his jaw. His entire face said, quite clearly, "YOU'RE CRAZY!"

"What are you talking about?" he cried. "Nothing exciting ever happens in Pinzolo. If someone's chicken lays an egg, the whole town knows. It's big news for weeks! Now in Chicago . . . "

Before Anthony could continue, a voice called out his name. A woman's voice. A very *old* voice.

The cousins turned around, and Paul found himself facing one of the oldest ladies he'd ever seen. She was hunched over, leaning on a wooden walking stick that someone had carved from a tree branch. The handle had been turned into a snarling monster's face.

How appropriate, Paul thought — and immediately felt like a jerk.

But the lady *was* creepy looking. Her face was creased and crumpled, like a dried-up apple. She had a little white mustache, and whiskers on her chin, too. And the craziest eyes!

"Ciao, Maria," Anthony called out.

The lady ignored him and mumbled something in Italian. Then — verrrry slowly — she pointed a knobby, bony finger at Paul.

Anthony answered her in Italian. Paul had no idea what they were talking about.

Suddenly, the lady's wrinkled face broke out into a hundred more wrinkles. Paul thought she might be smiling.

"Paulo!" she cried. And — verrry slowwwly — she hobbled toward Paul.

"She's a distant cousin," Anthony whispered. "Just say ciao."

"Ci-ciao," Paul stuttered meekly. He flashed Maria a lame wave. Her expression didn't change at all. She continued to hobble his way.

"You have to talk *louder*," Anthony whispered. "She's practically deaf."

"CIAO!" Paul shouted.

Several shoppers turned to look at the obnoxious American shouting "Ciao!" in the middle of the market. Even Maria seemed a little startled. But she grinned and addressed Paul in Italian.

Paul nodded politely and smiled back.

"What did she just say to me?" he whispered out of the corner of his mouth.

Maria was much closer now. And slowwwly leaning toward Paul. Her wrinkled lips parted slightly, revealing two lonely, rotten teeth.

Paul shrank back as she approached.

Anthony gave him a gentle shove forward.

"Go on," he whispered. "She said she wants a *kiss*."

Chapter Ten

"Yuck!" Paul said under his breath.

For the next five minutes, he couldn't stop wiping off his cheeks. *Both* his cheeks. They were in Italy, after all, and that was the way you got kissed. A double whammy.

For the next *ten* minutes, Anthony wouldn't stop snickering.

"You should have seen the look on your head," he laughed.

"Face!" Paul snapped.

"That's what I said," Anthony protested.

Paul didn't bother to insist.

The boys browsed through the market stalls and shops, but soon tired of it. Mostly because neither one of them had any money.

"I've got an idea," Anthony said. "I'll show

you the graveyard."

"Um, sure. That sounds cool," Paul lied.

He did not like graveyards. They were the one thing he *wasn't* curious about. But he didn't want his tough Italian cousin to think he was a chicken.

The graveyard sat at the edge of town. It was surrounded by a stone wall, too high to peek over. The only way to get in was through a rusty iron gate.

The boys pushed through and stepped inside.

The first thing Paul noticed was how *big* all the graves were. It seemed as if each dead person had his own life-sized statue next to his grave. There were crying angels and praying saints, usually staring into the heavens. Other graves just had giant, carved stones. Creepy, yellowed photographs of the dead person were usually attached to the stones under a glass cover.

"It'd be easy to get lost in here," Paul murmured. He heard his voice tremble. He hoped Anthony didn't notice.

"You're not scared, are you?" Anthony asked, giving his cousin a playful poke in the ribs.

"No!" Paul snapped. He tried to put Anthony

in a wrestling hold, but he was too slow.

"You'll never catch me," Anthony laughed, dashing behind a musty crypt.

Paul sprinted after him. Even as he chased his cousin, it occurred to him that there was a dead body inside that very crypt. Maybe a whole family of dead people.

He spotted Anthony at the end of a long row of graves and began racing toward him. Anthony tried to escape, but Paul's legs were longer.

Just as Paul reached to grab Anthony by the belt, the boys raced around the corner of another crypt.

And stopped dead in their tracks.

Blocking their path was the ugliest, hairiest creature Paul had ever seen!

Chapter Eleven

"Ciao, Italo!" Anthony called out, struggling to catch his breath.

Paul blinked in the bright sunlight. He realized he was face to face with the famous La Barba. The famous and *very hairy* La Barba.

Paul could tell that La Barba was old from the wrinkles on his face. But his hair was still as black as a young man's.

And what hair! La Barba had a long, thick beard that touched his belly. The hair on his head was a shaggy mop that fell past his shoulders. His arms, his legs, and even his hands were covered with a black fuzz so thick it looked like fur. It was gross!

Paul decided then and there that if *he* ever got that hairy, he would never go around wearing only shorts and a T-shirt.

Anthony began chatting with Italo. Just like Maria, La Barba soon pointed a hairy finger at Paul and muttered something in Italian.

Oh, no! Paul thought. If *he* wants to kiss me, I'll scream!

But La Barba didn't make any sudden moves. Anthony looked confused, though. He asked Italo a question.

Italo stared at Paul, long and hard. His beady eyes peered out from the tangle of hair that surrounded them like a forest. Then he turned to Anthony and shook his head.

After they said their "ciaos" and Italo shuffled away, Paul turned to Anthony to crack a joke. But he stopped before he even started.

Anthony was as white as a blank sheet of paper.

"C-come on," Anthony stuttered. His voice, normally loud and firm, sounded frightened. "Let's get out of here."

"What's the matter?" Paul asked. Anthony didn't respond.

They left the graveyard and walked in silence

for several minutes. Then, abruptly, Anthony stopped in front of an ice cream shop. A family sat at an outdoor table, laughing and sharing their treats. The youngest girl had chocolate sauce all over her face.

Anthony turned to Paul and grabbed his arm.

"I asked Italo if he remembered you from the other day," he said softly.

"So what?" Paul asked. "He didn't seem mad at me. And why should he be? I didn't hurt any of his cows."

"That's the thing," Anthony replied, his grip on Paul's arm growing tighter. "He said he's never seen you before in his life. He wasn't there the other day. *That wasn't his hand.*"

Chapter Twelve

"So what did you boys do today?" Mr. Alberti asked when they sat down to dinner that night.

Paul and Anthony had agreed not to say anything about the meeting with Italo in the graveyard. Just to make sure Paul remembered, Anthony gave his cousin a sharp kick under the table.

"Ow!" Paul cried.

"What's the matter?" Mr. Alberti asked.

"Um, nothing," Paul stammered. "I, uh, just stubbed my toe. On the table leg. I'm OK."

Mr. Alberti stroked his mustache curiously.

"Right," he said finally, but he did not sound convinced. He stared for a long time at Paul, then at Anthony.

Before Mr. Alberti could say anything else, Paul's grandmother brought out an enormous, steaming bowl of gnocchi. That's pronounced knee-yaw-KEY. They're Italian potato dumplings served with spaghetti sauce.

Paul had to struggle to keep himself from drooling like a wild beast. He found them *delicious*. Everybody dug in.

Two hours and five courses later, Paul and Anthony asked to be excused from the table.

"Have you been upstairs yet?" Anthony asked. Paul shook his head.

As usual, Paul had eaten too much for his own good. He felt too bloated even to speak, let alone climb stairs. Somehow he managed to follow Anthony up two whole flights.

At the top of the stairs, a doorway opened onto the flat roof of Paul's grandmother's house. A couple of folding chairs were set up there. The boys sat down.

The sun was starting to set, lighting the mountains from behind with a pink glow. It didn't seem possible, but the mountains looked even more impressive than usual.

"Wow," Paul exclaimed, adjusting his chair on

the roof. "What a view."

Anthony shrugged.

"I just like it up here because it's breezy," he said. "Now your Sears Tower in Chicago - *that* must have a magnificent view."

Paul slapped his forehead.

"Sure!" he said. "It's a magnificent view of a dirty old city! It's nothing like these mountains. I can't understand you."

"OK, OK," Anthony interrupted. "We will not agree for now."

Then he lowered his voice.

"I think you know what we really need to talk about," he said.

Paul nodded. "By the way," he added, rubbing his sore ankle, "you didn't have to kick me. I wasn't going to say anything."

"I was just being careful," Anthony shot back with a grin.

"Well, you didn't have to kick me *so hard*," Paul snapped. "So, what do you think grabbed me out there?"

He continued, nodding his head toward the

mountains.

"You think it could've been the . . . "

"There is no Orco!" Anthony barked.

He sounded like he was trying to convince himself as much as Paul.

"They've been telling me Orco stories since I was old enough to listen. And that's all they are. Stories! I can't believe you fall for that stuff."

He paused for a moment and began picking at one of the scabs on his arm. He had lots of scabs and cuts and bruises. Paul thought that made his cousin look even tougher.

Finally, Anthony added, "You're just like a little baby!"

Paul jumped up from his chair.

"I'm no baby!" he almost shouted. Remembering they were trying to keep a secret, he lowered his voice. "I want to find out what grabbed me just as much as you do. If you're so tough . . . "

He paused. He hoped he wouldn't regret what he was about to say. He plunged ahead anyway.

"If you're so tough," he said, "let's go back out there."

Anthony stared at Paul for a split second, then spat out, "Fine! It's probably a wild duck's chase anyway."

"It's *goose* chase," Paul corrected. There was a twinge of meanness in his voice.

"That's what I said!" Anthony snapped.

The cousins stared at each other in silence. Then, both at once, they laughed nervously.

"Let's not fight," Anthony said.

"OK," Paul agreed. They shook hands. "Friends."

But Paul realized that neither one of them would back down. The sun was almost gone behind the mountains now. They did not look as inviting as they had before. A cold breeze blew across the roof.

Paul shivered. Part of him didn't really believe in any old Orco. Part of him couldn't wait to go back and explore anyway.

But another part of him — the part that remembered that furry hand and its iron grip — was scared. He didn't say that out loud, though.

All he said was: "Don't worry, buddy. What could happen to *two* of us?"

Chapter Thirteen

Over the next couple of days, Paul and his dad went sightseeing.

They took a cable car to the top of the highest mountain, and drank hot chocolate in the refuge at the summit. They borrowed Uncle Freddy's car and drove to a nearby lake. It was too cold to swim, but they dunked their feet and ate at a fancy restaurant on the water. Paul snapped lots of pictures with his plastic camera.

At the end of the week, Mr. Alberti decided to get all of his visiting out of the way in one swoop.

He invited everyone he knew — cousins, in-laws, friends, practically all of Pinzolo — to get together for a huge picnic in the town park. Uncle Freddy started a fire and cooked polenta. That's pronounced poo-LEN-tuh, and it's a sticky yellow mush made out of cornmeal. It tastes better than it sounds, especially covered with cheese or stew. Uncle Freddy cooked the polenta over an open fire in a giant copper kettle, stirring it with a wooden ladle.

After lunch, Paul and Anthony got permission to go for a hike by themselves.

"We promise to stay on the trails," Paul said.

"And?" asked Mr. Alberti.

"We promise not to be too late."

"And?"

"Um..." Paul scratched his head. "I don't know. What?"

"Do you promise not to have any fun?" Mr. Alberti asked with a straight face.

Paul and his dad both cracked up.

"No," Mr. Alberti continued. "I want you to have fun. The only thing I want *more* is for you to be careful."

"I will, Dad," Paul insisted. "Really."

He and Anthony set off. They followed the same route Paul had taken on his first day in Pinzolo. All the way through town. Over the rickety-rackety bridge. And finally down the windy trail.

"See those painted rocks?" Anthony pointed to a rock by the side of the trail. Someone had painted a red blotch in the center of it. There were rocks like this every twenty feet or so. "That's so you can follow the trail and not get lost."

As they rounded a bend and headed toward the cow pasture, Anthony turned and pointed to a steep, overgrown incline.

"This way," he instructed.

The route Anthony wanted to take led right into the thick of the woods. It was definitely *not* the path.

"Why do you want to go that way?" Paul asked. "Whatever it was that grabbed me, it grabbed me over by the cows."

"Sure, but nothing's going to be there *today*," Anthony explained wearily. "It's Sunday. Italo's whole family comes up to his field on Sunday for a picnic. All of his kids and grandkids will be there, running around and scaring all the cows. We'll never see anything with all those people around."

"OK," Paul said. "You're the native guide."

As a native guide, Anthony was more used to

walking than Paul. Especially uphill. He was also better at dodging roots. And tree branches. And spider webs.

Paul stumbled twice. He scraped his cheek on a pointy branch and got a mouthful of cobweb. He puffed and wheezed from the climb. But the last thing he wanted to do was admit that he couldn't keep up with Anthony.

To make himself keep going, he stared again at his beat-up red sneakers. And concentrated. One foot. After another. After another.

Soon, his vivid imagination went to work and helped him pass the time.

He was a soldier. He'd been captured by the enemy and was being marched through the woods to a prison camp. They wanted to break his spirit. He'd had no food for days. They only allowed him a swallow of water from a dirty sponge. But he wouldn't give them the satisfaction of breaking. Not Paul Alberti. He'd keep walking. One foot. After another. Like a machine. An unstoppable machine.

A few minutes later, he *had* to stop. His imagination could give him only so much help.

"Anthony," he gasped, leaning against a tree, "hold on a second, I need to take a . . . "

Anthony didn't answer. Paul sucked in a deep breath and, finally, looked up from his enormous shoes. Immediately, he stopped talking.

Because there was no one to talk to. Anthony was gone.

Chapter Fourteen

"Anthony?" Paul stammered.

His words echoed through the forest. There was no sign of his cousin. Anywhere.

"Don't panic," Paul told himself. "You're just going for a little hike in the mountains. Nothing bad has happened."

He looked around. It was dark and difficult to see. The trees were so tall they filtered out the sun. The air felt damp. Green moss covered every rock. None of the rocks had red dots.

"Don't panic," Paul repeated to himself.

Then he panicked.

"ANTHONY!" he screamed. His voice echoed through the forest.

He spun around and ran back toward the main trail. Then he got confused. Was he going in the right direction? The area was hilly. Everything looked the same.

Anthony had been breaking branches so they could find their way back. But there were lots of broken branches.

No, this way wasn't right, Paul thought.

He turned and ran the opposite way. He slipped on a tree root and landed in the dirt.

Before he could rise, a hand gripped his shoulder.

He let loose a shriek of sheer horror.

Chapter Fifteen

Anthony cupped his other hand over Paul's mouth.

"Shut up, dummy!" he whispered fiercely.

"Anthony!" Paul cried through a mouthful of fingers.

At first he was delighted to see his cousin. Then he got mad.

"Where were you, anyway?" he asked.

"Up here," Anthony hissed. He led Paul to the top of a ridge. It was hidden by a cluster of trees and rocks.

"Look," Anthony said, pointing down the other side of the ridge.

Paul looked in the direction Anthony pointed. He saw a run-down cabin in the middle of a clearing. It was more like a shack, actually. It had a thatched roof and was made of different-sized stones that seemed loose and worn-out. Paul couldn't tell whether anyone lived in the cabin or not.

"That's why I didn't say anything," Anthony explained. "I was trying to be quiet, just in case anyone's in there."

"Sorry," Paul murmured. "You've never seen this place before?"

Anthony shook his head. "I've never even *heard* of people living up here. It's too hard to get to town."

He paused and thought and squinted a bit as he stared at the cabin.

"Well, I guess we should go down and check it out," he said.

Paul gulped. He felt his stomach twist up in knots. The polenta was like a boulder in his belly.

"All right," he heard himself say. "Let's go."

Anthony grabbed his shoulder.

"Wait," he said. He sounded embarrassed. "I, uh, want you to hold onto something."

He reached into a pocket and handed Paul something small and shiny. Paul held the object up to the light. It was his grandmother's gold wedding ring!

"You took Nonna's ring?!" Paul cried.

Anthony looked ashamed.

"I know those Orco stories are stupid," he said. "But, you know - just in case - I, uh, how do you say in English? I *borrowed* the ring this morning. She takes it off every night before she goes to bed. I snuck it out when she wasn't looking."

Paul remembered hearing his grandmother saying something about misplacing her ring.

"Borrowed it? You stole it!" he whispered fiercely. "I can't believe you just took Nonna's wedding ring. What if we lose it?"

"That's why I'm giving it to you," Anthony protested. "You have snaps on your shirt pocket, so it won't go anywhere."

"OK," Paul agreed warily. "I'll carry the ring. But we have to return it as soon as we get home."

"What do you think - that I want to sell Nonna's ring?" Anthony grumbled.

The cousins glared at each other for a moment. Then, without a word, they set off down the ridge, toward the mysterious house in the woods.

Chapter Sixteen

"Make sure you walk quietly," Anthony warned his cousin as they made their way down the slope.

Paul tried. But he couldn't help noticing every time he made even the tiniest sound. In the silence of the mountain forest, every snapped twig sounded like a giant cracking his knuckles. Every crunched leaf sounded like a stadium full of people all munching potato chips at the exact same time.

Finally, they made it to the cabin. Everything seemed quiet. The cabin was bigger than it had looked from the top of the ridge. The only window was too high for either of them to peep through.

They crouched next to the wall, directly under the window.

"One of us must lift the other," Anthony whispered.

"Well, I'm heavier," Paul noted, patting his belly for emphasis.

"Yes," Anthony agreed, "but I'm strong." He flexed his muscles. Then he laced his hands together, palms up, to make a step.

"Well, fine," Paul said. "I'll look. I'm not afraid."

He was lying, of course. Gingerly, he stepped into Anthony's hands and felt himself being lifted toward the window.

"Mama!" Anthony whispered. "You have some big feet."

Paul couldn't believe it. Here they were, risking their lives at this creepy old cabin in the middle of nowhere, and he was still hearing about his big feet!

He didn't have much time to dwell on it, though, because soon he was gripping the window ledge.

"Got it?" Anthony grunted.

"Yes," Paul whispered.

Slowly, he pulled himself up, until he could peer into the dark, shadowy cabin. It was hard to make anything out. He teetered on Anthony's hand, trying to keep his balance.

He squinted deeper, deeper into the gloom . . .
and then let go of the ledge and screamed!

Chapter Seventeen

Anthony and Paul toppled backwards into the dirt.

"Eyes!" Paul cried. "I saw a pair of eyes, staring out at . . . "

He was interrupted by a sound coming from the window.

"Meow."

Paul and Anthony stared up at the sill. A black cat was perched there, licking itself clean.

Paul felt himself turning red. He looked at Anthony — who looked just as red as Paul felt. Dirt covered Anthony's shirt. Twigs stuck out of his hair. A small cut shone scarlet on his cheek.

He looked mad.

"You!" Anthony grunted. "You!"

Paul realized his cousin was so mad, he'd forgotten how to speak English.

"I'm sorry," Paul stammered. "I just saw those eyes and thought . . . "

"You are the biggest baby I know!" Anthony yelled. "You see a little kitty-cat and you scream like it is a bear! I can't believe you are my cousin. I tell you to be quiet and now every mouse in this forest knows we are here! And look at me! I am cut up. I am filthy. I . . . "

But now it was Paul's turn to get mad.

"Don't call *me* a baby!" he shouted. "I'm the one who climbed up there, not you! And if you had been strong enough to hold me, we wouldn't have fallen down in the first place!"

"Oh, are you saying I was scared to look in that window myself?"

"That's exactly what I'm saying!" Paul yelled.

"Well," Anthony snapped, standing up and brushing himself off, "then I guess I'd better lead the way inside."

"Fine," Paul said. He stood up and followed Anthony around to the wooden door of the cabin.

"You made so much racket, if anyone was inside, he would've come out by now," Anthony groused.

He didn't sound so tough now that he was standing in front of the door to the creepy little shack. Paul didn't feel very tough either.

"Yeah," Paul agreed. "It's *gotta* be empty."

Anthony nodded. He grabbed the door handle and pushed.

The door didn't budge.

"There's no lock," Anthony whispered. "It's just stuck." For some reason, it seemed like the right time to start whispering again.

Anthony pushed the door again, harder. It still refused to budge.

"Maybe we should just leave," Paul whispered.

Anthony glared back at him.

"You think I'm scared?" he asked.

"No," Paul protested. "It's just . . . "

Before Paul could continue, Anthony turned around and slammed into the door with his shoulder, hard.

The door gave way with loud crash and swung open, and Anthony tumbled head-first into the darkness.

Chapter Eighteen

"Anthony!" Paul cried.

Without even thinking, he dashed in after his cousin.

Anthony lay dazed in the center of the room. Beyond that, the cabin was empty.

The old shack did not look as scary on the inside as it had from the outside. A worn-out bed occupied one corner of the room. A bare wooden table stood unevenly in the middle of the floor. A half-empty jug of wine sat on a shelf. Some old sections of pipe lay on the floor, and the corners of the room were filled with dust and cobwebs.

And that was about it.

"Are you OK?" Paul asked his cousin.

Anthony stood up angrily and brushed himself off, yet again.

"I'm fine," he snapped. But he seemed embarrassed about his fall. "This place is a dump," he added.

Paul nodded in agreement.

"You think anyone still lives here?" he asked.

"I don't know," Anthony said. "Everything's so old and dusty."

As if he wanted to emphasize the point, Paul sneezed loudly. All over Anthony.

"Sorry," he said. "I'm allergic to dust."

Anthony wiped off his face without a word. Then he dropped to his knees and peered under the bed.

"Nothing down here," he reported.

Paul turned to the shelf on the wall. Aside from the wine jug, there was a glass, a melted-down candle and a dirty kitchen knife. He picked up the knife and touched the tip. It was still sharp.

"Hey," he said. "Come look at this."

Before Anthony could respond, a horrible, high-pitched sound split the air.

Paul and Anthony both jumped about three feet into the air. Paul took a deep breath and looked toward the door.

The noise had come from the cat. Paul had never in his life heard a cat hiss that way. All of its black fur was standing on end. It stood by the open door, and seemed very scared.

Then it arched its back and screeched again.

"You think it's trying to tell us something," Paul asked.

"Yes," Anthony said. "Maybe that something's coming."

Chapter Nineteen

The cat continued screeching - uttering a high wail so frightening it made the hair on Paul's neck stand up like the cat's.

Paul and Anthony ran to the door and peeked outside. No one was around. Everything looked the same.

But different, too. The little bit of sun that had leaked through the thick tree tops earlier had disappeared. Dark storm clouds massed overhead. The air felt suddenly cold and damp.

Paul shivered.

"Something weird is going on," Anthony said.

"I know," Paul said. "Maybe we should really split this time."

"Split?" Anthony had a confused look on his face. "What should we split?"

Before Paul could start another lesson in American slang, they felt the first rumble.

Paul had read about earthquakes in California, and that's what the rumbling felt like. The ground beneath their feet was shaking. Not enough to make trees fall down or the cabin crumble around them.

But more than enough for Paul and Anthony to feel it.

Something really *was* coming. Every time they felt a tremor, they heard a stomping sound in the distance. It sounded a lot like footsteps. The huge, thunderous footsteps of something really, *really* big.

They heard the snap of branches breaking. The noise came from the top of the ridge. The trees up that way were shaking.

Whatever it was, it was close.

Then they heard the howl. It sounded like it was part bear, part wolf, and maybe part something else.

But definitely not human at all.

Chapter Twenty

The boys dashed back into the cabin and slammed the door.

The cat raced around inside the room, hissing wildly.

"Shut up!" Paul yelled at the cat. He turned to Anthony. They stood next to each other with their backs against the door.

"Do you think it's . . . " Paul began, his voice trembling.

"I don't know," Anthony breathed. The ground continued to shake. "We'd better block off this door."

The boys ran to the heavy wooden table and dragged it toward the door as fast as they could.

The terrible footsteps grew louder, the shaking of the ground more intense.

"All right," Anthony ordered. "Push it under the handle."

With a massive shove, they wedge the table under the door knob.

The rumbles grew more thunderous. The jug of wine rattled on the shelf with each approaching footstep. Whatever it was, it was getting closer.

"That's not going to keep anything out for long," Paul cried. He couldn't stop his voice from shaking.

"You're right," Anthony said. "The only other way out is the window."

The window. So tiny. So *high*.

It's our only hope, Paul thought. He grabbed an old, rickety chair from the corner of the room and dragged it over to the window.

The stomps were getting closer.

"You go first," Anthony said.

"No!" Paul cried. "You go. I'll hold the chair steady."

Anthony shook his head.

The stomps were getting louder. The wine jug was almost jumping off the shelf.

"You're stronger!" Paul shouted. "It'll be easier for you to get the window open."

Anthony thought for a second, then nodded.

"All right," he said. "I'll do it."

"Hurry!" Paul yelled.

Anthony climbed onto the chair. He tried the window. It wouldn't budge.

"It's stuck!" he cried.

The chair was bouncing with each thunderous footstep. Paul could hardly hold it still.

"Break it!" Paul shouted.

Anthony closed his eyes and punched the window.

"Ow!" he grunted. Blood dripped from his hand. He smashed away the rest of the glass and pulled himself through the window.

The horrible hammering of the footsteps approached. It sounded as if the next step would stomp the shack flat.

Frantically, Paul looked up. He saw Anthony's feet disappear through the window. He heard Anthony fall to the ground outside with a thud.

My turn, Paul thought. He stepped onto the

chair with one of his oversized red sneakers.

And immediately felt the old chair crack.

He tumbled to the ground. His glasses flew off and slid across the floor. The chair broke into a half-dozen pieces. Paul squinted up at the window. He could not possibly reach it now.

The stomping stopped.

Paul turned and looked at the door. The door started to shake.

Whatever it was, it was here.

Chapter Twenty-One

As he cowered in the corner, Paul heard the sound of a massive shove against the door. The table split apart and the door crashed open. Shards of wood flew across the room.

Paul covered his face.

When he opened his eyes, a blurry shape filled the doorway. Paul had trouble making it out without his glasses. But the shape was tall and dark, with two arms and two legs. It looked as if it was covered with a thick fur.

Paul could not see well, but he could smell. The shape smelled like a wet dog. Like a zoo on a hot summer day.

Like an *animal*.

Terror shot up Paul's spine like an electric shock. There was no doubt about it: He was face to face with the Orco!

Then the Orco roared. Paul thought his eardrums would burst. Even though he was all the way on the other side of the shack, Paul felt a blast of the creature's hot, foul breath.

I'm dead, he thought. There's no escape.

Another growl came from the shape in the door.

Paul was too scared to get up. Or try to run. Or even scream.

What would be the point? They were on a mountain. In the middle of nowhere. This wasn't a movie. No superhero would fly to his rescue.

The shape started to move. It bent down to fit through the doorway, and entered the cabin. And headed slowly — but surely — for Paul.

Squinting across the cabin, Paul saw that the blurry shape had something tied around its furry waist — a belt, perhaps, or a rope. A bulging sack hung from the belt.

Paul wondered if the sack contained treasure. Or the skulls of the Orco's victims. Or both. Maybe, to an Orco, a skull *was* treasure.

Paul flattened himself against the wall.

The blurry shape did not seem to have chicken's feet, he saw. They looked more or less like human's feet. Only hairier.

The Orco lumbered forward. I'm about to die, Paul thought. This is it.

He grabbed one of the broken chair legs. At least I'll go out with a fight, he thought.

Then he remembered his grandmother's ring!

The Orco was halfway across the shack now. He seemed to be taking his time. He paused to roar even louder. Paul's ears rang like it was a fire drill.

He fumbled with the snap on his pocket. The Orco took another step forward, snarling.

Paul ripped his pocket open and grabbed the ring. The Orco took another step. Paul thought he could see something dripping from the blurry shape's mouth.

Was he drooling?

Paul gulped. He had never had a great arm for football or baseball. But he hurled that ring as hard as he could.

The ring sailed through the air like a missile, straight and true. It walloped the shape smack in the center of its hairy chest.

Then it dropped to the floor and rolled into the corner.

The Orco growled and snarled and roared.

Oh no! Paul thought. I've made him *madder*!

Chapter Twenty-Two

Now Paul knew he was dead meat.

The Orco took another step closer. Paul was too scared to move.

Then, from in the doorway, Paul heard a scream.

"AIIIIEEEEE!"

The Orco heard it, too. He stopped in his tracks and whirled around.

Paul squinted at the doorway and made out a smaller shape. Anthony! It looked like his cousin was holding something small in his right hand. Something *glowing*.

As the Orco turned his head, Anthony hurled the object into the center of the cabin.

Paul saw that it was a tiny ball. What was Anthony doing?

Suddenly, sparks shot out of the ball. The Orco took a step back. A cloud of thick green smoke billowed out of the ball. The Orco howled and took another step backwards.

It was a smoke bomb!

Paul had bought some on the Fourth of July once. He didn't know they sold them in Italy. Or that Anthony had brought any along.

But he wasn't complaining! For some reason, the Orco was *scared*. He stumbled back to the wall and waved madly at the smoke.

This is my chance, Paul thought.

He scrambled to his feet and darted through the smoke to the door, to freedom! As he ran, he reached down and snatched his glasses off the floor.

From the midst of the smoke behind him, the Orco howled.

Anthony was waiting outside.

"Let's get out of here," he cried.

They heard the Orco thrashing around in the shack. But they never looked back. They ran up the ridge and back down to the trail, and all the way back to Pinzolo.

Chapter Twenty-Three

"He was *huge*," Paul huffed.

"He was *ugly*," Anthony puffed.

Mr. Alberti watched the boys. He frowned and folded his arms.

"OK, you guys really have to calm down," he said. "Nothing you've said so far has made any sense. Now, Paul, just take a deep breath and start over again. At the beginning."

Paul took a deep breath and started at the beginning. He told his dad about meeting La Barba in the graveyard, about leaving the path and hiking up the side of the mountain, about finding the old shack and going inside, about the clouds, the rumbling, the Orco, the ring, the . . .

"Hold it!" Mr. Alberti cried. "Where's your grandmother's ring now?"

Paul and Anthony looked at each other and gulped.

"Well, um, like I said, Dad, I threw it at the Orco," Paul said sheepishly. "But it didn't do anything to him."

"So where is the ring *now*?" Mr. Alberti asked. His voice was low and his teeth were clenched. Two bad signs.

"Um," Paul stammered. "Well, it bounced off the Orco's chest and, uh, rolled away. My glasses fell off, so I couldn't really see where it went. But I guess it's still in the shack. We didn't really have a chance to look for it, because Anthony threw in this smoke bomb and the Orco was roaring and waving his arms around and . . . "

"Enough about the Orco!" Mr. Alberti shouted. "I don't want to hear another word from either one of you about it. There is no Orco and you know it!"

"But Uncle, we . . . " Anthony began. Paul's dad cut him off.

"I told you not to go back to that mountain, but you did," he said. "You went to play silly games, and you took your grandmother's wedding ring and lost it. And now you've made up an imaginary Orco to make it seem all right. Well it's *not* all right! Do you know how your grandmother will feel when she finds out that ring is lost? Do you?"

Paul and Anthony both stared at their shoes.

Paul had never seen his dad this angry. Not even the time Paul had been trying to use Mr. Alberti's electric razor, just to see what it would feel like, and had accidentally dropped it into the toilet.

Mr. Alberti stared at the boys a few moments, letting them writhe under his gaze.

"OK," he said finally. "Let's go."

Paul looked up. Oh no! he thought. Were they going back to Chicago? Was his father that furious?

"Where — where are we going?" Paul finally stuttered.

"To find your grandmother's ring," Mr. Alberti stated firmly. "You are taking me to the mountain."

Chapter Twenty-Four

No amount of begging or pleading did any good. Mr. Alberti simply did not believe that they had encountered the Orco.

And so, after Anthony's cut hand had been bandaged by their grandmother, they headed back to the last place in the world Paul ever wanted to see again — the mountain.

They hiked in silence. Mr. Alberti was too angry to say much. Paul and Anthony were too scared to say anything.

They made their way along the trail and up through the mountain forest. Finally, they came to the clearing and spied the old cabin.

"Well," Mr. Alberti snorted. "At least you were telling the truth about *something*."

Paul was not really listening to his father. He

was too busy looking for the Orco.

What was that shape, there, behind the tree?

Oh. Only a bird.

Wait - there, behind Anthony, were two hands, about to grab him!

Oh. Only some branches in the wind.

"Well, come on, you two," Mr. Alberti said sharply. "We have some searching to do."

With that, he began to make his way toward the cabin. Paul and Anthony stared at each other, then reluctantly followed.

Mr. Alberti marched straight for the door. The Orco *can't* still be in there, Paul thought feverishly. Plus he only goes after kids.

Paul heard his dad say something in Italian.

Paul and Anthony rushed to the door of the cabin and peered inside. There, sitting on the edge of the bed, petting the black cat, was a man.

He looked like he was about Mr. Alberti's age. He had messy hair and a beard, and he wore shabby clothes. One of his toes poked out from a hole in his boot.

Mr. Alberti turned to Paul and Anthony. He

looked even angrier than before.

"Did you two destroy this man's house?" he asked. His voice was so low it was almost a whisper. A *very* bad sign.

Paul looked around. The chair lay smashed beneath the broken window. Pieces of table were scattered all over the floor. The whole place stank of smoke.

Paul gulped.

"I swear, Dad, it was the Orco," he began. Mr. Alberti cut him off.

"What did I tell you guys about making up stories? I don't want to hear it!" he ordered.

But the man on the bed had perked up when he heard the word Orco. He said something to Paul's dad in Italian.

"What did he say?" Paul whispered to Anthony.

"He told your dad that he's never seen the Orco before, but that he believes in it," Anthony said softly. "He told your dad that the moment he stepped in the door, he sensed something strange. Something *evil.*"

The man continued talking to Mr. Alberti, who could not get a word in edgewise. Anthony listened and whispered rough translations to Paul.

"He says his name is Gianni. He lives here all by himself, with only the cat. He says he came up here because Pinzolo got too *crowded*." Anthony snorted, then added in a sarcastic tone, "Oh, yeah, it's real crowded, it . . . "

"Never mind what you think," Paul interrupted. "What else?"

Anthony glared at his cousin, but continued.

"He hunts all of his food, and picks wild fruit and mushrooms. He hates modern technology. He's going to write a book about how much he hates civilization, but right now it's all in his head."

"What about the Orco?" Paul asked.

"I'm just translating. I can't control what he talks about," Anthony snapped. "Oh, wait! He's coming back to the Orco now. He says he used to think it was all just a story, but now he believes it. He thinks the Orco used to be a man, but fell victim to a horrible curse. Now he must roam the mountain forever. He can only feast on innocent blood — either animals or children."

Anthony gulped, then continued.

"He says he finds bones sometimes, deep in the forest, of deer and wolves. He can tell it's not the work of a hunter. And he says look at all the children who wind up missing every year. The papers say they got lost or kidnapped or ran away from home."

Anthony paused again and shivered.

"He thinks it's the Orco."

Mr. Alberti tried to cut in, but Gianni ignored him and continued his speech.

"I guess he misses talking to people," Anthony muttered. "Oh, he says he thinks the Orco has always lived on the mountain. That he's almost like a part of the mountain."

Anthony paused and gulped.

"And he says that if the Orco is after you, and he wants to find you — he *will*."

Chapter Twenty-Five

"See!" Mr. Alberti snorted after they'd left. "The only one who believes your crazy Orco stories is nuts himself!"

"Nuts?" Anthony asked, puzzled. "A person is the same as some nuts?"

No one offered to translate for him.

Paul's dad was still pretty upset. They had searched the cabin for over an hour, but they had found no sign of the ring. Gianni swore he didn't take it, and Mr. Alberti said he believed him. It was obvious Gianni did not care much about money or buying expensive things.

When they got back to Pinzolo, Mr. Alberti had to tell Paul's grandmother about the missing ring. She acted like it did not matter that much to her.

"I like you still," she told Paul over and over, patting him gently on the head.

But Paul noticed a teardrop glistening in the corner of her eye.

Uncle Freddy and Aunt Nat were more vocal. They decided, together with Paul's dad, that Paul and Anthony would forfeit their allowances every week until they paid for a new ring — *and* new furniture for Gianni's cabin.

Even worse, they decided Paul and Anthony should be separated for the rest of the visit!

"You two get into too much trouble together," Mr. Alberti said sternly. "You're lucky I'm not putting you on a plane and sending you right back to Chicago."

"But we're going to pay for the furniture and the ring," Paul protested. "Isn't that enough?"

"No," Mr. Alberti said softly. He sounded sad. "Actually, it's not nearly enough. That wedding ring had sentimental value to your grandmother. You can never replace something like that. Not ever."

Paul slunk back up to his room. His dad was right. He felt like a heel.

The next few days were horrible. Paul ate, slept, went for walks in town by himself. His grandmother never said a nasty word. But she moped around the house and did not sing and smile as she had before.

And word had gotten around Pinzolo about the ring — how Anthony and his American cousin had lost it while playing a silly Orco game in the mountains. It was a small town and news traveled fast. Wherever Paul went, he could feel people shooting him dirty looks and whispering about rotten American kids.

After a while, he started spending most of the day in his room, reading.

The family still ate lunch and dinner together at the big table in Paul's grandmother's house. There was only one difference — no Anthony. He had to stay home during meals. Afterwards, Uncle Freddy and Aunt Nat would bring him the leftovers for his supper.

One night after he had finished eating, Paul excused himself and went back to his room. He'd brought with him to Italy a thick spy novel from the grown-up section of the library. He had figured he'd be so busy having fun, the book would last him the whole summer. But now he was almost done with it.

Flopping down on his bed, he opened the novel to where he'd left off. Manly Manford, the British secret agent, was trying to defuse a bomb with one hand and beat the evil Dr. Crow in a sword fight with the other.

Before Paul could get back to the action, he noticed something odd. His bookmark had been replaced by a note!

As soon as he opened it, Paul knew the note was from Anthony. He could tell by the misspelled English words and awkward sentences. Anthony could speak English better than he could write it. He must have snuck into Paul's room while the family was eating dinner.

The note said: "PAULO — MEAT ME ON TOP OF HOWSE — TALK WE MUST — A."

Paul slipped out of his room and stood by the stairs, listening. The family was still at the dinner table, chatting loudly. Slowly, his heart pounding, Paul crept up to the roof.

Anthony was crouching in the shadows, watching the sunset.

"Hey," Paul said.

Anthony nodded. "So how has your vacation been?"

Paul rolled his eyes and sat down next to his cousin.

"This whole thing stinks," he said. "We lost Nonna's ring. Nobody believes us about the Orco. We aren't even allowed to talk."

"I know," Anthony said. "That's why we need a plan."

Paul's eyes widened. "What do you mean?"

Anthony blew back a wisp of hair that had fallen into his eyes.

"Well," he said, "the only way to make things better is to get that ring back."

"Yeah, but it's lost," Paul said glumly.

"Lost," Anthony asked, "or stolen? Did you notice a sack hanging from Orco's side?"

"Yes!" Paul exclaimed. "I remember. You think he took the ring?"

"Where else would it be?" Anthony said. "If

what Gianni said is true and Orco was once human, he might still like human things."

Paul's face fell again.

"But now we'll never get it back," he said.

"Why not?" asked Anthony. He reached into his pocket and pulled out a handful of tiny colored balls. They had fuses on the ends.

Smoke bombs.

"We know how to take care of that Orco," he said. "We can get the ring back. And if you bring your camera, we can prove once and for all that there is such a thing as the Orco."

Paul's stomach fluttered. Anthony hadn't gotten a good look at the Orco.

Of course, Paul hadn't really gotten a good look at the Orco either, without his glasses. But he'd gotten a *sense* of the Orco - and he sure didn't like it.

On the other hand, he wanted to get that ring back for his grandmother more than anything. And they had outsmarted the Orco before.

This time, they would be prepared.

And Paul's curiosity was rising again. He really wanted to get a better look at the Orco, no matter how scary it was. And a photograph! Imagine what a sensation that would cause.

His dad would have to believe him. His dad would have to *apologize*. The picture would appear in magazines and newspapers. He could write a book . . .

Then Paul thought of one small problem.

"How will we ever find the Orco again?" he asked.

Anthony nodded toward the mountains. The sun glowed pink behind them.

"We won't find him," he said. "We'll let him find us."

Chapter Twenty-Six

The next day was Sunday. It was also a big holiday in the northern part of Italy, the feast of some saint that Paul had never heard of.

Everyone in Pinzolo celebrated by taking the ski lift to a point near the top of the tallest mountain, where there was a hotel and a restaurant. They set up tents and games and an open space for dancing.

The festival was the first time in almost a week that Paul and Anthony were allowed to be in the same place at the same time. Of course, they still weren't supposed to play together. Or even talk.

But when they were on the roof, they had made plans to slip away from the party after lunch.

They met behind a huge rock on the far side of the hotel, where no one would see them. Italian folk music blared in the distance, mingling with the voices of the partygoers.

"You ready?" Paul asked.

Anthony nodded grimly and patted his pockets.

"I've got our weapons," he replied. "Follow me."

The cousins set off down a secluded trail Anthony said he had hiked before. The trail wound away from the hotel and restaurant, up toward the white peak of the mountain.

As they walked along, the trail became icier. Soon, they were surrounded by snow.

"How much farther?" Paul wheezed. They had not walked far, but he was already out of breath.

"It's not too far," Anthony replied.

About a half-hour later, they came to a flat, snow-covered clearing. It was a lookout point, where people often stopped to take pictures of the view.

Because of the party, no one was around today. A couple of stone benches stood next to a large metal plaque that was covered with dozens of names.

"What's that?" Paul asked, nodding toward the plaque.

"Those are the names of all the people who

have died while they were hiking up here," Anthony replied matter-of-factly.

Paul gulped.

"Look over here," Anthony called. He led his cousin to the edge of the clearing. Paul got dizzy as soon as he approached. He peered over a steep drop off the side of the mountain. He could not see the bottom. But he knew it was a long way down.

"I'll wait over by the benches," he stammered, stepping away from the cliff.

Anthony laughed. But he seemed nervous, too.

"This is the spot where my friend Anita said she saw the Orco," he said.

"Really?" Paul asked. "Is that why you picked this place?"

Anthony nodded. "She was hiking with her parents and they became separated. She was sitting on that bench. Right where you're sitting."

Paul glanced down at the bench and gulped loudly.

"She saw a strange shape move in those trees over there," Anthony continued. "She started to scream. Her parents came running around up the trail.

And then the shape was gone. Just like that. We all thought she made the whole thing up."

"Now we know better," Paul muttered. "So you think he'll show up today?"

"I don't know," Anthony replied. "He's found you twice already."

The third time's the charm, Paul thought grimly, and shivered. It wasn't because he was cold.

Chapter Twenty-Seven

Paul checked his wristwatch for the third time in five minutes. An hour had passed since they had arrived at the lookout point.

There was still no sign of the Orco.

"I don't think he's showing up," Paul said. He tried not to sound hopeful about it, but he couldn't help it.

Anthony paced back and forth near the edge of the cliff.

"We can't go back now," he cried. "Come on. Let's talk about something better. How about American cities!"

"I don't know why you're so obsessed with America, Chicago, the city!" Paul snapped. "It's way better over here."

Anthony shook his head. "You're crazy!"

"*You're* crazy!" Paul shot back. "It's so peaceful here!"

"Peaceful!" Anthony shouted. "Maybe if you're here on a three-week vacation. For me, it's boring!"

"How can it be boring?" Paul asked. "You could hike in these mountains every day."

"But there's no shopping mall," Anthony interrupted. "The only movie theater is three towns away. And you can't find a good hamburger anywhere!"

"A hamburger!" Paul cried. That was the last straw! Anthony shouldn't have started talking about food. "How can you compare a lousy old hamburger to the kind of feasts you have here?"

"Easy!" Anthony yelled. "I . . ."

Then Paul noticed something very strange. Anthony's mouth continued to move, but Paul could not hear him. All he heard was a loud rumbling. The rumbling was as loud as an eighty-person, all-drum orchestra. As loud as a jumbo jet buzzing two inches over your head.

As loud as if the Orco was coming.

"Do you think that's him?" Paul shouted. But

Anthony had turned completely white. His mouth moved, but Paul could not hear a word he was saying.

"What?" Paul cried.

Anthony pointed at something above Paul's head.

Paul whirled around and his eyes widened in terror.

"Avalanche!" he shouted.

Chapter Twenty-Eight

If you're ever caught in an avalanche, shouting "Avalanche!" probably isn't the best idea.

First of all, everyone around you already knows it's an avalanche. Second, there's a good chance you'll end up with a mouthful of snow.

That's what happened to Paul. For about a second, he got a look at the mountain of snow hurtling down from above.

It's like an all-white tidal wave, he thought.

Then the wave hit. And it sure didn't feel like water. It felt like a truck.

Everything around Paul became white. He couldn't breathe. He felt himself flying through space. Over the edge!

Seconds later, he slammed into something solid.

Then everything was still. And silent.

Paul opened his eyes and spit the snow out of his mouth. Dazed, he sat up and shook his head.

Everything still looked completely white. He wondered if he was dead.

Then he looked up. About ten feet above his head he saw the edge of the lookout point. He had landed on a narrow ridge just below.

He glanced over his shoulder at the edge of the ridge. Below him yawned nothing but wide-open space. If he fell again, he would not get a second chance.

He moaned in pain. Every bone in his body ached. He felt as if he'd just been pelted by a hundred snowballs. He definitely didn't feel like moving.

Maybe it wasn't a full avalanche, he thought.

Then a horrible thought struck him. Where was Anthony?

"Anthony!" he cried. He crawled desperately to the edge of the ridge.

"Anthony!" he cried again. His voice echoed between the ridges and peaks.

Then he felt a hand grab his shoulder.

"Oh, Anthony," Paul said happily, whirling around. "I thought you were . . . "

Paul stopped, mid-sentence, his mouth hanging open, the words frozen in his throat.

It was not Anthony he was facing.

It was the Orco!

Chapter Twenty-Nine

This time, Paul got a good look at the Orco. *Too* good a look. He was only inches from the Orco's face!

The Orco's face reminded Paul of pictures of cavemen you see in textbooks. A wide, high forehead set over thick eyebrows. A jutting jaw.

But, unlike a caveman, the Orco had a full set of yellow, pointy teeth.

And fur. Lots and lots of long, brown, tangly fur. On his head, on his cheeks, on his chin. All over his entire body.

Paul was close enough to see the twigs and bugs and flecks of dirt caught in the Orco's fur. He was close enough to stare into the Orco's beady, evil eyes.

Paul noticed all of these things in about two

seconds. Then he screamed.

The Orco wrapped one of his huge, hairy paws around Paul's arm and lifted him off the ground.

I'm dead, Paul thought. He tried to struggle free, but he could not break the Orco's iron grip. The long claws dug into Paul's arm.

I'm dead, he thought again.

He was eight feet off the ground, dangling like a fish on a hook, eye-to-eye with the towering Orco. A stream of drool dangled from the Orco's mouth.

The Orco began to slowly open his mouth, wide. Paul got a better look at those teeth. So yellow. So sharp. So *many*.

Suddenly, Paul heard a whistle.

Out of the corner of his eye, he saw something sail through the air and — SMACK! — nail the Orco right in the side of the head. Whatever it was exploded on impact. The Orco howled with rage.

It was a snowball.

It was Anthony!

Paul looked over to the far end of the ridge and saw his cousin, soaked from head to toe in snow, but still standing.

"Anthony! You're alive!" he shouted.

The Orco was greeting Anthony as well, but with a nasty growl. Anthony shouted back at the Orco. He was speaking in Italian, but it sounded quite rude to Paul.

The Orco roared louder. Paul's ears began ringing. He tried not to inhale the Orco's foul breath.

From the other side of the ridge, Anthony made wild gestures at the Orco with one hand and reached into his pocket with the other.

The Orco lumbered toward Anthony, still hanging on to Paul.

Anthony pulled out his secret weapon — the smoke bombs, along with a box of matches!

The Orco snarled.

"Drop my cousin, you ugly kitty!" Anthony yelled in English.

"I think you mean, 'you ugly *dog*!' " Paul called out weakly.

"That's what I said!" Anthony shouted. He sounded annoyed.

The arm from which Paul was dangling hurt badly. He *was* too heavy, he realized. If he got out of this alive, he'd have to go on a diet!

The Orco took another step closer. Anthony pulled out a match to light the smoke bomb. He struck the match against the side of the box. The match crumpled and bent in two.

With growing horror, Paul realized what was wrong.

The matches were all soaking wet from the snow. They would not light!

Chapter Thirty

The Orco tightened his grip on Paul and took another step toward Anthony.

We're dead, Paul thought for the third time.

Then his hand brushed against his pocket, and he felt a bulky object.

The camera!

Anthony looked up at the Orco. Step by step he backed away.

But there was only so far he could go before he came to the edge of the ridge.

One more step and Anthony would sail into the void and fall to his death!

Paul managed to grab the camera with his free hand. If only he could remember how to work the flash!

The Orco took another step forward.

Paul spotted a red button on the top of the camera. FLASH. That was it!

He jabbed the button with his thumb. A flash bulb popped up from the top of the camera.

Oh, no, Paul thought. It takes a second for the flash to activate!

The Orco towered over Anthony.

Anthony cringed on his knees, covering his face.

A light on the back of the camera started to blink. The flash was ready!

"Hey, you!" Paul shouted as loudly as he could, right into the Orco's ear. The Orco turned his head to face Paul and growled horribly.

Paul pressed the flash button. The light exploded inches from the Orco's face.

The Orco howled with rage. He twisted his ugly face until it was even uglier.

He also dropped Paul to the ground. He had been blinded by the flash!

"Grab the sack!" Paul yelled. Anthony leaped to his feet and yanked at the bundle on the Orco's belt.

The Orco could not see a thing. He swiped

blindly at whatever was pulling on his belt.

Anthony was too quick, though, and managed to duck.

The Orco was off-balance. He teetered right on the edge of the cliff! He stumbled, took a step back and stumbled again, waving around his arms desperately.

Anthony clung to the sack, trying to pull it off the belt. The Orco was starting to fall backwards.

"Anthony!" Paul cried. He grabbed his cousin by the leg.

The weight of the two of them together snapped the sack from the Orco's belt. Paul and Anthony tumbled backward into the snow.

With a terrific growl, the Orco fell in the opposite direction. Right over the edge. Right into the gorge.

His howl echoed through the mountains for a full minute before dying out.

Then there was silence.

Chapter Thirty-One

"And then," Paul huffed, "we climbed back up to the main trail."

"And then," Anthony puffed, "we ran all the way back here."

Mr. Alberti shook his head grimly.

"And you guys think this crazy story will make me forget that you two were not supposed to be playing together?"

"But we have proof!" Paul cried. He yanked the camera out of his pocket and handed it to his dad.

Mr. Alberti examined the camera for a moment and then shook his head.

"Buddy," he chuckled, "the only proof we have here is how forgetful you two can be. There's no film in this camera!"

"Oh no!" Paul shouted. "I can't believe it!"

"Wait!" Anthony interrupted. "The sack!"

It was true. They'd been in such a hurry to get back to their parents, they'd forgotten to check their prize.

"Hurry, dump it out!" Paul said.

Anthony emptied the sack on the ground — and the boys found themselves staring at a big pile of mushrooms.

"Hmm," Mr. Alberti snorted. "You guys found some pretty good ones."

Paul's heart sank. "I can't believe it. I . . . "

"Hey, wait a minute," Mr. Alberti interrupted. "I thought I saw something shiny."

He reached into the pile of mushrooms and picked up a small object. It was shiny. It was round.

It was the ring!

"All riiggght!" Paul and Anthony cried out at once.

"Well I'll . . . " Mr. Alberti began. Then words failed him.

He stopped and stared at the cousins.

"I don't know where you two found this, but

your grandmother is going to be very happy."

He stood up.

"In fact, I'm going to give it to her right now," he said. "Then I'll want the *truth*."

As he turned to leave, his stern look melted into a grin.

"In the meantime," he said, "I guess this means the ban is off. You guys are free to hang around together."

"All riiggght!" Paul and Anthony cried out for the second time.

After Mr. Alberti left, Paul looked at his cousin.

"So," he asked, "what should we tell them? They'll never believe the Orco story."

"You're right," Anthony said, shaking his head with disgust. "*Adults*. Well, we'll have to come up with something good."

"No problem," Paul replied. "We'll just think of something really boring. Adults are bound to believe that."

They looked at each other and smiled.

"Hey," Paul said, "when are you coming to

visit me in Chicago?"

"Maybe next summer," Anthony said. Then he smiled and added, "Now *that* should be an exciting vacation."

"I can't believe you!" Paul shouted.

"You are some nuts!" Anthony shouted back.

They clasped hands and grinned. And their laughter echoed through the mountains as the sun began to set.

DON'T MISS THIS NEW
SHIVERS

<u>NIGHT OF THE GOAT BOY</u>

Lights out, campers! Would a show-time summer for Nathaniel keep the illusion alive or was he in the real life role of goat food? He was one happy kid at Camp Spotlight, where acting was the way of the day. But at night, he and his tent mates didn't dare doubt the campfire story of Goat Boy. Half boy, half goat, and all teeth. Get real! There's nothing to fear. Or is there? Nathaniel was so confused. To be, or not to be — scared? That was the question. The answer will shock you.